ONE DAY UNDER THE GRASS

A SOUTHSIDE HOOKER NOVEL — 5

BAER CHARLTON

Rogena Mitchell-Jones, Editor, www.rogenamitchell.com
Cover Artist: Edith Antl
Cover Design: David L'Bearz
Laura Reynolds, Illustrator

ISBN-13:978-0-9971795-1-4 (paperback)
Published by Mordant Media, Portland, Oregon
10 9 8 7 6 5 4 3 — 2019 Edition

ALSO BY BAER CHARLTON

<u>NOVELS</u>

The Very Littlest Dragon: NEW 2019 Editions
(Newly edited editions available: an all-new full-color ebook, a paperback with coloring
pages, and a full-color Collector's Edition hardback)

Stoneheart
(Pulitzer Nominee 2015)

Angel Flights
What About Marsha?
Pirate's Patch
Dry Bridge of Vengeance

—

<u>SOUTHSIDE HOOKER SERIES</u>

Death on a Dime – Book One
Night Vision – Book Two
Unbidden Garden – Book Three
Boomtown – Book Four
One Day Under the Grass – Book Five

Southside Hooker Series: Books 1–5 Box Set
(Collector's Edition hardback & ebook available)

—

<u>THORNY WALLACE SERIES</u>

Death in the Valley – Book One
Light to Light – Book Two

CONTENTS

BOX

WORKING DOWNTOWN

If the girls had been a little younger, a little classier, a little prettier, and a little smarter, even as streetwalkers, they would work San Francisco or Los Angeles. But everyone has to be somewhere. Even in the night in downtown San Jose, there was a little something for almost any taste or preference.

The johns circled in their seven-year-old family cars—some too lazy to remove the child's booster seat from the backseat, others not caring. The color of their money and how fast they finished was everything to the girls.

The sidewalks were barely clean during the day. By night, the gutters collected fortified wine-laced puke, urine, feces, used condoms, and broken syringes, each a gemstone, jewelry of the broken dreams decorating the lives of those at the bottom, who only had lower to look forward to with each passing day.

The girls all knew each other, at least in passing. They knew who did what and who was really what or not. They all knew which block was theirs to walk. They also knew what was semi-clean to wear—and got the best responses—both in stops and spurts. They knew each other's names... most by their street names, some even by their real names. Some even shared cheap hotel rooms together—as the years, drugs, alcohol, and trade all took their toll. The one female there night after night was the one who seemed least affected by it all. Pete, short for Petunia, worked but not in the sex trade.

The dirty blonde ponytail hung to her shoulders. The gray-blue uniform jumpsuit matched her one blue eye. The red-brown of the thread on her nametag—Pete—matched her other eye. The uniform was loose and baggy—even on the woman her size. Her large pendulous breasts swayed unrestrained in the suit — her work-battered hands raw, callused, and with ropey muscle. The muscles played like piano strings as her hands moved, guiding the three-wheeled Westcoaster scooter, a dump bed on the back.

The mail carriers had the same scooter, but a shell protected them from the winter weather. Pete also knew, during the summer, the heat made the shells almost unbearable to drive in. The fiberglass shell also made them loud inside. Pete hated noise.

When she had originally gotten the job, she worked during the day. The noise and smell of the traffic made her almost quit. But, when a night shift came open, she begged for the job. By ten o'clock, downtown San Jose mostly slept—except the ten-block area where the girls walked.

Pete pulled the cart over to the curb in front of Original Joe's. Her eyes continuously moved. She took in everything around her. She once spotted a sparkle on the sidewalk, forty feet away. The streetlight had refracted through the stone— the diamond almost three and a half carats. The pawnshop traded it straight across for an eighteen-foot aluminum canoe someone had painted black.

The new concrete trash cans lining the streets of downtown had beauty tops. Pete found them to be an added annoyance. Every single can, she had to take the lid off, pull the liner up from between the concrete shell and the metal trash can, tie the bag off, and then lift and throw it into the back of her scooter. Then she had to lift the can out to put the new plastic bag liner on, stick it back in the concrete shell, and put the beauty top back on.

If anything was broken, she had to fill out a form to request the day unit come and replace the broken piece. Some nights she wanted to take the short pipe she carried for protection to the beauty top of every single one of the one hundred and fourteen trashcans.

The city-smart guys had mapped out her area and figured she could process one can every five minutes. This gave her plenty of time in her ten-hour shift to handle even the forms. It had not taken her long to figure out which cans were full, which cans were always only half-full, and even better—those which required changing once a week. Pete hated nosy people and hated worse those people who told her how to run her life or do her job.

The only manager who worked the night shift was under a truck or car in the garage. Pete knew him. Most of the night, he was asleep on the creeper. If he processed more than two or three vehicles in a shift, he had consumed too much coffee and needed to work it off. The paperwork was also pushed off onto the day shift. Pete had seen him rearrange the vehicles in the lot to make it seem like a lot was done—but mostly, it had been sleep.

With a boss like him, she didn't feel bad about how she did her job of collecting the city's trash.

Can after can, she moved methodically through the city. By ten o'clock, she was in the busy section with the working girls. This block was a quieter part on the north end. Pete knew the six girls who worked the block from Monday night to Saturday night. Her night off during the week had floated up and down from Tuesday to Friday. The one thing a woman in the city could never get was two days off in a row. Her boss never worked on Saturday or Sunday. One was sports night, and the other was the Sabbath. She was never sure what religion he claimed to be, so she didn't know or care which day was his religious day. Her lack of religion didn't matter—she got Sunday off because there wasn't enough garbage to collect.

Pete pulled the scooter to the curb. She turned the engine off and just sat looking down the street. Her eyes scanned the street, but a part of her mind was twelve hours and twelve miles away. The car pulled up at the end of the block—a 1960 Buick, four-door, a family man who should be using his money to buy better food instead of a blowjob on a Friday night. Pete could see the head of hair in the passenger seat.

Pete turned and opened the small utility box. Pulling her Roy Rogers lunch pail out, she got off the scooter and sat on the bus stop bench. The last bus was at nine-fifty. The next one would come just before dawn.

Her right hand reached into the back pocket of her overalls and withdrew the latex gloves. On the street, it was easier to put on clean gloves instead of finding somewhere to wash her hands. The leather work gloves lay on the seat of the scooter.

She opened the lunch pail and withdrew the thermos. She removed the top and set the cup down. Reaching into the lunch pail, she removed the sandwich and then the still cool can of cola. Prying off the pop-top, she dropped it into the can. Aside from the bubbles, the cola looked just like coffee when she poured it into the cup. Chugging the last of the can, she pitched it into the back of the scooter.

Pete pulled the sandwich out of its baggie and leaned back. Taking a bite of the sandwich, she chewed slowly and waited.

The footsteps were light, but the sound of how the heels thudded on the sidewalk disclosed the exhaustion. Pete knew the woman was only a little over five feet tall and wore a size four dress. The extra padding and breasts helped her fill out the stretchy dresses she liked. From the back, she was alluring, but her face showed her age and drug abuse. The woman was well past her street prime—but had nowhere else to go.

"Hi, Pete..." The voice was a little girl but was husky from age and alcohol.

Pete looked up at her. "Oh, oh, hi... um... Star. How are you?"

The woman came around and plopped mid-bench. Her sigh deep and mournful, she replied, "You know... same old same old."

Pete took a bite of her sandwich and slowly chewed as she leaned back on the bench and nodded. She nudged her chin at the scooter half full of bags of garbage. "Picking up for me... how about you?" She looked over at the woman. Again, she thought about how the body package was great, but the face was just a hole in the package where someone had scribbled crayon over the face, drawing Groucho Marx eyebrows and the hint of a mustache. Even the eyes were slightly crooked.

"Two so far..."

Pete took another bite. *Hope springs eternal.* Ten o'clock—the woman's chances of one more blowjob tonight were between slim and never going to happen. Two or three ten-dollar blowjobs a night was what the woman averaged and lived on. She shared an eight-dollar room with another whore who used it until midnight. The services she offered didn't work well in the front seat of a car.

"I don't know, Pete..." The woman sighed deeper as she looked up and down the almost empty street. "Sometimes, I just want to lie down and just never wake up."

"That's kind of a depressing thing to say..."

The whore looked at Pete. "It just doesn't matter anymore —my prince is never going to come and sweep me off my feet. Watch..." She saw a few cars coming. She hooked both thumbs in the stretchy top of her dress and pulled it down and under her teats. She sat back with both hanging out with no bra.

The three cars passed without so much as a head turned. The two women watched as the taillights flashed bright red for half a second when they got to the end of the block where two hookers with long legs and not much else but a smile stood.

Pete looked back at Star. The whore was pulling herself back in her top. "See... nothing."

Pete thought a moment and then pulled the flipper on the rubber stopper of the thermos. She pulled the stopper out and passed it over to the woman. "Here, you can have the rest of my coffee. I'm not going to finish it." She held up her red lid-cup.

Star took a sip. "It's a little old, but it tastes good after the last guy. I swear… I don't know what the hell people eat these days. His sperm tasted like a bad poop in a goat barn."

Pete continued to eat. She didn't want to know how the woman knew about goats—much less the taste of the animal's poop.

The occasional car drove past. Pete sipped on her soda and finished her sandwich. She reached over and carefully picked up the thermos where it had fallen on the bench. She poured out the remaining warm coffee and cyanide. She packed it in the lunch pail with the baggie.

Pete put the pail back in the utility compartment. Turning, she took the beauty lid off the concrete trash bin and pulled up the plastic bag. She tied off the half-full bag, pulled it out, and placed it on the end of the bench. She pulled the metal can out, inserted the new bag, and then put the can back into the concrete shell. Replacing the beauty top, Pete pressed her hands against her back and bent backward, stretching her sore back—as she looked around. The street was empty.

Bending, she pushed her shoulder into the dead woman's gut. She was lighter than Pete thought. She stood, took two steps, and tossed her into the area between the carefully arranged bags of trash. She reached and grabbed the other bag and tossed it on top.

Sliding down onto the seat of the scooter, she glanced at the large watch on her wrist. It had taken almost twenty minutes less than she had planned on. She turned the key and pushed the silver button. The scooter chugged and shuddered to life. Pete put the scooter in gear and eased from the curb. Looking in the rearview mirror, she hung a U-turn in the middle of the empty block. At the corner, the traffic lights had just started to flash red. Moonrise was still an hour away. The temperature sign on the Woolworth's building read eighty-one degrees.

The tiny red taillights of the scooter disappeared up Stevens Creek Boulevard. The whore on the second corner thought it was strange for Pete to be heading north when Pete was usually working south at this time of night. The end of the cigarette swelled hot red as she took another drag. By the time she breathed the smoke out toward the street, a car was coming, and everything else forgotten.

THE MORNING SUN was only half up as the heat of the day started to rise. The barrel-chested man stood in the black aluminum canoe as he pushed on the long pole. The sea of tan grass slid quietly past him. He stood steady in the boat—he had been standing in canoes and pirogues all of his life. The Everglades in Florida, the bayous of southern Louisiana, the sea of grass in the South San Francisco bay, all of them to Lane were the same—grass above, water, and mud below.

Lane saw the world as night and day. The sky, grass, and areas he moved in were day. The surface of the water was the demarcation border leading into the night. Lane remembered his mother telling him as a boy—when a body slides into the water, they are sliding into night. All the water in his life had been dark. His momma never lied.

He tugged at the binding bandage around his chest. He hated his chest. As a man, it betrayed him. The bandage helped flatten the shape, but at times, he felt like he couldn't breathe. He pulled the long-billed hat closer to his eyes. The shadow was dark, but in the early sunlight on the water, the reflection played in the blue and brown eyes. In school, he was teased about how he must be from Australia. Rarely did those mean children ever tease him again.

The canoe flowed on the freshwater river, which ran between the two saltwater marshes and grew full of salt grass and bulrushes. He knew what he was looking for, the area where the most crabs and ghost shrimp were—under the trestle. He tossed his head, and the short ponytail flipped off his shoulder and hung down the back of his neck to his shoulders.

He switched sides with the pole and started to turn the canoe into the grass. He looked up at the timbers of the trestle. He hadn't been to this spot since just after the New Year. He could name what was under the sea of grass—they had all been friends. Now they slept in the night of the water.

The back of his hands was ropey with muscle. He pulled back the trap. The woman quietly lay as if she were asleep.

Lane reached down and lifted the slightly built body to the edge of the canoe. Placing his left hand in the middle of the crossbeam, he lightly jumped the gunwale and stood in the shallow water and mud to just above his waist. The water wasn't cold, but it wasn't warm. He reached in for the body. Lifting, he turned and then slowly pushed the body under the grass and into the night of the dark water.

He watched the last of the legs and feet slip into the shadows and night. He whispered, "Sleep... Sleep well, Star."

FUNCTIONAL FORENSICS

Hooker, still a bit blurry-eyed, opened his bedroom door. The silence had woken him.

The morning was his time to sleep since he worked at night. Certain noises in the house were missing. No matter where he was sleeping—certain noises of life reassured him and kept him asleep. The silence wasn't one of them. The only sound was something irregularly and lightly hitting metal...

He rolled over, looking at the dimly illuminated clock. The forty-four card flipped over, making it nine-forty-five. No tiny red dot glowing—*morning*. Hooker lay listening. No murmurs of people talking. With four others in the house, there should have been talking.

Hooker swung his feet over the edge of the bed. Running his right hand over his face, he rubbed his eyes. He grabbed his pants off his socks and boots as he rose. Dragging his pants, he walked into the dark bathroom adjoining his bedroom, which made up his private suite.

He raised his arms and smelled his pits—he'd shower

later. Flushing, he pulled on his pants and brushed his teeth. He stood looking into the mirror, remembering he no longer drove Mae West—his giant 1959 Marmon tow truck. He thought about the five-ton truck parked out front. He groaned, turning off the light.

So much changed since he and the Squirt blew up the end of the San Jose airport, along with Mae West. The time in the hospital had been fairly short. The only surgery, this time, removed a large piece of cable shrapnel, which had whipped around and pierced his door and calf. The scar occasionally itched but didn't hurt.

He scratched at the old scars on his chest where the dimes had gone in. Padding out of his door, he still rubbed at his eyes as he took in three of the four other residents sitting silently at the table.

Manny leaned back and quietly sipped his mug of coffee as he watched the Squirt work on the toaster. Stella looked up. At seeing Hooker, she stuck her arm out for a hug— Hooker was capable of getting his own coffee.

Hooker folded over, hugging Stella and added a kiss on the top of her head. "Is the toaster broken?"

"Shhhh..."

Hooker put up his hands in surrender. Turning, he got his coffee. As he glanced at the clock, he remembered he was starting early for Don. His usual six-ish start would be when he got his first call after two. He looked out the window— thinking about working during the day. It paid better—but there were more people to deal with. More people meant more traffic in the way and more breakdowns and small acci-dents. The big stuff in the night had been his real meat and potatoes for over ten years.

Mae West had been the fastest of any tow truck in the five counties. Her booms and four-footed outriggers made her the most mobile crane for dead-drag recoveries and rollovers. She had proved her mettle on a recent train derailment with cars full of toxic chemicals. Even the Burlington Northern Railroad's twenty-ton Manitowoc rail crane couldn't do the rollovers needed, nor could it have lifted the hundred and forty-ton overloaded tank cars.

His golden girl had seemed almost indestructible—until the explosion ripped her into nothing left but the cab and front-end. The banner draped over the pin-up painting of the actress on the front read 'It's What's Up Front That Counts' never rang so true before. He was going to miss those eleven tons of hot, fast mama.

He returned to the arm of his other mama, or at least the one still here. His other surrogate mother, Stella's sister, wouldn't be up for another four hours to run the Night Dispatch as well as the city of San Jose. She only lent it back to the regular people to take care of it during the day...

Hooker leaned over and kissed Stella on the head again.

She didn't look up. "Hooker, you are either still asleep or slipping. You already gave me my morning kiss."

"This one was for being who you are."

Manny grumped at the other end of the table. "Then why are you stopping?"

"Manny T. Loverbe, you leave my boy alone. Some of these things take time to learn. In fact, I remember a day in 1956—it was a Tuesday in May, you left the house without kissing me goodbye."

Manny hid his face in his mug. Eighteen years and he still had never heard the end of it.

"You didn't come home either." She looked up at Hooker as the Squirt looked up from the toaster. "He was resting up at his other home—*the hospital*. A knife in the back can do that to you."

Hooker and the Squirt looked toward the retired detective in the wheelchair. Manny snorted. "Not up for the retelling. Let it be."

Stella wasn't about to stop. She leaned her head against Hooker's hip. "My lips ached that day—all day. And then there was still no relief while they had him in an oxygen tent."

"She went and kissed one of the K-9 dogs—ruined him from ever working again."

The Squirt coughed. "Okay, you just got a little too deep. I might have to go put my boots on."

Hooker frowned. The probing of the toaster had removed its bottom. Spread over a large sheet of white paper laid all the crumbs that had been in the appliance. The Squirt worked with tiny spatulas, brushes, and tweezers placed next to various magnifying glasses and a notepad.

"What is it you're doing, Squirt?"

Manny snickered. "It's a pop final exam in forensics."

Stella nodded as she got up to fix Hooker some breakfast. "I had the police lab clean the toaster out a few months ago— while you two were lounging about at Good Sam, chatting up all the wrong nurses." She gave him a stern eye.

She continued as she pulled out the omelet pan. "I have kept a record of everything I ever put in there. Now the Squirt has to replicate the list and the percentages of what was toasted."

Hooker moved around to look at the Squirt's list so far. The tiny crumbs were sorted into areas on the large white sheet of paper where he had labeled—white, wheat, sourdough, bagel, oat bran, and other. His notes were just thoughts about certain characteristics of the different breads toasted and why.

Hooker picked up a large magnifying glass and looked at the single curved seed in the area marked *other*. The side of his mouth facing Manny curled up. Manny cleared his throat, and Hooker put the glass down. He returned to one of the chairs on the other side and sat to watch the process.

Every crumb or crumb particle was examined, qualified, and sorted to its designated area. Some of the pieces were small enough to require the Squirt to pull down his head magnifier to look through for a super-enlargement. More than half of the tiny specs on the paper Hooker wouldn't even qualify as dirt—they were fine enough to be more like dust.

Knowing how Manny and his lessons were always about a much bigger picture than just crumbs in a toaster—Hooker was curious. He looked at the intent young man working. He had seen the look overtake the Squirt many times and knew he was beyond any distraction.

He turned to Manny and asked in a low voice. "This isn't about crumbs, is it?"

Manny put his mug down and braced his forearms on the armrests of the wheelchair. He pushed up and adjusted his body. Hooker waited as the retired detective became the teacher.

"When you go into a room having been trashed—you see a trashed room. With training, you start to see how it might have gotten trashed. A single person who searches a room methodically will leave a room trashed in a methodical trail. Two people create havoc, but it is a formal havoc. When there is a violent fight, there is nothing sacred, and so everything is swept up in the tornado of violence. With time and even finer training, the tornado aftermath can reveal how many people were in the fight, and even sometimes, the size of the combatants, or even their sex. Women fight a lot different from men."

"How so?"

"When they get angry, they throw stuff, but always in their mind, they are cleaning up after." He looked up at his wife. "Have you ever thrown any plates or crockery?"

"Only those ugly square Melmac we used to have." She held the heavy plate of her cherished Fiestaware to her chest. Her right hand absentmindedly stroked the smooth glaze.

Manny held out his hand to the proof. "They usually throw things they know won't break. Throwing dishes at a husband is something Hollywood made up. It's dramatic and shocking—but not based in reality—as a general rule. If the fight is for one's life, then all the rules are thrown out the window. Anything goes."

"So the crumbs?" Hooker took a sip of his coffee as Stella placed the plate in front of him.

"Once you determine what kind of a fight had ensued, you need to also see all the tiny details, right down to a hair on the carpet."

Hooker took a bite of the omelet and chewed. Swallowing with a sip of coffee, he frowned. He knew when Manny mentioned a detail, it was important—not a throwaway.

"You mentioned a hair on the carpet. It could have just been a hair. They fall out every day..."

Manny smiled. "So we know the fighters were a large man and a woman. The occupant of the apartment is a woman with short dark brown hair. A witness saw a bald man entering the apartment shortly before a neighbor called the police to report screaming. We presumably now have our two fighters. But what if the hair on the floor is about seventeen inches long and blond?"

"We have a third person of interest..."

"Bingo." Manny smiled and took back his mug as he leaned back in the chair.

Then all watched as the Squirt sorted out the last few chunks. He moved a sizable black something into the area marked other. He then grabbed his mug and sat back, evaluating his work.

Manny smiled. "Well?"

The Squirt pointed to each of the marked areas as he spoke. "Almost every day, ten pieces of wheat toast are made. Manny is diabetic, and the whole wheat provides the lowest glycemic problem. There are no crumbs from white bread because they don't have a heat tolerance and would be black char. You toasted sourdough about three times, which would match the three times in the last two months we have had French toast made with the thick-sliced sourdough. So you were toasting off the leftovers. The oat bran comes from Candy. She brings up her own bread the two days a week we all eat together."

He touched his tweezers to the large chunk of black. "The raisin is from raisin toast, which you got especially for Sissy when she came down with Claire and Norm to visit us in the hospital." He looked up at the smiling Stella. "You sent them back with the rest of the loaf to one, get rid of the evidence, and two, you hate raisins."

Stella clapped as she laughed. "Very good."

The Squirt turned to Manny. "And so we have come to

the final. What would have thrown me was this." He pointed at the tiny seed. "At first look, I thought it was a caraway seed. Logically it would have come from rye toast. The toast would fit with you two being Jewish, but I have never seen Stella slice a brisket thin enough to make a Rueben sandwich. Plus, I know you don't like sauerkraut, so Stella doesn't use it. The seed is similar to caraway, but the light and dark lines with stripes running the length are not color differences—so the seed is not caraway. I can only assume it is a wild card and was only thrown into the toaster to confuse or trip me up." He stood and walked toward the pantry.

Stella chuckled as Manny frowned at not understanding. She called out as he reached the door. "It should be the second shelf down and about the third one over from the left."

The Squirt returned a moment later. Opening the jar, he tumbled out a few seeds. With tweezers, he picked one up. With a magnifying glass, he took a quick look. He set it back down and smiled at Stella. "Bravo. Very close and easily confused, but fennel would never be used in rye bread. But it would be used for dill bread."

Stella, the consummate cook, frowned. "How would you make dill bread?"

The Squirt watched her with a deadpan face. "With some naughty dough..."

It took a few seconds until Manny started snickering. Hooker's mind wasn't far behind. Stella looked at her youngest baby and realized he was always a man—he just hadn't grown into his pants yet.

"You owe the swear jar fifty-cents... make it a dollar. You can pay for my having to repeat it to my sister." The four chuckled at the great but naughty pun.

IN THE SWING OF SUMMER

Stella picked up the phone and talked softly. The two men ignored her. Stella looked at the ceiling. "Sure, he can make it. He's in the shower, but he only takes a few minutes anyway. I'll tell him." She paused. "Okay, thanks, Karen." She hung up.

As she started to walk away, she felt the four sets of eyes on her. If she didn't know Box was outside lying on the deck sleeping in the sun, she knew she would have been feeling five. She laughed as she walked, shaking her head. "Stand down, gentlemen. It's only a flat tire."

"Yeah, that's how it all started with the shotgun..."

She froze, turning, her finger up and facing out. Her one eye was down, and her lips were set. "Don't you dare jinx this day..."

She pushed her way into Hooker's suite.

"Sweetheart, you have a T-wonderful. Karen is giving you three to get in the truck before she bangs it and starts the clock."

"Thanks, Mom..." The voice echoed off the tile walls. She

knew if she didn't leave instantly, his naked body would be pushing her out of the way.

She stood at the front door and waited. She counted the seconds, and she hadn't hit ninety when he came bustling out of the bedroom.

"I'll keep in touch, and if I'm clear, I'll pick you up a bit after seven, and we can eat at the hospital if you want."

The Squirt looked up at Stella. She snorted. "Leftover lasagna."

"Sure, seven sounds great."

Hooker kissed her on both cheeks and the forehead. As he walked through the plaza to the front gates of the hacienda, he called for his cat. "Box—go time." Stella watched the orange streak flash past the front arch and stop. He still looked for the giant Mae instead of just a large truck.

At least the large bench seat fit the box the twenty-pound cat rode in. The two were inseparable.

Hooker grabbed the strange mic. "1-4-1. I'm 10-8."

"10-4, 1-4-1, your T-1, flat tire is the right rear on a 1970 El Dorado, white. The woman member will meet you inside the Marie Calendars. She called this one direct to the shop, so it's a shop call." Hooker smiled. $9.57 straight in his pocket instead of only half of the usual $7.41, plus the fuel and truck was on Don instead of coming out of Hooker's half.

"10-4. Any word yet?"

"Hooker, you asked the same question at two this morning. When they locate him, they will let you know."

Hooker hung the mic looking at the cat already close to sleep. "Beans and wieners, Box. Willie should have told me where he was running off to."

The cat half-opened his one eye and then rolled over to

ignore Hooker. He had serious napping to do, and Hooker needed to stop whining. Neither one of them was happy with the truck—even if it was brand new. Don, his boss, had ordered it up for Hooker while he and the Squirt were in the hospital this last time. The part about them blowing up Mae West all over the north end of the airport, which shut the entire airport down for almost eleven days, was beside the point.

The city was still trying to figure out how to repay Hooker and the Squirt for saving a few dozen lives and one of the major county office buildings. The airport was screaming for Hooker's head, skin, and anything else. The city informed the Port Authority if they tried to sue Hooker, the city would pull the port's charter, or at least make any ideas of expansion difficult. The lawyers for American Airlines and PSA put it more succinctly—shut up, or they would both pull out.

Hooker couldn't figure out how the city could threaten the port when they owned it. It would be like holding a knife to your own throat, and then, with the other hand sticking a gun to your heart and saying... *go ahead, try it, and I blow a hole through your middle.* It just didn't make much sense. Dolly tried to explain it to him, and then, even she gave up.

The Cadillac sat near the front door. The heat was already in the high nineties, if not over one hundred. Hooker didn't blame the member for not standing outside to wait for the tow truck—even if they knew one would show up in fewer than twenty minutes.

There were few cars in the parking lot in the afternoon. The bar crowd would start in an hour, seniors the following hour, and finally, the dinner rush after six. Even with the solid air conditioning, Hooker knew people's appetite dropped off in the summer heat. He pulled into the two spaces next to the flat tire.

He left the air conditioner running as it was blowing into Box's face. The cat had his one eye closed and was leaning into the air. Hooker smiled as he left his partner to his comfort.

Stepping into the restaurant was a thirty-degree drop. The large muscular woman standing at the receptionist desk had a distinctive leather-braided ponytail. Hooker hadn't noticed any choppers in the parking lot, so he was a little confused.

"Did you put on training wheels, Max?"

The woman laughed and turned. "You're late, Hooker."

He glanced at his watch. *Eighteen minutes—slow but on time.* "Nope. Right on time."

"Your truck says if I want a quickie—"

Hooker's face turned sour. "Not driving my truck. I'm in a pig with only five hundred horses. The bean-herder can barely get out of its own way. I feel like you would if you had a Moped loaner."

Max laughed. "I heard. Sorry about your big truck. I liked the look of her. It fit you."

"Yeah, well..." He shrugged. "So is the Caddie yours?"

Max showed her hand at the tiny woman sitting on the long bench. "Hooker, meet my great-aunt Poppy. Her parents were some of the first florists west of St. Louis. They were in Hollywood when it started and were the florist to the stars. Poppy, this nice young man is Hooker."

The woman stood and smiled. "You're a hooker? Are you my birthday present also?"

Max laughed. "Poppy, behave. His name is Hooker."

Hooker laughed as he shook the elderly woman's hand. "I'm also a hooker, but not in the Hollywood sense of the word. I drive a tow truck, and it has a hook on the back."

"Well, then, let's stop flapping our lips and go flip the Firestones." She laughed at Hooker's face. "I may be eighty-four, sonny, but I know my way around a car or two."

Hooker smiled as he thought of a few people he knew she would fit in with.

As Hooker placed the flat in the trunk, Max handed him a twenty.

"I don't have change. Let me go inside—"

Max cut him off. "I was counting on it—in case you have a date for tonight. Stop by on Monday. I'll have chili, and it's slow—we can talk."

"Thanks, Max. I'd like that." Turning to the woman sitting in the seat with the door open. "It was very nice meeting you, Poppy. If you ever get up to the main library, you ought to look up a librarian named Maddie Robinson."

"Is she from the Salinas area?"

Hooker smirked and hung his shoulders. "Yeah, you probably already know her."

"Only know of her. For a number of years, she was the fastest woman in the world. I think her family built race cars or something. I would love to meet her."

Max looked at Hooker with a raised eyebrow. "And you know this woman...?"

"She's my aunt." Hooker smiled as he now knew what the topic of conversation would be the next night.

Hooker climbed back in the truck and rolled up the window as he did the paperwork. The truck may be a slow pig, but it did have a top-notch air conditioner.

"1-4-1." He called Night Dispatch for any commercial calls.

It was still the day shift, and Karen answered. "1-4-1, we have nothing, but I think the club just got one for you."

"10-4." Switching microphones to the auto club radio, Hooker checked in. "1-4-1, show me 10-98 on Blossom Hill."

The auto club was rarely busy on Sunday afternoons, so Jake was right back in his clipped rapid file style. "10-4, 1-4-1, holding T-3 at Granny's Attic, going to member's mechanic on San Jose Avenue. Red, AMC Pacer. Timeout: four-twenty-four."

Hooker was tempted to ask if it was okay to just drive the truck over the lemon car, but he was civil. "10-4, Pacer at the Attic."

The traffic was sparse on Blossom Hill and only slightly more once he turned onto Almaden Expressway. The real crowds would not be coming back from Calero reservoir for at least another hour or two. The heat would keep them in or on the water. The heat of summer kept many people indoors, out at the lakes, or away on vacations. Hooker still hated working during the daylight hours—it just meant more people, more traffic, and with the heat, heated tempers.

Hooker pulled up to find one such temper boiling over and kicking at not only tires, but the fenders, doors, and anything they could dent but not break. Hooker didn't even need to get close to hear the man swearing at the car.

"1-4-1, show me 10-97 at the Attic. I have a member, or at least someone kicking this car into just dents."

"10-4, 1-4-1. Member is male with the last name of Michaels." Hooker smiled at the syrupy voice that sounded almost like a twelve-year-old girl. He had met Bethany. She was built just like her uncle—who played for the San Francisco 49ers.

Hooker double-clicked the key on the microphone and slid out of the truck. He worked hard at restoring his deadpan face. With a Pacer, Gremlin, or Pinto, it was a hard thing to do.

"Are you the auto club member?"

Hooker eyed the dented panels of the car as he waited for the man to finish fuming. Some of the dents had rust along the creases—this was not the first time at the kicking rodeo.

The man fished the card out of his wallet. "You know Nick, up on San Jose Avenue?"

"Sure, he's right across from the Fly. An easy push when Nick can't fix it."

The man's head snapped up. Hooker swallowed. He knew he best remain quiet. Some people were sensitive about their cars.

The man leaned back against his Pacer, folding his arms across his chest. "Let me ask you. How many of these do you tow?"

Hooker's mouth drifted closed. With Mae West, the man would have been wondering why a truck nine times as big as his car responded to the tow. But Hooker knew what the man's question truly was.

"Compared to Fords and Chevys, they didn't make very many of these."

The man knew he would have to work for the right answer. "How many of these do you tow, straight to the scrap heap, instead of a repair place?"

Hooker was now in the corner. "About half."

The man curled his lips against his teeth. "My dad always drove Ramblers..."

"Good cars. Built like a brick. Simple and made for work. They ran like a Sherman tank—sometimes dependable and sometimes..." Hooker waited.

The man's smile was slow to come but finally got there. "Let's let Nick give the last rites."

"Where can I drop you off?"

The man looked at the sky, evaluating the day. "I live about a mile from here... I think I need the walk... and time to think. I need a dependable car. Nothing fancy, but it needs to run when I need it."

Hooker rubbed his jaw. "Nick knows a lot of people and a lot of cars. You tell him what you want to spend and what kind of car you need by nine tomorrow morning, and I'll bet he has three cars by noon for you to go look at."

The man was a little surprised. "Nick...?"

Hooker nodded. "It's his business... and he would want you in a car he knows will make you happy and will bring to him for oil and tune-ups."

"I never thought... makes sense. I'll call him tomorrow morning. God knows I certainly don't want to be taking the bus to Santa Clara every day for very long."

A half an hour later, Hooker was backing the car into Nick's apron. There were already three other cars on the large apron with only room for two more. Monday would be a busy day for the man.

"1-4-1."

"Go ahead, 1-4-1."

"Show me 10-98 on the Pacer."

"Did you get it started?"

Hooker laughed. "It was a T-7. It went to Nick Ivankovitch on San Jose Avenue."

"10-4. I have a T-5 stall... Might be a T-7 at Branham High. Don was going to get it, but his T-1 turned into a seven."

"Go ahead. Give it to me."

"It's a 1964 Corvair, red with white sidewalls. Member will meet you at the car."

Hooker pinched the bridge of his nose—it was turning into one of those days...

Actually, the little Chevy wasn't half bad. As Hooker nosed the large truck into the parking lot, the sun flashed off many afternoons of polish. The chrome package had been installed correctly and with flare. The young man was standing, not leaning against the car—a true sign of respect for his many hours of effort making the most of his car.

Hooker slid down from the cab. Box took the opportunity to use the large lawn. Hooker looked the car over. "This has got to be the nicest Corvair I have ever seen... You really take care of it."

The slight young teen smiled. "Thanks, I try."

"Well, it shows... which says a lot these days. What's the problem?"

"Twice today, when I went to accelerate, the car just dies. I wait a little bit, and it starts right up. I go gentle, and she runs fine. If I go up an incline or need to goose it to go around someone..."

Hooker thought a moment. "Did you install any extra fuel filters?"

"No, I've tried to keep it just the way I got it."

"Let's take a look."

A few minutes later, Hooker had the rear end up on the jack. He slid under and a minute later, slid out. In his hand was a small glass cylinder with two metal ends. The filter was inside. "Just as I thought... Whoever had this before you put in this little in-line fuel filter just in case. There is no fuel filter until you get to the engine—which is a bugger to get to. This one is a snap to clean while you change the oil."

A few minutes with the air, some gas, and the filter was clean and returned to its place. The kid had slid in from the other side, and Hooker showed him where it was hiding so he could clean it when he did the other maintenance.

Hooker tore off the receipt and handed the card and paper to the member, using his name. "Is Roc short for something?"

"Nope, just Roc. There was a boxer back in the fifties who my dad liked. Not a big one like Rocky Marciano, Battling Hays, or Max Baer, but good enough in the Bay Area. Dad just liked the name."

Hooker stuck his hand out. "Well, Roc Reed, it's been a pleasure to meet someone who likes their car enough to take good care of it. I apologize... I might have left a fingerprint or two on the paint."

The kid whipped around. "Where...?" He turned back around with a crooked grin and a chuckle. He knew he had been had.

Hooker was halfway up into the truck's cab. "You take care, Roc. I don't want to tow the bomb."

The kid waved and smiled.

4

HOW LONG IS YOUR CABLE

Hooker woke to the soft tapping on the door. "Yeah...?"

Manny opened the door and pushed in. The cordless phone was in his lap. He handed Hooker the phone.

Hooker sat up with his legs over the edge of the bed. He glanced at the clock—7:43 *in the morning*. "Maybe I need to drag a line into here..."

He put the phone to his ear. "Hooker... "

The conversation was short and sweet. "I'm pretty sure it's five-hundred feet, but even if it says three, I know they would wind more like four and call it shorter. I'll be in the truck in five." He hung up and handed the phone to Manny. "Someone drove off into the seagrass out near Milpitas way."

Manny nodded. "Stella already put some tuna on the floor, and she's wrapping bacon and scrambled eggs into some burritos. The thermos is already full."

Hooker started toward his bathroom. "Sorry to have woken..." He turned back and looked at Manny. By the face, he knew it had been one of those nights. "When...?"

Manny shrugged. "About three or so." The nightmares would wake him up, and the screaming would wake Stella up, and they would get up and play Gin until the sun rose, and the night terrors stopped. Hooker had his own terrors now to deal with. They had gotten good at playing three-legged Gin.

Hooker nodded and headed into his bathroom. "Tell Stella to give me about three minutes. I need to brush my teeth." He knew it was not going to be a short day.

"1-4-1, I'M 10-8 on Commercial, sheriff."

"10-4, Hooker. Captain Davis said he'll meet you at the bird sanctuary. There is a pumping station just north of there, and then the road continues north where the railroad tracks cross over to a ghost town named Drawbridge. He thought you might know where he was talking about. It seems there is a large rock or something out there..."

"10-4, I know the area intimately."

"He thought you did. Evidently, someone tried to cross on the rails last night. It seems they figured if they did it fast enough, it wouldn't be so rough on the trestle."

"How far across did they get?

"Into the seagrass, and the deputy figures it's a hundred yards to the dry land."

"He must have played football in high school."

"Played for the Raiders."

"I hope he wasn't a lineman."

"Running back... It's my second cousin, but we all call him Uncle Fester."

Hooker hung up the microphone. "Oh, great, Box. We have us an athlete."

The Night Dispatch radio squawked, "I heard that, Hooker. He actually has some brains, and he's a nice guy."

Hooker laughed. He thought about how he wanted to get to the bird sanctuary. There were areas Mae West, his usual eleven tons of sixteen-hundred horse-powered diesel truck, could go, but he wasn't sure he wanted to get Don's new baby stuck. He figured going in at Zanker Road was safer than where he used to go in just southeast of Moffett Field.

His sister and tribe roamed the entire mudflats, salt marshes, seagrass lands, and the buildings around there. Sometimes, he could talk to some of the street people in town, and they would know where she was—because they didn't want to be near her and her tribe of night denizens. Most were closer to the animals whose names they took, some a little more primal. His sister took the name Mouse—and like the old movie, *The Mouse That Roared,* she roared—making her the supreme power over the others known.

Hooker hauled on the steering wheel. The truck, a quarter the size of his big rig, was four times harder to steer, shift, or move down the road. He pitied the man who would eventually drive this truck—year after year.

Box got tired of being where he couldn't get his ear rubbed and jumped up on the bench seat. Hooker smiled, and his knuckles found the ear. The purring was almost instant.

The wildlife refuge was more like a mud bath stop on the west coast flyway for migrating waterfowl. At times, Hooker had been tempted to bring some shotgun shells loaded with birdshot instead of his usual dime load of a buck-forty in each barrel. But he also knew birdshot coming from the twelve-inch cut-down barrels of his Betsy would only be effective for about eight or ten yards, beyond which, the geese would just laugh at him.

He drove along the mudflats. If a person didn't know they were in the San Francisco Bay, they would have just thought the fields were some farmer's property. The smell was the only giveaway. Everything was rotting, especially the mud.

Hooker wasn't happy about coming out here in the heat of summer. The heat just made the small boring bugs, worms, and microorganisms more active eating and pooping. Sissy had explained it as a cycle. The big bugs rotted the big grass, the little bugs feasted on the rotting grass and the big bug poop, and then they pooped too, which fertilized the mud, and the grass grew better... a cycle. She was good at explaining those things, but he was sure she would get lost figuring out how the city and county were suing each other and themselves over Hooker blowing the runway up. A lot of things in Hooker's life made sense—and then there was the other stuff.

Hooker saw Chet standing out by the road, his cruiser parked and locked. Hooker smiled. They both knew every time they worked together, his cruiser got muddy, dented, or broken. Today, the CHP captain wasn't taking any chances. But why he was here in sheriff territory was beyond Hooker.

Hooker stopped. The passenger door opened. The older officer climbed slowly up into the rig. "I knew you probably got pulled out of bed, so I swung by the Whole Donut for some food. Mai Lin says you don't love her anymore. So how the hell are ya?" The friend and officer looked around the cab of the truck. "I hate what you did with the place."

Hooker grumped at the obvious. "Don't listen to him,

Box... He's always Mister Grumpypants. He just doesn't know this fine piece of shit like we do. He'll learn to hate it like a reasonable human being. Just give him time." Hooker looked up at Chet. "What kind of donuts?"

They eased down the road as it turned from asphalt to dirt to something little more than a track in the short grass. Hooker jammed the last half of the French cruller into his mouth and wrestled with the wheel. The truck lumbered off the road and around the pumping station and back up onto the small track, which ran around the slough pond covering a square mile.

"Is he this side or the Drawbridge side?"

"I think he said on the south side. The guy was coming from this side, and I don't think there is any way to tow him out of there going north..."

Hooker thought about the maze of tracks and roads laced in and around the ponds, flats, and sloughs of the bay.

"From Drawbridge, there are three ways to get out to Fremont. Two cross the floating island, and the other we would be walking the last five miles or so. This pig has no guts and only six wheels to carry the weight."

Hooker looked over at his friend. "I used to bring Mae in here all the time looking for Sissy. There were a couple of years they were north of Fremont and Newark. Most of the time, they were straight out from Union City. Occasionally, they would be up around Hayward because the salt crabs are cleaner there."

"How did you find them?"

"Mostly, I could get good information from Peter. Occasionally, I would take some food and troll north on Thirteenth or even go up to Newark. It's amazing what some of the broken bums would come up with for a warm meal. Usually, if the information was good, I'd go back and take them several days' worth of food. The food usually lasted about ten minutes. They aren't greedy—if they have food, they share with everyone else. They really understand what it means for all of them being in it together." Hooker nodded his chin at the officer who stood leaning against his squad car.

Chet laughed, knowing the nature of cars parked in nasty wet places. "There's your swimming partner."

Hooker glanced over with a smile. "Think he brought his wet suit?" Then Hooker remembered he was not in Mae West. His wetsuit vaporized into thin air along with the working deck of the truck when the bomb went off. *Beans in sauce, I'm going skinny-dipping.*

Chet read the sudden change of Hooker's face. "Did you just remember what part of the airport your wetsuit turned into?"

Hooker shot the laughing captain the bird as he slid out of the cab.

"What are we looking at?"

The deputy pointed out into the expanse of tan saltwater grass. It took Hooker a few moments to finally see the trunk and red plastic taillight of the white Cordoba peeking out of the grass.

"The guy had to be going well over a hundred when he hit the hump." They all looked at the tire tracks where they burst the top of the hump of dirt on the edge of the solid ground and road. The top of the hump was about seven feet above the top of the grasses. There was no track from the berm to the burial site. The car had gone airborne—flying at least two hundred feet.

Never to give a deputy a break, Hooker deadpanned the deputy who still looked like he was playing in the NFL. "I thought you called it in as one hundred yards?"

The man smirked. "I said approximately one hundred yards. The only thing to ever count is making a first down, which is only ten."

Chet chimed in and let his captain's bars carry the weight. "Did you bring your wetsuit?"

The deputy rolled his head to the side and smiled slightly. "Water temp is sixty-four. If I put my wetsuit on, I'd be overheated when I got out there. But it would probably fit you if you CHP pukes are so pansy." He started unbuttoning his shirt. Hooker noticed his black shoes were actually diver's booties.

"Rescue and recovery?"

The deputy wiggled his eyebrows as he opened his back door and laid his uniform on the seat. "I have an extra pair of booties, size twelve if you need them."

"Thanks. Mine are still at the airport."

The man stood up and looked at the young man as if for the first time. "You must be Hooker." He stuck his hand out and looked at the long scars racing into Hooker's hairline. "I'm Dina's Uncle Frank, but everyone calls me Uncle Fester." He finally took off the optional Smokey Bear hat to reveal a bald head. The smiling face took on a perfect mock of the TV character.

Hooker pulled the jumpsuit out of the side box on the truck. He looked in and saw there was another one in there too. He turned. "I have an extra jumpsuit if you want it."

The deputy stood in his bathing trunks and booties. "I'm good. The leeches and I are old friends. I used to keep a few dozen at home. Feeding them controlled my polycythemia. Now I just go bleed once a month at the Red Cross."

Chet frowned. "I thought you could only donate once every eight weeks."

"They only take the red cells. I produce too many, which is no good, and the cells can collect and cause a blockage."

"Clot?"

"No. Clotting is coagulation. This, they crowd the artery to a standstill. So they take out the extra and give it to other people who need them, like people with anemia."

Hooker swallowed. "But you put leeches on you to purposely suck the blood out?"

"Sure. They've been doing it for centuries. And because I did it at home, there was no doctor record of it, and I could play ball."

Hooker finished tucking the pant legs into the booties. "Let me pull up here, and if you can bring your cruiser down here about thirty yards, I can turn this pig around."

"Aren't you glad you don't have the big rig right now?"

Hooker looked the man in the eye. "If Mae was here, I'd just drive her out there, snag on, and haul the Prom Queen off to the dance."

Fester held his look for the count of three. He wasn't sure if Hooker was pulling his leg or if he really was crazy enough. The big truck was amazing enough to deal with two feet of muck under three feet of water. He took the low road and moved the cruiser.

Chet chuckled as he watched the two vehicles swap

places. He wasn't sure if Mae could or couldn't, but he knew better to not bet against Hooker and the amazing Mae West.

The sun was low, but the heat was still working. Chet climbed up into the cab and grabbed some more coffee and a donut to watch the show from a safe perch. Box barely opened his one eye at the sound of the door. He was happy in the cool cab with the air conditioner running.

The water wasn't warm, but it wasn't the coldest Hooker had endured. The hot water bottle ballooned up with air and kept the heavy cable eye afloat after Hooker ran out a hundred feet of cable and coiled it at his feet. He swung the cable and heavy-duty balloon over his head in an ever-widening arc and finally threw the cable almost halfway to the car.

Hooker laughed at where the cable end landed with the balloon. "Hah, two hundred twenty feet at the most." The deputy in retribution had pushed him into the bay water. Hooker swam through the sea of grass. It was like a frog walking the mud and pulling himself along with the grass. Suddenly, there was a canal of open water. He looked down the canal both ways.

"They call it a river in the grass." The deputy swam up alongside him. "There are some old-timers still paddling canoes through the rivers for shrimp and to fish for crabs. The rivers are where the fresh water doesn't mix with the salt-water of the bay, and it just cuts through. The grass lives on the salt and alkali, so where the freshwater is, the grass doesn't grow."

"Personal experience?"

"Third-generation crabber from Hayward."

"Make money at it?"

"Not a real living—not anymore. The Dungeness crab was once plentiful, but overharvest has killed off much of the population. We used to have a good-sized shrimp, but now it's just the smaller ghost shrimps and tiny ones like the flea shrimp. There is a growing population of the Mitten crab, but not enough beyond maybe just sport-crabbing. Plus, the restaurants have to want the crab to make it marketable to go after."

Hooker finally grabbed hold of the back bumper of the Cordoba. He tried to push and wiggle the wreck, but it didn't budge. "Looks like I'll need to get the shovel and release some of the mud suction. The mud cushioned the landing, but also stuck it too."

"What can I do?"

"Maybe see how bad it is on the downside. See if the tire is buried while I wrap the cable around the pumpkin and axle. I don't want to have to come back out here when I start pulling."

Hooker moved the tie on the blown-up water bottle. He figured about twenty feet of cable should make a complete figure-eight around the differential. He took a deep breath and closed his eyes. He knew he could open his eyes in saltwater. He just didn't like the idea of trying to see in the muddy water. He felt his way to the pumpkin and started feeding the cable end around and over the axles.

As he hooked the fast clips to secure the cable, he knew his time was up. He reached for the back of the gas tank and pulled his way to air. As he stood in the mud up to his knees, he pulled on the cable. The wrapped cable cinched and held. He was ready to pull.

"Hey, Fester... what did you find?" He pulled himself around to the side of the car.

The bear of an officer stood in water to his waist. His demeanor was a calm tension. His tanned face was now blanched white.

"What's wrong?"

"I don't think we can tow the car..."

Hooker frowned. "Because it's connected to a submerged train...?" The old trestle ran almost overhead, but Hooker knew smaller trains still ran across the flats once a day.

Fester bent down and felt in the water. As he rose, his hands were full of a blob somewhat in the shape of a basketball, but with long stringy hair. "No... I think we have a crime scene."

Hooker could see flesh was still attached to the skull. The ghost shrimp, leeches, worms, finger crabs, and spider crabs were still busy on the surface as well as in and out of the openings, which had once been eyes, nose, and mouth.

The man dropped the head. "The rest of the body is under the car—I felt her. The car cut the head off or just disturbed it. We need divers out here."

Hooker's detective mind took over from the shock of going from a tow to a crime scene. "How long do you think it's been underwater?"

The officer thought, but Hooker knew the third-generation crabber answered. "With all of these guys feeding—not more than maybe a few days... a week at the most."

Hooker thought and then pulled himself back under the car to unhook his cable. He wouldn't be towing this Prom Queen any time soon. The water recovery team wouldn't touch it until the sun was up.

As Hooker stood winding the cable back in, Fester explained the situation to Chet. They dried in the last of the sunshine and then just wiped the last of the goo off. Hooker called Dolly at Night Dispatch while Fester called the sheriff's office. They both knew dinner was going to be late.

5

WE HAVE ANOTHER BODY

Ace and Hooker sat on the back of his working bed. Ace drove a one-ton, so it was easier for them to get up on it. Chet and Fester stood as they all chewed on large Togo's sandwiches.

Hooker washed his mouthful down with some chocolate milk. "How did you hear about us out here?"

Ace smiled with his huge teeth. "I had a commercial up to Sacramento. I had just cleared the curves out of Pleasanton and had reception, so I grabbed the mic. Only, I grabbed the shop mic instead of the club. I called in, and Dolly knew what had happened. She asked me if I wanted to come over for Wednesday night dinner, and if so, I needed to run by Togo's tonight. I knew where the tracks run across because my great-uncle lived over there in Drawbridge. I used to fish those rushes for crab and shrimp when I was a kid." He pointed out where a team of six divers was searching the area for any other parts or clues."

"How much do I owe you?"

Ace wagged his head. "Did you know Dolly has a tab at Togo's?"

"No."

"Neither did I, but we know it now." He wiggled his eyebrows.

"That is the last tab I would want to mess with if you know what I mean." Hooker took another bite and chewed while he looked out across the grass.

The sun was down, and the gloom was setting in. The divers had water lights and would work through the night if need be. The Sheriff Tactical Support truck had shown up over an hour before and backed the mile up the road because the officer did not think he would find a place to turn around. They shifted vehicles around, and the support truck now had a rack of large field lights run up and would soon light up the area like a baseball diamond.

One of the divers surfaced, and a red balloon popped to the surface next to him. He was about twelve feet from the corner of the car. Fester hung his head. Hooker could tell he was swearing.

Ace leaned over. "What happened?"

Hooker pointed at the diver and the balloon. "The second balloon means they found another body. It just went from homicide to serial killer."

Ace looked at Hooker. "Isn't that where you take over?"

Hooker gave him a dirty look. *The truth was...*

Both of their attentions were distracted by the sound of another diver standing up. He was almost sixty feet from the car. There were two red balloons floating near him.

Chet turned around and looked at Hooker. There wasn't

going to be a recovery tow tonight—probably not even this week.

The diver in the support truck, who was taking a mandatory rest period, started pulling down the yellow nylon cord used to grid off a large crime scene. Hooker knew the ten-foot-long orange stakes would come out next. He was afraid to guess how big the grid would become. His night was done. All he needed was to have the original deputy release him.

Fester walked along the tow truck. His face was dark and angry. "Hooker, they have five bodies now. Your tow is now the center point of a crime scene. We'll send you a letter when we either finish here or retire."

Hooker's head ground around to face the bald deputy. "Sorry about the events. I know you don't get relief until the big boys get here."

Fester scowled and flipped his head toward the support truck. "There are bunks in there..."

"I'm headed back..." Hooker glanced at his watch in the stadium brightness. "At this hour, probably to Dispatch... You want me to let anyone know where you are?"

"Nah, we'll keep a lid on this until we know what's going on. Maybe we get lucky, and the killer tries to stash another body..."

"Makes sense." Hooker backhanded Ace's shoulder. "You off or on?"

"Off."

"Want to go get some ice cream and call the girls?"

The two laughed about the effect the French vanilla ice cream had on their voices. Dolly hated it and called it the bedroom voice. She knew it made her girls squirm and get distracted, which made Hooker do it even more.

When Hooker had started towing, his mentor, if he had one, was Ace. The man had taught him a lot about what to do and what not to do. But they both had the habit of driving with the window open and the heat on full blast—all winter long. It was Hooker who got Ace started on eating ice cream in the middle of the night. They both had a reputation for showing up at a crash while just finishing a large cone.

Of course—when they show up on a call, they are required to call in their position...

They had dumped Ace's truck back at the tow yard, and the two were having fun like old times. The tape deck Don had ordered in the new truck ran through the stereo with an extra speaker. Ace had brought one of his new mixed tapes, and it was filled with all the old songs and singers. The two drivers caterwauled about sixteen tons of coal as they finally cleared a locked car and made it to Thrifty's for some ice cream—just before midnight.

Ace grabbed the auto club mic and called them in. "1-4-1."

The new dispatcher, Stephan, answered. He learned the voices, and even with Ace using Hooker's numbers, he knew who was who. "Go ahead, 1-4-1, Hooker Ace... or is it the Ace Hooker?"

"10-4. Show us 10-98 on our T-6. Also, put us in the log for an El Dorado in under ten seconds. Note it as a fully enclosed window with a Slim-Jim down the glass."

"You two do know we don't keep records like—"

Ace laughed. "Please. And Andy only weighs in at one-twenty."

"Does Hooker confirm the time?"

Ace tossed the mic into the air as he laughed. They both

knew Andy would still be there and the last man out the door. Hooker snatched the mic out of the air.

"I confirm Andy is a slender three-hundred, and it was actually just over six seconds. My hand was on the handle as I watched the clock. Ace beats Mike's time by three seconds for any El Dorado newer than 1972. Also, show us 10-7 for a short coffee break."

"10-4, Hooker… and just for the record… has anyone tried to beat your record on opening a hotrod Plymouth?"

"Not enough nuns driving those around…"

"Good thing… and good night in 5-4-3-2…" The radio squawked a double click of his microphone key as he signed off the auto club. For the rest of the night, all the calls would go through Dolly's company—Night Dispatch.

Dina's voice from Night Dispatch tinkled through the cab. "Midnight, Night Dispatch." The baton had been passed. Hooker looked over at Ace. The two giant smiles were evil—like two little boys getting into trouble. It was time for ice cream.

Hooker reached down and picked up the little red dish as his left foot nudged the door open. The orange streak knifed between the seat and his calf. Box was looking for a patch of grass.

"Did you wash your truck in hot water and tumble dry on high heat?" The tall young woman stood in the open doorway. Holly was studying to be a nurse along with Hooker's girl-friend, Candy. Raised on a truck farm, she had a tight strength about her, but Hooker always thought she looked more like a surfer with her liquid movement and the slightly splayed legs and hips. They looked like she rode a surfboard— or horses. He had never thought what the rotation of the hips from bending over could do when you spend hours a day planting and then weeding.

Her hips were the only thing giving her body curves. The rest was as straight up and down as a water glass. But her quick undercutting humor was her best feature—in Hooker's opinion.

"Mae overheated, and now I'm trying to get this little pup raised up with all the cold air you're letting out."

"Just waiting for my boyfriend..."

Hooker frowned, and his head snapped around and looked at the huge toothy smile of Ace.

"Oh, in your dreams, tow boy. I only have love for a man who wears a fur coat on a hot day and never sweats."

Box walked past the two men. His tail was straight up and waving like a flag—except for the kink at the tip. Holly bent over and put her hand out with the palm down. Box sniffed and then let it pass from the top of the head, down the back, and loosely up the tail.

"Good evening Mister Box... Your reserved spot on the floor awaits you."

She stood with her hand out for the little red dish. Her smile was as large as Ace's, but the teeth were smaller. Hooker still found it warm and inviting. He was glad she and Candy were becoming fast friends. Their studies to be nurses had brought their two worlds together—Holly's large family working on a collective family farm, and Candy's scattered, anything but family foster homes, and worse—the two had grown to understand a larger universe through understanding each other.

Hooker followed the parade of Box and Holly. Ace brought up the rear. "Where's Randy?"

Holly waved her head toward the back. "Trying to figure out the day shift's inventory sheets." She placed Box's dish in the same spot she did any night they showed up.

She stood and watched Hooker as she scooped triples of French vanilla into sugar cones. There were certain things you could always rely on—the sun rising in the east, pumpkins harvest after corn, and a triple French vanilla in a sugar cone. As long as she had known Hooker and Ace, their order never changed. If it ever did, she or anyone who works the night shift would know right away that something was wrong, and the world was coming to an end.

"Sorry about your truck. I know you loved her. But how are you and John doing?"

Hooker took his cone and put the dollar bill on the counter. "Thanks, maybe someday she will live again... but for now..." He looked out the window at the seemingly tiny truck, which was a beast by most standards.

"And John?"

"Oh, he's on the final parts of the academy."

She frowned. "I thought he graduated last month?"

"He did... but he's doing some extra work most only come back to. He wants it all out of the way before he makes his choice."

Ace took his cone and left his bill. "Is he still leaning toward the PD over the highway?"

"It looks that way. Manny has him figuring out all sorts of stuff, so I don't know if he's interested in ballistics, forensics, or he's just going to ask straight up for a gold badge."

Holly cocked her head as she closed the ice cream case and took up the two dollars. "Gold badge?"

"Detective's badge—something you might get after many years of fieldwork…"

Holly chuckled, "But because he hangs out with you…"

"Hey, he's worth more than a couple of plugged nickels…"

Ace snorted. "Yeah, not a bad tow bunny for such a two-bit kid."

Holly stiffened. "He may be only a little more than a pair of dimes, but he is a stand-up guy and a gentleman when someone throws up in his boots." She turned red under her jaw, but Hooker was proud to see she was becoming less embarrassed by her slip when she saw the fresh scars laced across the kid's body.

"Holly?" The voice came from the rear of the store.

"Yeah, Randy?"

"Is Hooker there?"

"He's just leaving…"

"Tell him he has a roll-over northbound 101, just north of Story. Tell him Dolly said he isn't supposed to even touch the mic until all of the ice cream is out of his mouth."

"10-4, Randy." He stooped to fish up the red bowl. Hooker and Ace pushed through the door. "Next time, Holly."

"Good to see you too, Ace—stop in more often."

Hooker looked at Ace as they got in the truck. "Doesn't she know you're on days now?"

"Guess I might have to start making some late-night ice cream breaks."

Hooker looked over with an evil smile. He handed Ace the mic. "Dolly only said I'm not supposed to call in…"

Ace controlled his laughter and breathing. He rumbled

up his deeper voice and keyed the mic. "1-4-1, 10-8 for 101 rollover."

They only got a stutter of mic keys in answer. It sounded like both women on the board had keyed over each other. Both men knew there would be some hell to pay on Wednesday night after dinner—but some things were worth it.

6

WEDNESDAY DINNER

Candy rolled over to find a warm bed and pillow, but no Hooker. She listened, and then the shower started. She didn't need to be up for a while yet, but a shower that starts with sitting on a wooden stool either scrubbing Hooker's back or him scrubbing hers sounded like a reason to get up. She padded into the bathroom to find Hooker standing naked—waiting for the water to get hot.

She bent to get a closer look. "I think before you get in the shower, you might want me to get those leeches off your back."

He turned and then looked in the mirror. Four large engorged leeches were attached to the area he couldn't feel—right where the bra hooks would be—if he wore one.

"And I took at least two dozen off last night..."

Candy took the rubbing alcohol out of the cabinet. "I guess I better check you all over..."

AS HOOKER STROLLED into the kitchen, he was smiling.

Stella gave him a side hug as she was scrambling the eggs. "Looks like a good long shower this morning did you some good."

Manny looked up to see Candy coming out of his bedroom, buttoning the last couple of buttons. Manny laughed. "Looks like your shower theory just got blown out into the back forty."

"Hush your mouth, and clean up your mind." She turned and folded Candy's head into her large chest. "This is my favorite daughter you are talking about."

Hooker wasn't sure who was doing the laughing to cause both of them to jiggle. He turned and ignored them all and poured two mugs of coffee. A hand reached over his shoulder and took one of the mugs. "Candy might want a mug also." Hooker glanced back. He hadn't even heard the Squirt walk in.

Hooker poured another mug and turned to give it to Candy. As he leaned back against the counter, he took in the white sidewall haircut and the slick-sleeve blue uniform with no designations. "Boy, they are still putting you in the yoke? At least towing, I allow a white T-shirt."

Stella rolled her head over and gave Hooker a stern look. "A white T-shirt *is* your uniform."

Hooker laughed. It was true. "At least I am lax about whether he uses starch or not."

Stella laughed. "You think I have your shirts marked. You both wear the same large shirt. I throw a dozen into the wash and iron a dozen with light starch. Six go in his closet, and six go in your closet. The same goes for your pants—you two are a matched set, right down to your socks and under-wear. Only thing changed is now he has a real uniform, which just makes me feel young again. I get to pretend I'm ironing Manny's uniform when he was just back from Korea."

She scraped the eggs out of the pan into the large orange Fiestaware serving bowl. She nodded at the bowl and at the table. Candy pulled the last of the four pieces of toast out of the new commercial-sized toaster, and they all gathered around the table and sat. Other than silverware on Fiestaware, the room was silent. Manny and Stella were in heaven—breakfast with all of their children at the table at one time. Everyone healthy, happy, and...

The phone in the office rang.

A second later, it was echoed in the sunroom.

Hooker rose and headed for the office. Stella laid her fork down. The phone ringing in the morning was never a good sign. She sipped her coffee as she eyed the Squirt. The tempo of his fork had increased in speed and the size of the bite.

"You do know you're going to school today and not out to play with Hooker?"

The Squirt hesitated for only a half-second and then continued.

Candy gently put her mug of coffee down. "John?"

Her brother looked up.

"Our mother is talking to you."

He shoveled the last bite into his mouth, and while he was chewing, he stood, took up his plate, kissed Stella on top of her head, and put the plate in the sink. As he passed the table, he grabbed his coffee mug. As he walked toward the office, he sang out, "Manny, could you please explain the nuances of forensic investigation." The office door closed quietly behind him.

Hooker was just hanging up the phone and turned to face the Squirt. His face was deadpan.

The Squirt sat and sipped on his coffee. Neither one was going to blink. The first to open their mouth was the loser.

Finally, the Squirt lowered his mug. "Seven hundred forty-two million, fifty-one, and twenty-three."

Hooker knew it was a puzzle he should know how to answer. He knew it had nothing to do with anything other than the two of them. It was a Squirt-Hooker puzzle. "Fifty-one is how much change we share."

"The turns of Mae West's tires we have shared... The amount of change that almost killed us... and how many times we have stopped for French vanilla ice cream in a sugar cone." He didn't have to say anything about the four tiny white scars on the back of his left hand. They had started everything— Hooker burying his fork through the Squirt's hand. They had shared a lot. More than most friends share in a lifetime.

"How did you figure the revolutions?" He knew if the Squirt said it was true, it was true. Hooker didn't question the figure. He was only curious about the math and how the kid got there.

"Miles divided by the circumference of the thirty-six-inch tire. Give or take about one or two miles."

"I don't keep a log."

The Squirt tapped his head. Hooker smirked. He knew if the kid had seen it, it was forever in his memory bank and ready for quick, if not instant, recall.

The kid looked at the phone and then back at Hooker.

Hooker had stalled long enough. "It's not a call out. It was just an update. You rushed through your breakfast for nothing." Hooker stood. "Now I'm going in and finishing my breakfast and enjoying my family." He opened the door.

As he walked through, the Squirt rose and muttered, "Good luck with that."

Hooker's eyes went to Manny. The man had his elbows on the table and the coffee mug to his lips. He was working hard at ignoring anything near his office door.

Hooker started silently counting down from sixty. The two men returned to the table and sat. As Hooker silently hit three, Manny cleared his throat. Stella put her fork down next to the last three bites.

Hooker glared at Manny. "Jeez in the breeze... you couldn't let her finish this one time?"

"Is she going to get upset?"

"No."

"Are you going to share about the phone call from Dispatch?"

"No, it was just an update. They still don't know where Willie is." He looked over at Stella. "You can finish eating. I'm just worried."

Stella looked up at the large grandfather clock. It was nine-seventeen. She knew she had just been lied to, and she wanted Hooker to know she knew and was remembering the time.

Hooker slumped back into his chair. Candy watched the battle that only these two could play. The Squirt sensed a shift and rose to get the coffee carafe—breakfast just got longer.

Hooker slid down in his chair—defeated. "Karen also gave me this morning's body count."

Manny sat up, and the Squirt froze halfway through filling Stella's mug. "Body count for what?"

Hooker turned as Stella slowly put her fork down. There was one bite left on her plate. He turned to Manny. "Are you familiar with the old ghost town out in the seagrass off Milpitas and Fremont?"

"Where the old train trestle crosses and heads over to Newark? Sure, there was a shooting out there in 1958. The guy killed three people and then wounded four officers before they got him. What about the place?"

"There's a body dump just east of the trestle, just north of the bird sanctuary."

Manny's first urge was to ask how many bodies, but he could feel the anger radiating from the other end of the table. He sipped on his mug. "And why are they calling you?"

"I have an El Dorado nosed into the grass and mud about seventy-eight yards into the grass. It's the hub of the search."

Candy snorted, "And where those leeches came from..."

"You had leeches?" Stella started to rise.

Hooker waved her down. "They went down the toilet. The nurse gave me a clean bill of health."

Manny laughed. "Very clean."

Stella growled. "Manny P. Romero, you now owe the naughty thought jar a full buck."

"Why a full buck?"

"To cover me telling Stella later." She turned. "You too, Hooker—you are up to a buck, also."

They all laughed as the Squirt fished out a dollar, and Candy threw out two dollar bills. The goodness of the morning was restored... right up until the Squirt tripped getting up and spilled coffee all down the front of his uniform.

He never even yelped. But he did fish into his pocket and added another dollar to the pile.

A few minutes later, he returned wearing his other uniform. As he threw the leather jacket over his shoulder, he looked at Hooker. "My other uniforms are in the wash. Karen can call the academy and let them know."

Hooker sighed and stood. He kissed Stella on the head and walked around the table to Candy's head. She remained deadpan as he kissed her neck. Fishing for a laugh, he placed his hand on top of Manny's head and then kissed the back of his hand. There was only a small chuckle from Stella. Hooker knew Candy had seen right through his talk about the body dump.

"Box, go time."

The two men and cat walked out the large hand-hewn door. The sunlight in the courtyard already had the heat up over a hundred—it wasn't even noon yet. The peak would hit about five. The summer heat of San Jose was fierce and unrelenting, even though Hooker's leather jacket was already in the truck.

Hooker drifted the truck down off the Hill of Stupid. The five-ton truck was a third the size of Mae West, but stock, it was a pig to drive. It made Mae's eleven tons and twenty-eight feet handle like a sports car in the curves. He and Uncle Willie had worked to make the giant truck the most nimble as well as the fastest in the five counties of the Bay Area. Hooker knew there would never be another truck like her. The other big diesel rig tow trucks made the five-ton look like a Chevy Nova—not great,or easy to drive.

The Squirt cleared his throat. Hooker had been waiting for it.

"Twenty-seven and thirty."

The kid watched the fake English Tudor manors slip by as they rolled down a street with a Spanish name. His mind was not even registering the houses. "Bodies and feet or yards?"

"Yards—they were just starting the next ring this morning at daybreak."

"And we are headed...?"

"Coroner's office. They found something on one of the bodies."

"What?"

"Her driver's license."

The kid leaned his head back. "Tracking down Willie, my ass."

Hooker's head snapped. "You owe—"

"I paid ahead." They both laughed at the idea of paying in the morning and having free rein in the afternoon when you need it.

Later, as they drove down Stevens Creek, the Squirt looked longingly out the window. "We need a better tape deck in here. Tex Ritter sounds like Roy Orbison."

Hooker laughed. "Ass... it is Roy."

7

WHO IS JOYCE JACOBSON?

"Jesus, Hooker." The man in the white smock pulled him over against the wall. The man held his head down, and his voice barely more than a harsh whisper. "What the hell are you doing bringing *that* kid here? Do you even know who he is?"

Hooker looked at the assistant coroner. The frazzled mess almost vibrated. His long hair hung stringy and greasy like he hadn't showered in days. As Hooker got a good whiff of the guy, he changed his estimate to at least a week. "He's my brother. Who do *you* think he is?"

"He's been burning up the academy and pushing..." The guy's eyes popped wide. He looked at the Squirt and then back at Hooker. "Your brother...?"

"Well, sort of. His sister is my girlfriend, and our parents are... Well, it's complicated. What did you want to show me? And don't worry about the Squirt. He is mine, and nobody else's unless we agree."

"But he's—"

"Going to be a cop... Right now, he is my partner. What I

learn—he learns. It's how we solve problems. My mind works one way and his works... Well, different. Forget what you've heard and just tell us what you've got."

"If he knows every—"

"Quinton, you're talking eight years ago. The kid was eleven and didn't even live here then. There is no reason—yet —that he would know about the dope in your trunk, the meth in the glove box, or the six grams—"

"Okay, okay... In here." He led them through a back hallway to the examining room. The room's temperature hovered in the fifties. But even the chill did nothing to mask the smell in the room, and what it was used for by the second day it was running—thirty years before. One of the old cops explained the facts about morgues to Hooker—they never stop using old morgues. They just burn them to the ground and move on. Standing in the room, Hooker could believe the truth in the joke.

The Squirt leaned in close to Hooker. "Why is he so squirrely?"

Hooker silently harrumphed as they watched the man open one of the refrigerator doors and pull out the cadaver tray. "Meth, cocaine, dope, too much coffee, and he recognized you from the academy."

The Squirt looked at Hooker with a face of horror. "There is such a thing as too much coffee? Say it's not so."

Hooker remained deadpan as they stepped over to the body. Quinton drew back the sheet. "We haven't done an autopsy yet for a good reason—as you can see, there are no GSWs, ligature marks, lacerations, or punctures. By the swelling and deformation, we estimate the body to have been in the water since either Saturday or Sunday." He smiled and stepped back and stood silently.

Hooker's mind raced. A lot of information there—for having not done an autopsy yet, but also, what wasn't being said. He looked at the Squirt. The kid stood with one eyebrow raised watching Hooker.

"You've already figured this one out, haven't you?" The kid nodded slightly. "And you're just going to stand there and watch me screw it up."

"What is the obvious question?"

"What's the cause of death...?" Hooker frowned as the kid just kept moving his head back and forth.

"He told you what wasn't there... but he also gave you some hard facts."

There wasn't much the assistant coroner had said... Hooker's eyes opened wide as he snapped his fingers. "Saturday or Sunday... and we pulled her out yesterday... so how do you know?"

Quinton pointed at Hooker and smiled. He turned to the Squirt, "Care to tell him? While I push her back in and turn on the fans..."

The Squirt smiled. "Take a last smell."

Hooker frowned. "It smells like Stella baking for Christmas."

"Chanukah, but same season... what is she making?"

Hooker tried to remember the few baked goods Stella made to give away. Sweets in the house stopped at small amounts of tidbits, and the orange sherbet because of Manny's diabetes. One of the few cookies she made and also allowed Manny to eat—the cookie with a nut in the middle of the top. "Almonds." And as he said it, he realized how strong the odor was.

The Squirt grabbed at his sleeve as he guided them away from the area. "And...?"

"Cyanide... cyanide poisoning."

Quinton smiled. "Exactly, but with the body being in water, there was no telltale white foam about the mouth. So when the examiner started to perform the gross exam, he became overcome by the cyanide off-gassing and collapsed. Lucky for him, I came in when I did and found him on the floor."

"He died from breathing in the cyanide gas from the body?"

"He didn't die... but yes. There are high levels of cyanide in the body. He will, however, be at Valley Medical for a couple of days in an oxygen tent until his system is flushed."

"So let's go back to how you figured out when she died."

"Oh, time of death is still undetermined. But we do know she was in the water more than a day and less than three."

Hooker looked at the Squirt with a frown.

The kid smiled softly. "Because of the Fiddle crab. There are no marks from her being chewed on. The cyanide was still toxic, so she was oozing poison and killing the crabs who wanted everything off her bones. In the saltwater, the cyanide is toxic for about seventy-two hours. But the saltwater also causes other abuses to the flesh, so they knew she had been in for at least a day, but the crabs hadn't started in on her—so it was less than three."

"So, boy genius, what is your best guess at the time of death?"

"I want to know what they found in her clothing first."

The examiner smiled. "Now I see why you are striking fear into the black hearts of the academy. This line of question is exactly the right idea." He turned to a file cabinet and opened the middle drawer. He took out a box and opened it on the desk. Reaching in, he withdrew a plastic bag with a driver's license in it. "We found this stuffed in her panties, under her pantyhose."

The Squirt snapped his fingers. "TOD was late Friday night."

Hooker lowered one eyelid. "How did you figure...?"

"After further examination and investigation, they will find she worked the downtown area of San Jose as a streetwalker. My guess would be her stock-in-trade was the blowjob. So they need to start asking around near Stevens Creek and First, and then circle out."

Quinton leaned back against the wall. There was a short smile on his face. "Yes, they figured she was turning tricks—but how would you know the rest?"

"Her ID was in her panties. If she turned regular tricks, she would have a purse, and the ID would have been in it. But she didn't have or need a purse. She had a great hot body, but you saw her face... it was a train wreck looking for a place to happen. So the john gets to look at her great body and behind while he gets sucked off—and never has to look at the face."

"But how do you come up with Friday, and why late?"

"If she died Thursday, she would have had the crabs start working the body over. With early Friday, it might have attracted attention... but late..."

Quinton chuckled. "The crabs don't work on the weekends?"

Hooker snorted and mock punched at the kid. The Squirt

knew it was also Hooker's way of showing he was proud of him. *They had come so far together.*

"The fiddler crab is very sensitive to toxins. They would wait for the cyanide to leach out into the saltwater before they would go near her. The mud worms, on the other hand, went straight to work and died. I noticed tiny bite holes on her underside, but they had not lived long enough to get around to the top."

The Squirt turned to Hooker. "The killer buried her under the water so she could, in theory, see up through the water. He didn't dig in the mud and then just throw her in. She was on top of the mud, under the grass..." He nodded for Hooker to continue.

Hooker would have expected the same from Manny, but from the kid, he was caught off-foot. "Could see the sky... umm..." He searched his memory for all the lessons learned from Manny and Willie... and then he remembered his first conversation with Dolly. He had to drop off some paperwork. He didn't expect a woman three times his size and a couple of inches shorter. Her muumuu and bare feet caught him off-guard. Her voice over the radio sounded like warm honey, but standing with her nose two inches from his, he could taste the razor-sharp teeth in the honey.

In his youthful way, he became bored waiting for her to finish talking to someone on the phone. She kept calling them *hon* and *sweetheart* as he snuck glances at the size of the woman. He wasn't sure he wanted to even know who she was talking to. As kids will do, his fingers danced along the edge of her oversized desk. And then he actually wrapped his hand around the handle end of the large limb on her desk. Carved into the limb were the words 'The

Stick.' It was the stick Dolly—and only Dolly—used to stir shit up.

He never heard her say good-bye. She simply hung up and then appeared in front of him. She never huffed or puffed. Her voice didn't raise. In fact, it lowered—somewhere down into the bowels of the earth.

Quietly, she explained about respect and honoring other's property. He never touched the stick again.

"He respected her, or at least, had empathy for her. He didn't bury her. He laid her to rest in a spot where he could show he respected her. Where she could watch the sky."

Quinton frowned—the side of his mouth curled up in a snarl. "She was dead. How was she supposed to watch anything? Especially under the muddy water?"

The Squirt sighed. "Brackish... not muddy."

"What?"

The Squirt turned from watching Hooker. He looked at the assistant coroner, who was only maybe a year or two older than Hooker. "You said muddy water... the water in the south bay is brackish saltwater. For the most part, it will be hazy to clear."

"But we cleaned a lot of mud off her, and there was muddy water in her mouth and upper throat—"

Hooker held up his hand to hold off the Squirt. "John is right. The water was clear... until I put my foot into the mud. By the third step, it's all just muddy water as the mud floated in the disturbance I had created. Some of the other remains probably won't show as much mud since the guys were floating as they looked and worked the grid."

"Oh." The hand stroked the stubble just above the white smock. He looked up. "What kind of mud?"

The Squirt stepped in. "It's called float mud because of its tendency to float. The sediment is so vegetation dense that it should be called grass clippings or something. But it captures the fine silt, which will stir up with the least movement of the water. Once it is trapped by the vegetation fibers, the color is the mud, but it all floats like the grass clippings. The reality is it never packs down because most of what we see as two feet deep of mud is only about four inches' worth if you took a core sample and dried it out. But what you would find is about six-inches of worms, beetles, sea mites, slugs, leeches, and other hen ways."

The examiner furrowed his brow. "What's a hen way?"

Hooker laughed as he slapped the Squirt's chest. They needed to go. As they walked out, Hooker called back, "About two or three pounds." The large doors swung shut on the young examiner's swearing.

In the truck, Hooker looked out at the large parking lot. He sat quietly thinking.

The Squirt clicked his seat belt. "What...?"

Hooker turned the key. "Did you get the name and address?"

The Squirt pulled his hand out of his pocket and held up the driver's license.

Hooker took it and looked at the photo. "We need a good photo, man."

"There's a guy at the academy, but then, I'd have to say where the ID came from."

They sat at the light. The heat of the day allowed for no breeze. The fan in the truck was going full blast but barely pushing cooled air. Hooker looked at Box, who was draped upside-down in the box, trying to get rid of his body heat through the moving air over his tummy.

"My next truck is going to have real air-conditioning."

The Squirt snorted. "Heavy-duty enough to run with both windows still open?"

Hooker laughed because it was so true about him. "Of course."

The Squirt pointed at the white airplane a few thousand feet above them. There was a large dish floating above the fuselage. Everyone in the South Bay knew what an Orion P-3 Sub Chaser looked like. It was headed for a landing at Moffett Field Naval Air Base.

"You could be up there—the temperature, while they are on station, is about minus twenty degrees. They turn on the heaters once they clear land and don't turn them off until they land."

Hooker watched the white plane with the red tail as it crawled along the sky. They were pointed in the same direction. The light changed, and he turned right on the parkway. He pulled the auto club mic from its clip. "1-4-1."

The new voice of the club radio came back. Hooker knew it sounded like an eight-year-old girl, but he was willing to bet lunch at Togo's that she was over thirty and at least a hundred pounds larger than her voice sounded like. "1-4-1, go ahead..."

The tiny woman released the wiggle key. Her feet didn't reach the floor, and she had just celebrated her twentieth birthday. Hooker would have lost on all accounts but would still buy her lunch.

"Show me on a commercial T-5. Can't start at Moffitt Field."

"Can the toy truck you're in jump-start one of those sub hawks?"

"One engine at a time, Jenny. One engine at a time." He hung the mic and smiled at the Squirt. "She sounds like something you might date."

"I'll stick with Beth right now, thank you."

THE TINY WOMAN spun sideways on her swivel chair. Her arms were outstretched to grab the armrests. She looked at Jake—the old hand at the club.

He noticed the change out of the side of his eye. His head snapped over to confirm the change and then snapped back to scanning the three calls in front of him they were currently working. Nothing was running the clock—he could talk.

He turned back. "What's the question?"

"What does Hooker look like?"

He laughed. Few club dispatchers ever meet the drivers and the other way around. "How do you picture him?"

She thought a moment. "How I imagine him and what he looks like is probably the same difference of what he thinks I look like, and me."

Jake thought as he acknowledged the voice on the radio calling to say he was 10-97 or finished with his call. "10-4, 1-7-1, board is clear at this time."

The radio squawked. "10-4, dispatch. Show me 10-7 for lunch at Chiaramontes."

Jake wiggled the double key to give two clicks on the radio. The one-second delay from broadcast to receive and back into the dispatch gave a static echo to the two clicks of his key. He turned back to the young woman.

"You've handed off the radios to Dolly—try her."

"Voice alone... she sounds about average height, say about five-foot-six, but she has some husky power there, so I'd say about one-sixty or one-eighty."

"How old?"

"Forties, but then, her voice has some edge... so I'm going to hedge at young fifties. Have you met her?"

He nodded. "Night Dispatch, for years, has thrown an open house from about eleven-thirty until about two in the morning, on New Year's Eve. If you wait for midnight, there isn't a parking spot within two blocks of the building. I've seen cop cars and tow trucks from as far south as Salinas and north of San Francisco. One year, I met one of the senators there. Everyone here is invited, but few make an effort."

"So was I close?"

"Not even... you're off about three-hundred pounds, and I think she's in her sixties. She's taller than I am, and I'm five-eight with shoes. She's always barefooted." He looked at the dwarf next to him, and how she sat in the chair. "You could use her custom chair as a bed."

"Whoa." The word was barely stronger than an exhale. Her eyes were wide. She knew exactly where she wanted to be on New Year's Eve.

"So try Hooker..."

"Kind of a mix of Mickey Dolenz and Michael Nesmith—tall, but has some thick muscle to him. He has a certain... um... seriousness about him, but also, he has a fun laugh in his voice." She looked over at the frown on Jake's face as he sat back, staring at the run sheets. "What?"

His face cleared, and he looked over. "Nothing... I just never thought about Hooker and his voice. For the playful side, throw in Davy Jones, but only part of Peter... Hooker is no goofball. The guy is one of the smartest drivers out there. And if you ever meet his partner—the human one—the Squirt, hang onto your hat. The guy is a walking landmine of knowledge."

"Landmine?"

"Poke his mind, and the eleventh-grade science department will blow up, and you get the whole years' worth in ten minutes. It's freaky."

"So if he's the human one...?"

"Biggest orange cat you've seen who wasn't a lion or tiger. Actually, I'm not sure he doesn't have some tiger in him. Rumor had it a few months ago, he attacked a hundred pound Kai dog, and in less than two seconds, the throat of the wild dog was missing."

The radio squawked. Jenny and Jake listened. Jenny took the call and pulled the slip of paper, passed it through the time stamp, and spun it into the done box.

8

MOFFETT FIELD PHOTOGRAPHERS

The gate at Moffett Field was the usual small white building with glass all the way around. Hooker always wondered if there was a short toilet in the back somewhere—just in case. But with two people running the gate, he figured they just ran somewhere or used the small shrubs along the fence line.

The khaki dressed guard stepped out of the booth. Hooker squinted as they rolled up. The man looked familiar, somehow.

Hooker was expecting to be asked about his business, but instead, his truck fell under immediate exam. Both guards began to look the truck over. The second had brought out a measuring tape and started checking the height of the tires. He shook his head at the first guard.

Finally, the man looked up at Hooker. The blackout wrap-around glasses showed no sign of the eyes, only reflections of Hooker in the window.

"Did you wash this truck, sir?"

Hooker frowned. "Hmm... yes... Of course. It gets dirty every day. I like a clean truck."

"Did you wash the truck with extremely hot water, sir?"

"No. I used the hose... What's this about... um... Sergeant?"

The Marine continued. "Have you recently put this truck on a diet, sir?"

"Diet?"

"Can you explain the unusually small size of the tires, sir?"

"They are standard for a truck this size..."

"Yes, about that, sir... can you explain why the paint job is not the regulation nature with a hot woman draped along the door? Or did she take off when you blew the other half off the truck?"

Hooker squinted at the man as the guard removed his dark glasses, and the smile swept across his face. Hooker was fairly sure who the man was. He turned back into the truck. "How much did we throw into the swear jar this morning?"

The kid began to laugh. "More than enough..."

Hooker's head ground back around. "Screw you, Marine. You have been twisting your fucking hat on too tight." He smiled broadly and was mirrored by the marine.

"You've been hanging out with my brother-in-law and Willie Knight way too much." He stuck his hand up. "I heard about you blowing your girlfriend up. Sorry about your loss."

Hooker bit on his lip. "We saved many lives that day." He didn't mention the two who had died.

"I take it you're here to see the captain?"

"Actually, I need help with some photography."

"Best to see the captain first..." He glanced at his watch.

"Chow call is in about twenty minutes. He can introduce you to Snaps over some good old Navy chow." He pointed at the low white building at the north end of the base offices.

Hooker saluted with a Cub Scout two-finger and let the clutch slip as he edged off. He parked at the far end of the building, and they walked back up toward the entrance.

"The guy is..."

"Sue's brother. Micha is his brother-in-law. I met him a few years back when he was out for their tenth of July barbecue. I think he had just gotten out of boot camp or something. He was a lot thinner then."

"Tenth? You mean the fourth?"

"Nope—we all work on the drunk days. The tenth is their anniversary."

They entered the cool building. No matter how tight budgets got, the government always had solid air conditioning.

The yeoman at the desk looked up and smiled. "You look just like a guy we blew up last summer." He stood and stuck out his hand. "Sorry about killing your sister."

Hooker smiled. He figured the whole Navy base had been in on the performance. "She's in a far better place now."

"It still sucks about her friend."

"I think he did what he planned to do all along. It wasn't like he was ready to settle down in the suburbs with a car, wife, and the two point five kids, including the dog."

"Do I see a dead body walking?" The voice boomed down the hallway. The khakis had crisp knife-edge creases, and the man walked with a smile.

Hooker turned. "Hello, Captain."

"Hooker, how are you?"

"Alive and well, John. John, I'd like you to meet my Squirt. John, this is John—also known on base as Captain Jacobs. He's the one who worked hard to kill me while I was killing Sissy, and you were chasing nurses."

The Squirt stuck his hand out. "Just call me Squirt, it's easier. And don't pay attention to the man. He hasn't been the same since he died... again."

"Great to finally meet the famous two-bit Squirt. How are the classes at the academy going?"

"Done and almost done. I'm staying on for the extra credit in forensics. I figure it will help when I interview."

"You're planning on skipping patrol and just jump right to detective?" The man laughed until he noticed the Squirt wasn't. He sobered. "You're serious."

Hooker notched up his one eyebrow. "We told you he was special, John." Then thinking, he smiled. "How many bills do you have in your front pocket?"

The man frowned. "A few." his hand dipped into his right front pocket and fished out three ones, a five and two tens.

Hooker nodded to hand them to the Squirt. "Now, your driver's license, a military ID, and maybe a credit card." Hooker looked at the Squirt, who nodded as he looked over the last bill and folded them and exchanged them for the man's wallet. He opened the leather, and his eyes scanned over the information on the two forms of identification. He pulled out the three credit cards and the base PX card. He glanced at both sides and returned them to the wallet. Folding the wallet, he held it out.

The captain smiled as he took it back. "We had a profes-sional magic guy here who memorized three or four bills... so this will be amazing if you do as much."

Hooker ignored the Squirt. "Did we catch you before your lunch?"

"Was just going to go roust Alex and head over to Capri's for lunch. They have a great chef's salad we both like."

"Can we talk a moment before we go?"

"Sure. What do you need?"

The Squirt held out the driver's license. "About twenty eight-by-tens of just the photo."

He looked at the ID. "Is she missing?"

"No... dead."

The captain held Hooker's eyes for a few heartbeats. Without looking away, he held out the card. "Yeoman, we need headshot only, standard print. Tell Snaps I need one-hundred prints right after lunch."

"Color or black and white, sir?"

Hooker swung his head around to the yeoman, who was already turning to walk away. "Black and whites are just fine, thanks." The yeoman was already through the back door and gone.

Captain Jacobs bit his lip. "Let's go get Alex."

As they waited for their food, the Squirt made a fast pass at Captain Alex Romanoff's wallet as well. The two captains were smiling. They were keen to see how well the Squirt did. Everyone loves a show.

Lunch was bright and lively as the two captains enjoyed telling the Squirt about setting the stage to blow up the world and help Hooker kill his sister. The Squirt kept sneaking glances at Hooker. He could tell Hooker liked hearing how it had been set up, but he also knew there was still some leftover trauma from the fatal night.

He looked at the ribbons on John's blouse. "You were a SEAL?"

The captain nodded. "It's where I know Bill Knight from —he was my commander."

Hooker chuckled at the Squirt's frown of confusion. "Uncle Willie."

The Squirt's face cleared, and then he dug back in. "Did you ever lose anyone?"

The man held up three fingers.

The Squirt nodded. "You don't talk about them." The man slowly shook his head, and his eyes lowered. "Yeah, sorry... but you see, the night... Hooker was there to save two people. No matter what the man named Dog had in mind, Hooker's mission was clear... and he lost a man."

The point hung in the air.

"Okay, who had the grilled cheese sandwich, and who had the barbecued beef?" The two salads dropped where they always did on a Wednesday, and the other two were sorted. "Anything else?"

The Squirt cleared his throat. "Could I see your order book a moment?"

"This?" The woman screwed up her face. The Squirt took it and looked at the back, and then peeked at the inside of the back.

Handing it back, he winked. "Thanks. How many dollar tips have you gotten today?"

She reached in her apron and took out four. He took them, looked at each, and returned them. "Thanks."

She smiled, but she wasn't sure what had just happened.

As the Squirt picked up his fork, he turned to Alex. "Did you opt for a Corvette or a Camaro?"

Alex laughed. "Neither. I already had a Nova with a 327, which was blown and polished. I wasn't interested in a slow car." He pointed at the other uniform.

The Squirt laughed. "No, John is too easy. He didn't do Annapolis. He was up through the ranks, so he has a low-end Hemi—probably a 340 in a Dart."

"You pegged me for a Chevy and nailed him with a slow car?"

The Squirt looked at Jacobs, who was very busy eating his salad. The Squirt reevaluated. "Actually, I think I have to go with no flash, so it would be a Belvedere, but it has a 383 Willie reworked for you."

The man laughed as he wiped his mouth. "Close... it's a 340 made into a 390. I would have gone for the 440s, but it would have made the engine a little too... um, weak—easier to break."

Hooker smiled. "I remember the discussion with Willie and Maddie. She took it out to Stockton when they were finished with it."

Jacobs smiled. "I was there. She brought home some good money from Stockton. First, she won the bracket, then there was some kind of open run, and then, finally, she staged against a rail job and still won."

Hooker nodded. "The open was a challenge from one of the guys she eliminated earlier, but they were friends. He just didn't want to pack it in for the day. The rail job was a not so friendly grudge match, which had been brewing for a few months. She would have preferred to run the race on a motorcycle, but Willie had taken it down to LA and sold it to some undercover cop friend of his to use as a fast chopper."

The rest of lunch danced quickly through gears, tires, and

gasoline. There was no more talk of blowing things up or killing people. Hooker watched the Squirt—the kid was still over a year away from buying a legal drink, but he had developed into an adroit guide of conversation and people.

The waitress brought the check. She held it to her chest. "So, what was the business about looking at my ticket book?"

The Squirt smiled and nodded that it was time. "Gentlemen, time to get your wallets out." He started with Captain Jacobs.

"Wait, that's not one of the numbers," the man protested.

"Look between the PX card and MasterCard. There is a county library card."

John looked. "Not the number either..."

"No... the library card number is seven-three-zero-two-five-eight. The number I told you before is the phone number for Sally on the back of the library card."

The man looked and turned red. "Oh, so that's where I wrote it down. No joy now—it was a year ago."

The Squirt smiled and turned toward Alex. First came his ID card information and then the PX and credit cards. The Squirt smiled and then continued through the man's insurance card, two business cards, and the name and address on a receipt, as well as what the man bought and how much. Turning, he started with the information on the back of the waitress's book, then stopped. "Let's leave the man's name and phone number out of it. But the other numbers are interesting."

The waitress roared with laughter. "It's my new son-in-law, and those are the measurements I needed to rent the tuxedo he's wearing for my son's wedding next week."

The Squirt chuckled and then recited another phone number.

"It's our phone number here..." She looked at her ticket book.

"It's on the back of the menu." Hooker laughed.

The Squirt smiled and pointed a finger at Hooker and rattled off a medium number, and then a long number.

Hooker's eyes got big. "The first is my driver's license, but the second...." His mouth dropped open. "Bells in the wind... Mae's VIN number?"

"How do you...?" Alex was astounded.

Hooker snorted. "Pay the bill, and he'll tell you."

The captain reached out. "Oh, no. This was too enjoyable. I've got this lunch."

Thirty minutes later, Hooker swung the five-ton up onto the freeway. The Squirt was looking at the enlarged photo. "This guy did really great work. He cleaned it up too. She almost looks happy."

Hooker looked over. "Maybe it was just one of those days..."

The Squirt looked out the window. The large photo hung in his hand. "Yeah... the kind everyone should get... more than they do."

9

WORKING THE STREET

"Where do you think we should start?"

"Let's start by returning the driver's license and handing over most of the prints. I don't know about you, but my math says there are only three of us in this truck."

The Squirt started laughing.

"What?"

The kid leaned over and held one of the photos up for Box to look at... the cat rolled over and went back to sleep. The Squirt sat up. "He wasn't impressed and doesn't want to ask around."

Hooker snorted with an upturned smirk. He leaned forward and grabbed the shop microphone. "1-4-1."

"Go ahead, Hooker."

"Any PD at the table tonight?"

Karen chuckled as she looked at the ten people on the dinner roster other than Hooker and now the Squirt. "You mean other than the Squirt?"

Hooker pulled the key on the mic once—his only response to honor the comment.

"Aligo and his girlfriend..." Sergeant James Aligo, notorious for serving many tours of the King & Story Road turf wars. When he finished his one year and was given his choice of any duty he wanted, he said he already had a beat and home—just needed a partner. The man was a giant Filipino who made most Irish look small. He had a quick smile and a bigger heart that had turned to affection for the beaten-down area of the city. When he finished his third year staked out at the Gun & Knife Club, they asked again—his answer was still a dog. Now he had a partner he could respect.

He hadn't liked the long Phoenician name. He reached an agreement with her, and she became Zap.

Mexican, Vietnamese, White, or any other language, they all understood the power and meaning of Zap. Zap was rarely on leash. The gangs knew and respected her as much as her partner.

"1-4-1?"

"Go ahead, Karen..."

"Did you need someone else? Because there's a pair of fillers on here who can be—"

"No... we're good, Karen. See y'all in about an hour." He knew who the fillers might be, and he didn't want them getting away.

He swung the truck toward the off-ramp and, at the bottom, turned right. He wanted a little time to sit and think without driving. He looked over at the Squirt. "Do you shoot pool?"

The kid wrinkled his upper nose. "I can sink a ball or two, but it's a motor skill set I haven't really mastered. Why?"

"We're going to go shoot some pool."

The Stick and Balls was a low-lying bar with a large parking lot in the front and an even larger one in the rear. It was Hooker's guess most of the patrons preferred to park out of sight in the rear. This left the front with plenty of room to park the large tow truck.

As they slid down out of the truck, Hooker sized up the one section of the parking lot. If the coffee and food were as good as Max promised, Mae West would have no problem snuggling up into the wide berth at the end of the building.

Hooker looked back in the cab. "Well? You need grass or not?"

Box rose from his place on the seat, thought, and almost shrugged as much as a cat can. He strolled to the edge of the seat and slid over more than leaped. Hooker chuckled softly at the casual masculinity of the twenty-some pounds of orange tabby.

After a brief stop on the tiny strip of grass, Box caught up with the men as they entered the door.

The dim interior was brighter than Hooker expected. Each of the eight tables was lit by their own low hanging table light. Hooker wasn't an expert on tables, but to his eye, they were all high quality. One thing he noticed was the lack of any quarter eating hardware. Gentlemen's tables, you pay the house for your time.

Hooker's eyes flowed down the row of tables. Every table was different—some heavily ornate, a plain-Jane, and the rest in between. As his mind figured out the differences, the Squirt muttered a low warning. "I don't think we're welcome here."

Hooker saw a dozen women slowly moving down the

room. Some with pool cues held at a casual ready, and two slowly spun their sticks in a show of weaponry. Hooker held his hands up in front of him but said nothing. The air rapidly grew thick with tension.

The Squirt was nervous, and his mouth started muttering smartness as fast as his mind worked. "Let's go play some pool, he said. Just a friendly game with some friends, he said. Maybe have some coffee with our cracked skull, he forgot to mention. Hooker, don't you think it's time we backed out of here?"

Box slid between their legs and advanced. His saunter was of a wildcat ten or twenty times his size and weight. The tail whipped back and forth. It had been more than a few months since he killed or beat-up anything at least four times his weight. Hooker could see the bunching in the shoulders—Box's tattletale he was ready. The cat was looking forward to the fight mere seconds from starting—and a few seconds more from being over. The approaching woman in the work shirt, jeans, and biker boots had no clue how close her life, or at least her face, was now hanging in the balance.

Hooker decided to end the standoff. His voice was calm but loud enough to reach everywhere in the building. "Max... does your liability insurance cover death by twenty-pound cat? Because you're about to lose one of your customers, and by the look of her clothes—a fellow biker."

Everyone froze as they heard the heavy desk phone slam down in the office. "God damn it, Hooker, don't... I'm coming." The large woman whipped around the corner. Her massive gray braid continued and swept the air to circle around her neck, with two feet continuing around to fall onto her chest.

Max took in the scene of her patrons. They thought they were about to take apart two men who stupidly walked into a lesbian bar. It was not common, but usually, the fantasy of stupid men who hazarded the thought, *If only they tried me just once, they would go back,* ended more often than not with a trip to a hospital for the man. It had happened only four times in the fifteen years she had owned the bar. Usually, it was just broken bones, but twice, there were knife wounds. The cops searched for the long thin knives, but nobody ever thinks about an old woman hiding throwing knives in her braid. The six knives were what made the braid move and swing so heavy. In a close-quarter fight, Max had even used the weighted braid as a bludgeon.

"Girls, meet my good friend Hooker. The cat is named Box, but I would not suggest trying to snuggle with him. He killed a man-sized wolf-dog a few months ago. It only took him about..." She looked to Hooker.

Hooker blinked. "Five seconds... plus or minus a second. His favorite signature—dog or man—neither hits the ground with their throat in place. Box usually drops it on their chest as they lie gasping on their end, right before he stands over them and pisses where the air is trying to be drawn in."

The woman in the lead smirked. "That is so much bull shit."

"I'd be more than happy to give you the name and phone number of the vet who pronounced on the last dog. As for the two men, I can give you the name of four county coroners who can show you photos. We had to knock Box out to pull dental impressions that matched the few bite marks, but it wasn't until I watched him kill the wolf-dog I understood how he rips the throat out. He sinks his claws into the sides of the eyeballs or ears and shreds the throat out with his hind legs."

"A cat doesn't have enough strength." She was now leaning on her pool cue instead of getting ready to use it as a weapon.

Hooker looked at the sturdy chains supporting the large lights running two-thirds the length of the tables. The top of the old stained glass fixtures was almost seven feet above the floor. To get to the fixture, Box would have to clear the end of the table so the jump would be almost ten feet of vertical angle.

"Box... top of the lights over the table... Do not touch the tables."

The orange fur shimmered and then was a flash. The hindfoot touched the edge of the light fixture as the rest of the cat streaked out in a show of energy. He raced down the five-foot fixture and leaped into a high arch carrying him to the next fixture twelve feet away. Fixture by fixture, he raced to the end of the building. At the end, he leaped out directly toward a stunned woman who shrieked and dropped.

Box hit the wall behind her. The weight of his impact knocked a cube of chalk into the air. As he backflipped off the wall, his hind paw smacked the cube, and it flew into the air in a higher arch.

As the cube arched toward the second table's light fixture, Box dove under the first table. The orange exploded out from under the other end, only to arch up and land on the second table's light fixture just as the chalk cube arrived. He caught it in his mouth and raced once more the length of the fixture, only to dive to the floor. He disappeared under the third table, back to the top of the fixture of the next, and then repeated the up and down until he got to the last fixture. As he leaped off, he leapt over the head of the woman he had been kept from fighting. As he flew over her, he spit out the cube. It hit her in the face as she ducked. If she hadn't flinched, it would have only hit her shoulder. He knew she would flinch.

He bounced off the floor and landed on the bar. He stopped next to the woman he recognized as in charge. He sat and started cleaning his paws as if to say *the top of the fixtures needed dusting.*

Max smiled at Box's style and size. Slowly, she looked back at the stunned group. "Any more stupid questions?"

A tall, good-looking blonde near the front of the group notched her chin up. "If the cat is Box, and he is Hooker… who's the squirt?"

The Squirt snapped out his hand onto Hooker's chest as if to say *I've got this.* He smiled at the woman. "Exactly, my name—the Squirt."

The woman next to the blonde laughed and jabbed at her shoulder. "He got you on that one Mindy."

The blonde ignored her friend and stepped forward. "Is that true?"

The Squirt nodded with a quirky smile and a shrug. "Real name is John, but everyone calls me the Squirt. It's slang for—"

She cut him off and stuck out her hand. Her voice was lower. "The fucking new guy in the cop car." She smiled. "Are you a cop?"

"Not yet. I'm just finishing the academy. You?"

"Nah, I went the nurse and EMT route. My dad and his two brothers are cops. Two of my cousins are cops up in the city, and one is a firefighter in Santa Clara. I figured one of us needed to learn how to patch up the rest of them."

The Squirt snorted. "Sounds like my sister." He jerked his thumb at Hooker who was talking to Max. "And his girl-friend." He shook her hand. "It was Mindy?"

"Yes, nice meeting you. A bit bizarre—but nice. What are you guys doing in here, anyway?"

"You mean because it's a... girl-girl bar?" He shrugged. "You'd have to ask Hooker. He told me we were going to shoot some pool and have some coffee... but I think there is more to it."

Max looked up and spotted Mindy. She waved them over as she looked for another. "Hey, Carol." The brunette who had been teasing Mindy looked up and laid her pool cue down.

They stood around as Max showed them the blown-up photo. "You ever see this woman up at Valley Med or over at Joe's?"

Hooker helped. "We think she worked the streets downtown."

Mindy looked up and studied Hooker's face. She reached over and moved some of his hair to reveal the long scars running back along his scalp. She smiled. "I thought I recognized your voice." Then her eyes got really big as she turned on the Squirt. "That's who you are. You're the two-bit kid. You have dimes and pieces in you too."

Her shoulder's sagged. "It's also where I've seen this cat before..." She glared at Hooker. "You left the Squirt catatonic one night."

Hooker laughed as he remembered visiting the Squirt with Willie and they had snuck Box into the hospital in a shopping bag. The blonde nurse caught them. "A small world."

Mindy pointed back at the photo. "She's dead?"

Hooker nodded.

The blonde turned and looked at the room again. Not seeing who she was looking for, she turned and tapped the photo. "Can you leave this here? If Sonia comes in—it won't be until after eight tonight—maybe she knows something."

Max lowered her voice. "I thought she worked up around Stanford or the city?"

"Not since she lost her driver's license."

Hooker could see on Max's face the same look he often saw on Dolly and Stella's—all mother hens with huge hearts looking out for their broods. She would make three in his life, but he knew the world was short too many. So many chicks fall through the floor of the coop only to get drowned in the waste below.

"Sure, and if it would help, we have a few dozen more in the truck."

Max's eyes slowly left the photo and softened around the edges. "Any idea on the cause?"

Hooker nodded. "She was murdered. Cyanide."

Hooker noted a collective pause in the heartbeats of the two women. Violence, car accidents, and gunshots—those areas the two had intimate familiarity with. A specific poison so targeted is a wild card usually only experienced in a movie —and even then, rarely.

"Are you sure? Cyanide?"

The Squirt nodded. "They recovered the body soon enough, but even with the other bodies, they were able to pull trace from the bones."

"Other bodies?" Max's eyes were surrounded by compressed dark. "Where?"

Hooker glanced at his watch. "Up near Bridgetown, in the seagrasses. Look, we've got to go, but you can have a handful of photos to ask around. We need to know what happened the last night."

Max smiled wanly. "Thanks. I'll walk out with you."

The three walked across the front parking lot toward the tow truck. Max glanced with a smirk at Hooker as she looked at the size of the five-ton truck.

"This is going to get some getting used to. Do both of you fit in the clown car?"

Hooker turned to the Squirt. "Do I have any credit left in the swear jar?"

"Nope." The kid laughed. "You used it all up on the jarhead."

"Well, he deserved it."

He turned back to Max as he opened the door. His face took on the look of Uncle Willie at his sweetest intoxicated level when his Nancy was dancing as hard as his dress was ugly. "Sweet thing, you certainly are special." He stalled. Finally fishing into his pants, he pulled out a wadded bill and threw it at the kid. "Fuck you, Max. It hurts enough as it is."

Max smiled. "Dude, been there. I'm sorry about you losing her. We followed it all in the paper. But you two saved many lives that day. If I thought I could help, I would... a lot of us would."

Hooker sagged. "Thanks, Max. I know you were just teasing, but it really does hurt. I miss her like you could never know."

She nodded as she took the stack of photos. "If you ever

just need to talk… or just coffee…" She rested her hand on his upper arm and squeezed gently. "And as for the swear jar? Leave the civilized crap at home. Around here, everyone would be broke by Tuesday if we threw a buck in."

"Hey!" They all looked back at the bar's door. Mindy stood there as Box sauntered toward them. "I don't think anyone wants to play pool with him. He doesn't use the chalk fairly."

They all laughed as the three males climbed up into the cab of the truck.

Max raised her hand. She watched them leave. She turned back to her bar and shivered as ice ran down her spine, even though the day's heat was still over ninety-seven degrees. Even at three in the morning when she finished closing, it would still be over eighty degrees, but she shivered from the cold thought of poison.

10

WHERE HAVE YOU BEEN?

Wednesday evening dinner at Dolly's was a dance of politics, power, and friendship. Dolly's needs or wants dictated a person getting an invitation to be one of the anointed at her long table. Dolly positioned and paired until the seating met her critical orchestration. Many political careers began or ended at the table.

On her desk lay the stick Dolly used—and only Dolly—to stir shit up within the South Bay Area. Most people focused on the stick as her scepter of power—but they were wrong. The table and Wednesday night dinner were the true embodiment of her power.

Dinner was at six sharp. Don't be late.

If you ever decline an invitation—and aren't in the hospital—don't ever expect another.

Hooker sat at the head of the table as Dolly's anointed one and complaisant ringmaster. His only nod to the warm season —his leather jacket hung on the back of the chair. Summer dinner attire—starched white T-shirt. Along one side sat the Squirt, but almost everyone else was an interesting mix.

The previous year, Dolly started mixing things up a little. She called it stirring. What had once been a table of testosterone now occasionally enjoyed the spice of hormone harmony. Tonight was more than a spice—more like a dose.

The two sheepish diners were at the sacrificial end of the table. They sat the farthest away from Hooker, but still under his direct view. Uncle Willie and his constant cohort, Maddie, squirmed just a little. Some would even find it interesting the two squirmed at all.

William Knight was a retired Naval Intelligence Captain. As a SEAL, he led an escape from a Vietnamese prison camp. After hanging from a meat hook for four days, he worked himself loose, killed the guards, and led the rest of prisoners over one hundred miles to safety. Six commanders of the returned prisoners, and every prisoner, to the man, wrote letters directly to the Joint Chiefs of Staff recommending him for the highest honor the country could bestow.

Hooker found the medal and sky blue ribbon in the back of a drawer one day. Willie had left the White House, took off the medal, and he never wore it again. Personal grandeur was not his style.

Hooker had the medal and certificate framed then hung it by the door they used the most. Hooker did it to remind Willie—and everyone else—he had paid the price and earned the right to wear any dress he wanted, love the man he wanted, and be the person he took pride in being. Not one person in the land could say else wise.

Maddie, a librarian, grew up wearing bib-overalls more than anything resembling a dress. Her father and three brothers raised her in the family business, making fine moon-shine, building fast race cars, and driving them even faster. For a few years, she held the world speed record as the fastest woman. She enjoyed it at the time but knew technology and younger women would eventually take the title away. With only a summer sprinkle of salt in her pepper hair, she was still the only woman Hooker knew who was as comfortable driving a car at two hundred as she was going to the store for milk and eggs.

To the others, the couple sat calmly. To Hooker's trained eye, they would give anything to be elsewhere.

Along the one side sat the anomalies. The table's normal mix of guests were officers of the law, politicians, firefighters, tow truck drivers, or other customers of Dolly's answering service or radio dispatching. Rarely did anyone fall outside this scope.

Hooker watched the small, yet powerful, Japanese American woman everyone knew as The Fly. Her wrecking yard and truck repair had grown into the largest auto body repair shop in the South Bay—possibly the entire Bay Area. The back storage yard, Hooker's impound, and the haul-to yard were over three-acres alone. The building hulking between the yard and the rail docks was another two acres under one roof and the kingdom of the one-legged yard boss commonly known as Dog.

The fluorescent light reflected softly off the pecan-colored bald head of Dog. His goofy smile told Hooker he had no idea why he got cleaned up and escorted The Fly and her daughter Mai Lynn—his live-in girlfriend. All he probably cared about was the dinner in the offering.

Mai Lynn, more Americanized than her mother, was tall

enough to have played basketball for Branham High. Her taste in colors still ran to the blue and white of the school she graduated from over ten years before. Her voice was like honey, as she small-talked with the other person of Asian descent in the room—Officer James Aligo.

The large Filipino had a booming quality about his voice, which could make you feel good and warm with his friendship or freeze you in your tracks when he caught you on the street. The dog at his feet was only there for back up. Zap didn't give a rip about the dinner. She knew when and where her dinner would be placed and in what bowl. Everything else was work or didn't concern her.

The Fly sat chatting with one of the usual suspects and close friend of Hookers. Ace almost went to work for The Fly more than a few times. Like Hooker, towing was the only job Ace had ever worked. Even mowing his small lawn, he hired a neighbor kid.

The two men at the end of the table next to Uncle Willie were the ones Hooker couldn't figure out. The older one wore a red and white checked seersucker shirt. The fringe of white hair ringed his head. His voice was low as he talked to Willie, and the younger man with the butch cut hair just sat and listened. His white short-sleeve shirt looked like it was usually pinched at the throat by a tie. By the strained edge of their seats demeanor, Hooker could tell they were also clueless about their presence at the table.

Hooker looked up at Dolly, making herself busy ignoring Hooker as she served up the plates of spaghetti with Sicilian sausages from the deli on North 13th Street. Hooker would just have to let the evening play out.

As the dinner wore on, the talk landed on fishing. At first, it was innocent enough as the conversation involved pulling ten-inch stocked trout from Calero Dam. The conversation changed when the man in the seersucker shirt asked Aligo if he had ever done any deep-sea fishing.

"I've gone out a few times."

"Where?"

"I have a cousin down in San Diego, and we've gone out of there, and a small place in the Baja."

The younger Texan drawled, "Ensenada or San Felipe?"

Aligo's eyebrow rose with interest. The man knew of both places. "We usually make a long weekend of it and went out of San Felipe."

The man swallowed his mouthful of sausage and wiped his lips on his napkin. "Gotta love the long, slow ride down the sea of Cortez—sand on both sides of the dead flat sea— unless y'all are with Zeb here. He gets antsy and opens up all four diesel engines. Thirty-two hundred horses and our old PT boat flies down the Cortez. We usually clear the end in about ten hours."

Uncle Willie gently put his fork down and patted at his lips. He watched the older man named Zeb turn red as he tried to ignore Willie. "You told the Navy the PT sank."

The man whined. "Jeez, Bill, they'd just scuttle her anyway. She's the best the Navy ever had."

"Where did you hide her?"

"Con Son Island off Bac Lièu down in the Mekong. I friended a couple of French pirates who needed a boat for a while. If it happened to have some machine guns and a torpedo or ten—so much, the better."

"And they gave it back?"

"By sixty-nine, things heated up all over the peninsula,

and they needed a bigger rig. One day, they asked where I wanted it parked. I thought they were joking... so I said San Felipe. When I got home a month later, in the mail was a picture of her, parked in a slip for life. At first, I was afraid to go near her. She sat for six months." He jammed his thumb at the younger man. "One day, Junior here said he wanted to go fishing. I figured what better trolling machine than an old PT boat. At worst, we just kick off a depth charge or two and see what floats to the surface."

Hooker choked as Dolly walked by and slapped his back. She leaned in near his ear. "Keep up, Hooker. This man is the mirror of Willie, Maddie, and Manny."

Hooker took a sip of his coffee as the entire table looked after his well-being. "They left live depth charges on the boat?"

Junior snorted. "Oh, they was just the starter package. I'd just gotten back from 'Nam, and there was stuff I never seen on even the new Surface Effect boats. Even the heavier armed Swift boats, which replaced the old PT boats, didn't have this stuff."

He smiled at his father. "The racks of torpedoes were larger and held about four extra. They installed a shielding on the outside of the racks the Navy never even thought about. The old twin-thirties were replaced by a pair of mini-guns off a gunship or Cobra."

Willie smirked. "What did the locals think?"

"They paid the local police captain to clean and take care of it for us. We figured they went out for the occasional joyride, but they worried about who we were. They never shot the guns or touched off a fish or can."

Junior snorted. "They also never tried to pick the lock on the forward locker."

Aligo laughed. "What was so important in a locker?"

The father and son looked at each other and sized up where they were. "Because the rent was in there."

"Rent?"

"For the use of the boat."

"I assume more than a couple of baskets of old fish..."

"Hardly. It was more than any bank would loan us to start our business."

The Fly was quickest with the smart mouth. "Which wasn't a sport fishing business done with explosives?"

The younger turned toward the woman. "No, ma'am. We design and build prototype specialty vehicles—usually for the government, or mining and exploration."

The man's voice was soft and quiet, but for Hooker, he might as well have screamed it at the top of his lungs. The weight of his words cleared up many questions.

Hooker leaned forward as he watched both heads of Uncle Willie and Maddie drop. "And how long is it going to take to build the special new tow truck?"

The Fly swore softly in Japanese, and Mai Lynn's head snapped up in shock to look at her mother. Hooker had his confirmation the small woman was in on the surprise. He ignored the woman, as well as the glowing red faces at the end of the table.

"Well, shoot... Mr. Knight here said we had until about Thanksgiving. We could even have until the first part of December if we did the wild custom paint job he gave us photos of—"

Zeb backhanded his son's chest. "You can stop talking any time now."

Junior frowned at his father, then seeing Willie and Maddie blushing and not looking up the table, he looked at Hooker. "Oh, shoot. I done ate the wrong end of the armadillo, didn't I?"

Hooker nodded with a smile. He was just happy to get his girl back—even with a new dress. Revealing Willie's disappearance was only a bonus. "I'm assuming you have done a little work with Marmons before?"

"Yes, sir. We designed the slip-shift for the Desert Eagle. We had a bunch of other modifications the government never seemed interested in looking at, but we still wanted to test bed." He looked back at his father and then looked down. "I think I'm going to say a bunch of hush-up now."

Dolly patted him on the shoulder as she poured him more coffee. "It's okay, Junior. You aren't the first to lose the lock on your lips around this table. And just so you know... nothing ever leaves this room—or the person would answer to me."

"Yes, ma'am. Very good, ma'am."

Dina's whistle shrilled from the other room. "I have calls."

"Ace, you have a T-Wonderful in Willow Glen.

"Aligo and Zap are needed at the academy, and please take the Squirt with you.

"Micha, your backup just went 10-7 at the Monterey Steakhouse for dinner. Your dispatch requests you head for the north 101 and work from Story to the breakers.

"Fly, Mai Lynn, and Dog, nice to finally meet you three. Please, do not touch your dishes. Monitor is showing clear. Oh, and Hooker, you have a phone call on line two from a woman named Max." The Squirt and Hooker looked at each other. The pleading was in the kid's eyes. Hooker gave him a *shooing* motion with his two hands.

The slow, gentle rumble of laughter migrated from the large Filipino as he hid his face and bent over to collect his partner.

The table erupted in directed chaos as Hooker left for the inner office.

Uncle Willie started to move. A growl from behind him settled him back down. "I think you four could use some more coffee. It may be a long night." Dolly smiled at the two gentlemen from Texas. They both recognized where command stood and who was on the working end of the shit-stick.

Hooker hurried past the door. "Dolly, cut 'em loose. Karen, I'll call you in about an hour to go 10-8." The door opened and closed in one heartbeat. The Squirt stood with his mouth open, and his finger outstretched—he had just been cut out of the investigation.

11

WE WORKED TOGETHER

Hooker backed the tow truck into the end of the parking lot. A few cars sat in the front lot as he walked across. He figured many more hid in the back lot. The music was thumping on the wall. As he opened the door, he realized the walls were thinner than they looked, and the music wasn't as threatening as it sounded.

The general attitude had changed in the few hours. Some of the women stood with their hands draped from their pool cues. Others glanced up and went back to shooting the balls on the table. The hostility toward a man walking in ratcheted down. Hooker still felt sensitive to being the interloper.

"Where's your cat?"

Hooker sized up the stocky woman. The haircut almost as short as his, but the bulging arms revealed a much more physical day's labor than his. Hooker recognized the work shirt and figured her for a yard worker or drove one of the larger forklifts at the canning plant.

His glance took in the tattoo on the right forearm. He smiled at the logo for the Arm Wrestling Association. "Box doesn't arm wrestle... and you beat my right arm before I got through the door." He stood passive waiting for the response.

The woman thought and then smiled. She turned her forearm in and rubbed at the tattoo. "Made it to the finals five years running." She pointed at the large lightning bolt scar running up her left arm from the mid-forearm and into the short-sleeved shirt. "I used to be a lefty—until they chased my bicep back up into my shoulder. When the muscle is under tension and tears away from the elbow..."

Hooker smiled. He understood pissing on the backside of the barn. He sloughed off his jacket and pulled up his shirt to expose several scars, and then ran his hand up along the scars leading into his hairline. "Dimes—from the mouth of a shotgun."

She laughed, and her chest shook but didn't jiggle. "You win. And, yes, I already knew who you were... as well as the dimes." She stuck her hand out. "Tawny. I'm Max's little sister."

"Hooker, and I left Box with his girlfriend. He and I both hate the truck I'm driving... for now."

Max came out of the office. "Oh, good. Now you know the whole damn family." She flipped her braid around to her back. Hooker got the distinct feeling it was her way of uncocking a gun. She lowered her voice. "Tacky, can you go quietly get Shawna, please? Bring her into the office—it'll be quieter."

She waved Hooker into the back. "You want some coffee?"

"I'm good."

Hooker took the offered chair. "Can I ask a question?"

Max sat and gently drew her braid around where she

could reach all parts of it. In the light, Hooker could see the leather bindings dyed to match and blend into the hair and hide the arsenal of knives. "Sure... but I'm assuming it's about Shawna hanging out here, but her working as a prostitute. You're wondering if she's a lesbian."

He nodded.

"The short answer is yes. The longer answer is—you should never confuse a person's sexual leanings with what they need to do sexually to make a living—or for many, to stay alive. When I was in my twenties, I was married. The man was my closest friend in high school. We knew each other's secrets, and we loved each other."

"What happened?"

"One night, he was leaving a bar up in San Francisco, and four thugs jumped him for his jacket. I sat in the hospital, holding his hand for two days while they tried to control the bleeding in his brain."

"I mean... you were married?"

"Conveniences—society said you marry—my mother wanted a son-in-law. Harold needed a wife who understood, and I needed a husband who also understood. A little two-bedroom house in Milpitas can go a long way toward hiding many secrets."

Tawny knocked at the door. Max waved them in.

Shawna was already made up for work. Only the short dress was needed. Hooker rose and put out his hand. "I want to thank you for talking to me. My name is Hooker." Suddenly, he started to blush as he realized, for the first time, his name could be awkward.

The woman laughed. "Down, sport. Every working girl in town knows about you, who you are, and the big-assed tow truck with Mae West on the side." She sat down. "So, what's on your mind?"

Max pushed the photo across her desk. The woman glanced at it and then picked it up. "This is Star." Her face crushed in realization. She looked up at Hooker. "What happened?"

"We're trying to figure it out."

"But you're not the police."

Max interceded. "No. No, he's not. But tell me... would you rather talk to the police about work and how you know her?"

The woman thought it over. She looked sadly back at the blown-up driver's license photo. "This is an old picture of her. She was prettier then."

"It was the driver's license she had on her."

"I remember thinking then how young she was. But then... we all started young." She cautiously looked up at Max for support. "I was fourteen when I ran away. I met my first pimp the next day at the bus station in Salt Lake City. Two fast years before I was in San Francisco." She rested her elbow on the desk and her head in her hand as she softly rubbed or scratched at the pancake makeup on her forehead. "It seems like a couple of lifetimes ago."

Max pushed her hand out flat on the desk. She didn't touch the woman, but the gesture was there. The woman read the offer. She looked up at Hooker. "What do you want to know?"

"We're trying to figure out when she went missing and from where."

The woman looked at her small silver watch and thought.

"I need some food, and then Toni will be uptown about nine or so."

Hooker stood. "This guy Tony is her pimp?"

"She's too... she doesn't have a pimp. Toni is another girl—they room together." She didn't have to explain why a forty-two-year-old woman didn't have a pimp—there wasn't the potential for enough money.

"What do you want for dinner?"

"Food."

Hooker looked to Max for guidance. She only shrugged one shoulder. He smiled back at the woman. "Steak at the Bold Knight or pizza at VIP?"

"Pizza. Too much meat upsets my stomach."

"VIP, it is."

She knew who she was and what it could look like. "Are you sure?"

"Unless you prefer Original Joe's."

"No, nothing uptown." He knew she was thinking about being seen. He gave her a warm smile.

"What kind of pizza do you like?"

"Anything out on the by-the-slice table."

"I think I can spring for something more than just a slice. I'm hungry myself," he lied.

WEDNESDAY NIGHTS WERE NORMALLY slow nights, especially after the usual dinner hours. A couple of other tow truck drivers still hung out and shot pool in the backroom. Some old black and white movie played on the screen. Hooker focused on the woman, ignoring the screen. Knowing the owner, it was an early Hitchcock mystery. They took a quieter seat, Hooker knew.

The leftover of a medium mushroom, ham, and olive pizza, sat next to a half-full pitcher of root beer. The two talked sparingly about life on the streets for the working women. Hooker knew some and wasn't really surprised by the new revelations. What surprised him were the backgrounds of the girls who drifted into the world.

Shawna sipped and then blotted her lips. "You would think broken homes, foster kids, and beaten or molested girls would be the majority... and in a way, they kind of are. But there are also ones like me—a good home, bored, and running away to seek excitement. I was probably looking just to make my parents pay attention—but what I got was a pimp and turned out by five businessmen by the end of the next night. Afterward, I was afraid to leave. I didn't even think making a phone call from a payphone would be safe. It wasn't until Michael got stabbed to death by my next pimp I realized he didn't have real control over my life.

"But to answer your question, girls aren't always in trouble when they walk away from home—but trouble finds them. Once a girl in San Francisco—a rich trust baby going to Stanford—worked along Polk St. She worked Polk dressed like a young boy. Her johns were businessmen in town for meetings or conventions looking for something they would never get in Ohio."

"A young boy?"

"Exactly, and she was good. They never knew the boy blowing them was really a girl."

"What if they wanted more?"

"That's how we found out. The john beat her because she

wouldn't have anal sex. If she'd just dropped her jeans enough in a dark alley, everything would have been fine. But when the guy didn't find a young boy, she ended up in the hospital."

Hooker frowned in confusion. "Were you working Polk Street?"

"No. I was the other hospital bed in the room. They were putting my jaw and seven broken ribs back together."

"Your pimp?"

"Wrong pimp—jumped by four other girls who wanted me off Market Street."

"Tough competition."

She snorted. "They were nothing compared to your sister and gang."

Hooker froze—a small piece of pizza halfway to his mouth. "My sister?"

"Your sister... The Mouse... wasn't she..."

Hooker returned the pizza to the plate. His interest in food finished. He nodded. "How would you know my sister... or she being my sister?"

Shawna leaned back and thought. She realized Hooker had no real idea of the darker side of the streets and how his sister and her army of cockroaches worked.

"When I was young, I wouldn't talk to the person panhandling for dimes and nickels. As you get older, you realize you're just another animal on the street. When you're so old, a pimp won't keep you—your only defense is every set of eyes on the street. We older girls look out the best we can for each other, but the invisible people are the best watchers."

"But how did you know about her being my sister?"

"Those little tow trucks... what? Fifty or sixty in this

city?" Hooker nodded, and she continued, "The size you're driving now...?"

Hooker thought a moment. There were only a few big rigs in the four counties. "Seven or eight... maybe."

"And how many trucks the size of Mae West dolled up like she was?"

"One."

The woman put her finger on the tip of her nose as she laughed. "Everyone on the street at night knows your truck. At first, you recognized the yellow, then just the size and shape of her as she slides by. After a while, I could hear you, two or three blocks away, and know it was you. Most of the girls do. We call you the Knight in Yellow Shining Thunder."

"And the Mouse?"

"The members of her army knew you too. They always kept tabs on you. After a while, I asked why. I knew who The Mouse was—she preserved a certain quiet on the night streets. The lack of violent types was good for us, but even more so for her people. The quiet left them unmolested as they could scurry about and collect food and stuff. I miss those times. We miss your sister and what she did for the city."

"Has it gotten more dangerous?"

Shawna twisted her mouth around her answer. "After..."

"She was killed."

Shawna studied his face. "There were stories about how..."

Hooker realized the street had its news, and the woman looked for full honesty from him. "I shot her, and well... a big explosion."

She nodded. "If they weren't afraid of your shotgun before, they have no doubts now."

Hooker wound his finger in the air. "You were saying about after..."

"There was quiet for several months. But this spring, things are changing. Much of the army doesn't come into town anymore. But those who do are, well... skittish. There is something out there they are afraid of, which is strange because they used to be the scariest thing on the streets at night."

"How so?"

She studied his face for any duplicity. "You do know they're cannibals, don't you?"

He thought and nodded. "Not all." He shrugged. "Or at least, I don't think they all partook."

"Your sister...?"

He rolled his lips into his teeth hard. "I would be just lying to myself and you if I said not. She may have even started it."

"See? Worse than getting beat up. They made people disappear."

"Is Star the first you can think of to have disappeared from the streets?"

The woman shrugged as she rolled her eyes and head. "Girls come and go. If they moved to LA or up to the city, did they disappear? Or did they just move?"

"So how would you know?"

"All of us have friends. If I moved, say, down to LA and Hollywood, I'd tell my friends Connie or maybe Tawny and Max. It's a safety net of sorts. Once I got there, I would call back and give Max my phone number in case anyone needed to get ahold of me."

"Like my sister and her people keeping track of me."

Shawna smiled. Her eyes wandered all over his face as she took her time. "I think she loved you more than you knew."

"I knew." He looked toward the unmoving front door.

"It... it must have been hard to kill her."

Hooker nodded and looked back at the woman.

His damp eyes were not from what he knew the woman would think, but it would work.

Even so, he missed his sister.

"We should go."

Hooker looked at his watch. It was late enough. The woman Toni would be working the street.

12

WHAT HAVE WE GOT?

Manny sat in the office with his giant professional-grade headphones on. Hooker glanced in and guessed Brahms was rolling on the large tape recorder with the sixteen-inch reels. Sweets got Manny the tape deck while he recovered from the gunshot wound ending his detective career.

The professional set-up was a few years old, so the radio station replaced it. Sweets told the owners about Manny, and they sprung for brand new headphones, and a lot of music Sweets knew Manny would like. Sweets and his brother Danny spent days and nights putting together several dozen tapes containing eight hours of music each—almost all classical.

Hooker wandered into the kitchen, finding Stella pulling the last loaves of fresh bread from the oven. The smell filled the large hacienda.

Hooker snickered as he kissed the top of Stella's head. There was a voice—seeming to come from the large pantry, "Do we smell fresh baked bread down here?"

"The children are restless... and when did you start baking bread?"

Stella turned on Hooker and gave him a stupid look without the zombie head roll. "When I was about six."

"No, I mean... Oh, never mind. It smells amazing." He looked at her with eager eyes.

She pointed at the Squirt just coming out of the pantry. "You better go bring your posse up to speed. I'll bring some in when it's cool enough to slice."

His shoulders sagged, and he put on a grumpy face but turned. She popped the towel on the back of his jeans and made him laugh. It felt good to come home to a busy house.

Hooker pointed at the office but looked at the pantry and the Squirt.

"We're going through the anatomy. They have a test tomorrow."

Hooker knew any book the Squirt read was committed to ironclad photographic recall. The Squirt probably read Candy's nursing textbooks out of boredom, but would now be a great study partner for his sister and any other nursing student.

"Are you two going to talk out there all night, or are you coming in here like gentlemen?"

Hooker lowered one eye looking at the Squirt. They both smiled. The Squirt held up his one finger. "His voice is louder than needed—which meant, the music is still playing, and his headphones are on."

Hooker nodded.

"But standing here, he can't see us or even know we are here."

Hooker snorted. "Trust me—he knows. It's a Manny

thing. And if I drive the rig up to the Bold Knight without ever saying anything, I can count on the phone ringing before my steak gets there."

The Squirt nodded in resolve. "Because it's a Dolly thing."

"Welcome to the family."

They turned to find the man in the wheelchair sitting in the doorway. "Well, we having a meeting or not?"

"Just working out logistics, Manny."

Stella walked up behind Hooker and took his left hand. She slipped the syringe into his hand as she looked him in the eye and smiled. "I always wanted to say this—shoot him." She turned to retrace her steps back into the kitchen. She called over her shoulder, "Challah bread and fixings in ten minutes."

The bread, cream cheese, jam, and butter left only tiny marks on the plates or at the edge of a lip. A moment of reverent silence descended over the three men. But as long as they kept staring at the squiggles and lines on the chalkboard, they could pretend they were still brainstorming.

Stella knew better, as she gathered the evidence of her fourth superpower—the ability to knock out a whole brain collective with her cooking. At the door, she decided it was humane to turn the mental switch back on. "Anyone ready for seconds?" She was met with six glassy eyes. She made a mental note to check Manny's blood sugar in another half hour. *Let him fly with the kids for a little bit.*

The Squirt was the first to re-track. "So Toni saw Star get to her block around nine, and then Toni hooked up with three businessmen who wanted her kind of party." He turned and frowned at Hooker. "Which is exactly...?"

Hooker looked over at Manny, whose head was back, and

his sight was down his cheeks, and over one of his famous Manny teaching smirks. He waited to hear Hooker explain the extreme level of what the street offered—without providing a number to call for an appointment to a specially rigged house or basement.

The Squirt continued naively, "Three guys on one woman sounds like gang-rape to me..."

Hooker snorted. "You have your penetration and receivers all backward. Toni is just short of six foot before she put on her tight thigh-high black boots with nine-inch heels and four-inch toes. Then there is a tight one-piece leather swimsuit thing laced up the back. Hanging off her Sam Brown belt is a curled six- foot whip and a shorter cat-o-nine-tails. I didn't want to know the contents of her large black leather bag. I imagined a portable dungeon gear set or some such equipment. She was reaching into her bag and talking about a perfect mask for me when I asked her not to. I just needed to ask her about Star."

Manny just smiled as the Squirt did the three-second catch-up and snickered.

Hooker growled. "I set you up with a date for Saturday night at ten to go over the contents of the bag. She promised she would let you go by Tuesday."

The Squirt squirmed and blanched, but still giggling, "Can I bring Beth along?"

Manny and Hooker's mouths popped open in round exclamations. They were either bested in a comeback or made privy to his love life. They both knew there would be no confirmation either way.

Manny cleared his throat first to stop the laughing. He

loved getting out of hand with the boys, but he also knew they had serious work to do.

"So Friday night, and you found the body on...?"

"Tuesday." Hooker pointed to the redheaded pin in the marsh. "Where the train trestle crosses over to the old ghost town of Drawbridge. Last I heard—twenty-seven skeletons or, at least, those are the complete ones. The skeletons a little east of there, bits and pieces having been worked over for many years. Those might go back fifteen or twenty years."

The Squirt added, "Toxicology on the ones they looked at so far have high traces of cyanide in the bones. The older the bones, the more leach, but they're checking the sternums as well as the rotators of the shoulders and hips."

Manny nodded. "As the blood stops pumping, the highest concentration is in the arterial. If the lungs survived, they're high in the exchange. Next are the extremities where it makes it to the pinch-points of the shoulder and the hips. The concentration of blood leaks into the bones as the cyanide breaks down the platelets and the blood thins. The cyanide binds with the thin plasma, leaking through the artery wall and finally pooling in the joints—forming the concentration they're looking for. Once they knew it was cyanide, they look in the joints... any joint. If it had been arsenic in slow doses, they would be looking at hair and fingernails. Every poison has its tattle-tell. People think it's clean, but there is just as much trace as the lands and grooves on a bullet."

Going back to the downtown map, "So maybe from ten o'clock on she's on...?"

Hooker stopped mid-sip. "Santa Clara. Just off First."

Manny studied the photo. "Hmm, still a good body but

needed the darker to hide the face. Do we know what she was doing?"

"Oral."

Manny nodded. "The john can touch and watch the back and legs but doesn't see the face. It's the end of a career. When they're down there, the better money is gone. If you're lucky, you're making rent in a cockroach motel off Monterey Highway or in Milpitas."

Hooker rubbed his face to stay awake. "I think she was moteling with Toni. Toni needs someone dependable to lace her into her rig. I didn't notice any side zippers or anything—she's the real deal. Plus, she was angry she'd been in the rig for four days straight. She had me loosen the laces right there on the street."

The Squirt snickered. "And that's all?"

Manny smiled at Hooker's expense.

"So Star getting into a car for a date. This gets her off the street and away from prying eyes. But how do we slip her cyanide? In my years, hookers weren't the most trusting people—especially with johns."

Hooker's lips rolled in. "I think if we figure it out, we will have our killer. So who do you think the girls trust?"

The phone on the desk made them all jump. Hooker frowned, and Manny looked at the clock. The Squirt raised his hands as if to say it wasn't for him.

Manny swept the hand unit off the base halfway through the second ring. "Romero."

There were a couple of heartbeats of silence. "What time?" Manny nodded. "He'll be there." He hung up.

Hooker knew of only one other person so short in words. "What time is breakfast?"

"Three."

The disc jockey Sweets was blind. His brother Danny was his bodyguard, driver, and anything else he needed. Hooker once joked Danny was rationed to only seventy words a day. His joke didn't go down well, but they were all good since.

Because Sweets worked from Midnight to six, he went to work around nine in the evening. His mother, Lovey, would make breakfast for her three sons—her two biological black sons and the one she referred to as her ghost son. Because Hooker usually worked the night shift, he never had a tan of any kind.

Hooker pushed his T-shirt up his arm. The tan line was more of a shadow and only visible in the right light.

Manny snorted. "Nope—you're still a ghost."

13

BREAKFAST WITH SWEETS

ooker's head was buried down in the dark cleft of Tilly Sweets' chest. He could feel a laugh or giggle working its way north. But for the moment, she was looking at the tow truck parked at the curb.

The colors were right. But the size...

She held onto Hooker's head harder. "Danny... Danny, you get out here right now."

"What, Mama?" The giant of a man loomed up behind her.

"Look out yonder. What do you see?"

"An itty-bitty tow truck?"

"And I have your ghost brother, my ghost child, clenched to my breast." Hooker squirmed with her laughter, even though it was at his expense. She clenched her large arms even firmer. "Hush, Hooker. I'm talking here with your brother."

She looked back at Danny. "So if Hooker is in my breast, what is at the curb, and what does it mean?"

"Means someone stupidly washed Mae West in very hot water and then dried her on high heat. She done shrunk, Mama."

Tilly grabbed the back of Hooker's hair and pulled his head out of her breast. "Shrunk is exactly what it looks like. Did you not pay attention to our years of explaining the facts of real life, and you done washed her in hot water?"

Hooker was laughing so hard, he fell into her and nuzzled her fat neck until she giggled and started pounding his back.

Danny, understanding his job as straight man for his mother tormenting Hooker, was done, turned, and returned into the depths of the house. Ever the logical man, he growled back at his mother, "You're letting the expensive air-conditioned cold air out the open door."

Laughing, the two closed the door and supported each other down the hall. Tilly finally turned serious. "I am awfully sorry about Mae. Can they fix her? I heard she was cut in half."

"Oh, the whole back two-thirds were vaporized by the blast. Her rear-axle cluster took out the runway light controller, went through the storm fence, and ended blocking traffic four football fields away on the parkway. The sleeper on the back of the cab was what saved me and the Squirt from being flattened like little bugs."

Danny stood his full height as he held four large plates. "You are a little bug."

"Says the man who never eats enough so he shrivels away until his mother can hardly recognize him..."

The voice from the other room was accompanied by the sounds of a braille book being dropped on a coffee table. "Did I hear some strange skinny guy say breakfast was served?"

Hooker could hear the crinkle of the starched white dress shirt before Sweets came around the corner. The man turned as his tongue clicked its ubiquitous sounding tick as he located where people were. He stuck out his hand—directly at Hooker.

The fact a totally blind man knew exactly where he was had long ago stopped unnerving Hooker. He took the man's hand. "How's it hanging, Sweets?"

"Bright, sweet, and beautiful, Hooker, like it should be." They shook and then sat down at the table. There was not much protocol in the Sweets house. This was breakfast. Tilly cooked, Danny served and cleared, and the guest was expected to only be there.

Hooker looked at his plate as Danny set it down. "Oh, Tilly, I don't know how you knew what I woke up this morning thinking about. Stella was cooking bacon, but Candy had some flowers in the bedroom or something, and quiche floribunda was all I wanted."

"My sister Stella didn't make it for you?"

"When I got out to the kitchen, the bacon was gone, the eggs were gone, and she was headed for town. I thought about stealing a piece of bacon off Manny's plate... but you do know he still hides his 357 bulldog under his crotch."

The three snickered at the thought of Manny stuffing his old service revolver between his crotch and the wheelchair seat. Sweets was the first to sober. "I thought his nightstand weapon was a Glock 17, nine-millimeter automatic?"

Hooker smiled at being called out on his joke. "Hmm, yeah, I guess it wouldn't fit, would it? What with them giant cast-iron detective balls of his."

Tilly leaned over and placed her hand gently on Danny's

arm. "Honey, after breakfast—not now, but after breakfast, call Willie and let him know the swear jar is a dollar richer."

Hooker protested. "I don't owe a dollar. I only used the word balls once."

She smiled evilly as she held up her two fingers. "What about the other fifty cents?"

"Oh, honey... I'm going to use it up when I talk to Stella later this afternoon."

Sweets held his napkin up to his mouth to laugh. "Hooker, you never learn. You were had the moment you met Mama. She is always going to win."

Hooker growled as he took another bite. "Nothing new in my life, Sweets. Dolly, Stella, Maddie, and now Candy—these women are all on the same team, and we are just the water boys."

Tilly smiled and nestled her hands under her chin as she made goo-goo eyes at Hooker. And then she sat up as she snapped, "Nope... the line sounded good, but you still owe the dollar."

Sweets tapped his finger on the table near Danny's right hand. The big man growled, "What?"

"Give Hooker a buck. It was a great line, and it did make up for the balls line."

Hooker protested, "I don't need—"

"Shut up, skinny," Danny growled with a wink as he tossed a ten over from his pocket. "The man has spoken."

Hooker held up the bill. "But this..." The look on Danny's face had snapped to cold and hard. Hooker gave up.

Turning to Sweets, Hooker took a sip of coffee to wash down the last bite of quiche. "I know I wasn't invited here just because you needed a sparring ball to bounce back and forth."

Sweets calmly wiped his mouth and refolded his napkin. Feeling for the edge of the plate, he aligned the cloth to the knife and plate edge. His left hand found his coffee mug, and his index finger dipped in and found the mug empty. He pushed it toward his brother, who filled it from the carafe and placed it back in Sweets hand. Sweets head dipped almost imperceptibly as he raised the mug to his lips. Sipping, he placed it back on the table.

"I'm not sure where to begin. None of what I have been seeing makes any sense. I almost dismissed it, but then, it started to repeat."

Hooker cleared his throat. "What was first?"

"Mud. To be more exact, it was you covered in mud."

"Mud?" Hooker knew better than to help.

"I could taste salt... but it tasted nasty like it was old or contaminated."

"So salty mud."

"No. Like saltwater and mud. There was grass or something, also... but it was gray or brownish tan like it was dead or at least not alive. It wasn't green."

"Could you see what I was doing?"

Danny growled quietly. "Towing a crab."

Sweets' head swiveled loosely toward his brother. The face never changed. Danny got the hint and retreated into silence. Sweets' attention returned to Hooker.

"You were supposed to tow... but you didn't. There was something in the grass."

Hooker watched the man. It was time. "Bodies."

Sweets' head rose less than an inch. "Ah..."

Hooker cleared his throat. "Well, actually skeletons... and remains."

Tilly held her fingers to her lips as she gently closed her eyes. Hooker knew this part of her *adopted* son made her uncomfortable, but she was coming to grips. It was just the fact of it coming to roost in her dining room and at her table. Hooker knew she loved him as she loved her sons by birth, but he also knew this side of Sweets' life only came with him and his involvement with crimes, as they seemed to find him.

Hooker's voice softened. "Anything else?"

"Plenty. There are scattered dots of things. I feel a woman who is also a man... or is it a man who is really a woman? I am above the water, gliding along..."

"Like a bird?"

"Closer to the water, but not too close... It's like a small river in the grass... it winds."

The slender black man shifted in his chair. "I can feel... It's like I have been here before... the internal war, the hatred, the self-loathing... I can feel the large stick in my hand... I'm pushing..."

Sweets sat back. His shoulders droop as if his strength has suddenly drained out of his feet. Like a deflated balloon. Hooker knew to wait.

The voice was Sweets but from a great distance. "You need to go talk to your sister."

Hooker thought about his sister. The marshlands and the salt flats of the edge of the bay had been her domain—her empire. She had ruled upward of a hundred people society would not recognize as one of their own. She was the manifest of a goddess, a queen, and a mother to all who had been cast aside. The reach of her minions had ceased to amaze Hooker. From the depths of the salt marshes in the southernmost tip of the bay having stretched sixty miles north, she had exhibited knowledge of things going on in the northern parts of Marin County and as far up the Sacramento River as Sacramento itself.

Hooker had figured out over the recent years why he never saw more than a few dozen of the tribe at a time—because the others were traveling and gathering information. His sister was intelligent and knew information was power. He recently discovered she even had a resource for checking out and reading hundreds of books from the Santa Clara County Library system each year. He remembered her capacity to consume vast quantities of the written word, but never thought, while living among the scrub brush in a hole or cave, how she would continue to devour so much information.

Hooker thought about the sea of grasses and the nature of Star's work and life. Maybe it was time to go up to sit in the cool shade of a large tree and pick his sister's wealth of information.

Hooker looked to Sweets. "Anything else?"

The man nodded slow and slight. "This is the part I have a problem with. I have a sense of a ponytail. Not a big one, but just long enough to be one—but I have no sense of it being a man or a woman."

"Any color?"

He shook his head. "No... but for the first time... even right now, I keep getting a smell. Not solid, but just whiffs here and there."

"What kind of smell?"

Sweets turned to his brother. "Danny, could you go get the garbage from under the sink and take it to the front door? Not just the bag, like you usually do—but the whole can."

The man rose and silently followed his brother's bidding.

He walked past the table carrying the can—with the garbage exposed to the air. He reached the front door and stood.

"Okay, now slowly take it back to the kitchen."

As Danny passed the table, Sweets' finger came up and pointed at where the man and garbage had been a second before. "There. *That* is the smell. Just like the smell of the garbage can—a little... and then more. It's not old and rotting, like when we are near the dump or when a garbage truck passes with all the old smell and rot... but the fresh smell. Fresh garbage—but it comes and goes... "

Hooker's nose wasn't as sensitive as Sweets, but he did finally get the smell. "And this is the first time you ever had a smell connected to one of your visions?"

"Well, yes and no. Back when I was in the hospital, I was getting crazy memories and kept smelling oranges and occasionally, grapefruit."

Danny snickered.

Sweets' head jerked, and then he snickered and was followed by Tilly. "One morning, I was still asleep. But for some reason, I always knew and still know when Danny is in the room or close. In my sleep, I knew he had come in and quietly sat down. I didn't know Mama was with him.

"Suddenly, I got a strong smell of—" he looked at Danny, "How much did you give Hooker just now?"

"A five or something..."

"Good, because... I smelled a lot of shit." They all laughed. "I woke up and asked Danny if he had just shit his pants or only farted. I was only seventeen and still had a high school smart-assed mouth on me."

Danny snorted, and Tilly continued with a smirk. "He didn't know better. During the night, he had gotten a roommate. The old man had one of those bags on his stomach because they cut into his bowel."

Hooker nodded at what was coming next.

"The poor man had something wrong, and he blew the bag open, and it was all over him, the bed, and the floor. He was so embarrassed."

Sweets wiped down his face with his one hand. Hooker had seen him do this at the radio station when he needed to be serious and maybe do the news. At times, it was scary to watch. Hooker had watched him go from a full belly laugh with tears in his eyes to reading the news about someone killed in an auto accident, in the space of a couple of heart-beats and a hand swiping down his face. *Training and focus.*

"It was the last time I smelled anything when I was seeing something... until now. My guess is—it must be important."

Hooker shrugged and played down the heavy nature of what they were talking about. "Or it means I forgot to take out the trash this morning and will pay dearly later when I get home. Maybe I should go stay with Willie for a few days."

Sweets snorted, and then he was serious again. "Or maybe you better go see your sister."

"It's been a few months."

Sweets leaned back. "Any word on Mae West?"

Hooker looked at the blind man hard. "What do you see?"

Sweets shrugged with a twisted mouth. "Bits and pieces, but she is coming together. It's strange. Some of it's close, and some feel far away."

"The new frame and stuff are being custom-built in Texas. I can only assume the Fly is working on the body here."

"When?"

"By Christmas, I think."

Sweets pursed his lips and pulled at the cluster with his one hand. "I have a feeling... you're going to need her sooner."

"How soon?" Hooker knew in his heart he needed to, and *would*, trust in what Sweets was seeing—in his strange way of seeing—what was happening or what was coming. Those visions had never been wrong, nor had they let Hooker down.

"I can feel Halloween. Not in the past, but close."

"October?" The sooner timeframe was sounding better and better to Hooker, but only if Mae was ready in time. Hooker knew what Sweets was seeing was not the completed Mae, but Hooker's need for her. The two could be mutually exclusive—or have no relationship at all.

Sweets nodded. "I don't feel a conflict, but I also don't see why either."

"But... I need to go see Sissy." Hooker's head snapped up at the sound of Danny's low growl. Hooker focused on the large man whose shoulders and upper arms looked more like someone had parked a large steer in his starched white shirt. "You may not like her name, but she has granted you until this Christmas to come up with a name you like better. I don't get a say. She doesn't get a say... but until then, she can be Mouse, Clair, or Sissy, and you have nothing to say about it... nor are you allowed to growl or grumble. So you either play by her rules, or I will let her know you're misbehaving when I see her soon."

Hooker held the man's hard look. Finally, Danny sat back and held his hands up in surrender.

Hooker nodded. "Good... because I certainly don't want to be the one who has to tell her something that could really piss her off."

Sweets snorted a short laugh and then thought about Hooker's world. He was surrounded by women who it'd be wrong or dangerous to anger. Sweets moved to defuse the situation. "Give her our love when you see her."

14

APPLE FARM WITH SISSY

The working masses of San Francisco, and the elite who manage them, herd them, prey on them, or provide legal ramifications for or against them are separated by the long expanse of the Golden Gate Bridge. The living refuge to the north is where the three-piece suits slip off their Bill Blass slippers and strap on their heavy hiking boots. For many, the shoes are changed in the city to the south before the march to their BMWs or Porsches. Then it is a race to the snail line of metal coffins being pushed north by the thoughts of a glass of wine, a joint, and a soak in their hot tub.

Many workers were painfully aware of the true separation being a few minutes before four in the afternoon. With still a full hour of work for the working bees—the Marin County evening migration begins to build up mass. In the middle of the early wave of German sports cars, the fire engine red of the 1938 REO Speedwagon stood out among the muted greens, silver-grays, blues, and blacks.

When Hooker asked Uncle Willie for the use of a car to run up and see his sister, Willie took the opportunity to have

Hooker also deliver an engine to a client in Santa Rosa. The large eight-hundred horse-powered engines with all of its shining parts—either powder painted or chromed—rested snug in its transport crate under the secured tarp.

Hooker glanced right at the side mirror and saw the self-important black Porsche attempting to pass the *old* truck. He smiled at the sleeping bundle in the seat next to him. Box had his form of fun, and Hooker had his. The ramp ahead narrowed from two lanes to only the one. The three-piece suit in the sports car didn't want to be slowed by some old codger in a broken-down piece of old Detroit iron.

Hooker looked back at the empty ramp with a nasty fifteen miles per hour right hook at the end. He was sure the sports car could take the corner at maybe twenty or even twenty-five if the guy was good. Hooker also knew, even with the massive engine in the back of the truck, he could drift the Speedwagon through the turn at well over thirty.

The German car dipped its nose as the maladroit driver downshifted to make his move. Hooker snorted and just mashed down the gas pedal. The five-hundred horses grunted a muted roar, and the red truck shot toward the turn. As the truck's rear end started to drift, Hooker snuck a peek at the mirror—he was almost fifty yards ahead. As he cleared the curve, Hooker shot ahead to merge with the light traffic. Glancing in the mirror as he blended, he snorted when he saw the black Porsche almost spin out as it tried to take the corner too fast. Hooker's smile pulled to one side as he thought about the driver trying to explain to his insurance broker how a fifty-year-old truck could make the curve, but he fish-tailed and smashed into the signpost that said fifteen miles per hour.

Box, Hooker, and the old truck calmly rode north to Santa Rosa.

IN THE EVENING, after dinner, Hooker took his sister's hand. They strolled through the long grass toward the two Adirondack chairs under the gigantic Queen Anne cherry tree on the west slope of the large yard. The long grass of the lawn felt good between Hooker's toes. He couldn't remember the last time he had walked barefoot on a lawn—but he was sure his sister might be able to tell him.

"Remember the last time we walked in tall grass?"

"Together?"

"Okay..."

Her laughter tinkled in the dusk air. Hooker smiled. It felt so complete—her laugh, the smell of the grass mixed with scents from the apple orchard, and the wet grapevines. The evening air was thick with information for all of his senses. Even his eyes were tantalized by the twinkling flights of a few early bats.

"You don't know, do you?"

His silence was covered by his smile. They eased into the chairs. Both of their heads fell back against the gray wood of the rustic furniture.

"Fifty-six."

Hooker thought a moment. "Mentone."

Sissy nodded in the gathering gloom. They rarely used the names of the foster people who had cared for them. The few names they used had been special people, and from a young age—before they were sold into abusive and twisted circumstances.

"The man left to take care of his mother somewhere, and the lawn grew long and un-mowed."

"She lived in San Diego. He went for almost a month. But he had to go back, which is why we moved down to Redlands."

Hooker sat silent. They didn't have to say anything. They both knew when their foster care became abusive—the man who paid extra attention to the nine-year-old Sissy, and the woman with a penchant for using a wide leather belt on the young Hooker. The same year the blanket tent thrown over four chairs became a fort and refuge.

The two were only beginners at preying on children. Mostly, they were agents of a sort—they found children in the system they could make disappear into an underground organization. The children were sold from one pedophile to another, if not to another torturer.

They sat under the giant tree like it was their old blanket tent. Hooker's hand curled to hold the tips of his sister's hand, which was stretched over his. Even in the dusk, Hooker could see the glow of her skin begin to show in the last light of day. *She must have been out in the sun today—to glow this bright.*

The two drifted in their silence, letting go of the old and bad, celebrating their bond and being together. The few bats became many as the summer evening dimmed. Tiny bits of darker dusk flittering about in the only slightly lighter dusk. The occasional tweet of a tree frog syncopated with or counterpointed the rhythm of the night's cricket choir.

"Neither one could have children." Her voice sounded like part of the valley breeze. Hooker's thoughts froze. He wasn't sure he heard the words. "He studied mental health because both of his parents had become so bad, they were institutionalized. He was afraid it was hereditary—he volunteered to be sterilized at nineteen."

Hooker realized she meant Norm Osofsky, who she now lived with for his medical and psychological expertise and care. Norm married Clair, Stella's best friend and maid of honor. The bonds of family and friendship ran deep. As Manny and Stella became Hooker's family, Sissy's problems meant she would always be Norm and Clair's family.

Hooker cleared the stiffness in his throat. "But he is fine…"

"Time occasionally has a way of proving you right or wrong."

"They could have adopted."

"Still would have been a gamble. What if he provided a nice home only to become deranged?"

"But they always wanted kids?"

"It wasn't an option… until now."

"You." Hooker's head rolled toward her as she nodded. He squeezed her glowing hand lightly.

Her face was self-illuminated from the phosphors her body produced. It made her soft smile literally glow. "Now I know how you feel about your Uncle Willie, Manny, Stella, and everyone else. I feel so complete now. More complete than when I was the goddess and mistress of a hundred minions."

Hooker wanted to pull her back from where he would need to take her later. "Don't forget my brother Danny…"

"Ho no." She giggled. "Danny is mine now. I'm counting the days until Christmas when he is to give me my new name."

Hooker mused about the deal she had struck with Danny

the previous Christmas. Her real name was Clair, the same as Norm's wife. Hooker had always called her Sissy for sister since he was only four. When she became the goddess of her tribe of night people or animals, she became The Mouse.

Danny hated the name Sissy and became agitated when Hooker used it. He believed it was disrespectful because of the other connotation of the word. So when she finally met Danny, she gave him until the following Christmas to come up with a name he liked. She would officially change her name, and all would abide by his choice. Hooker was sure she had also been a bit captivated by the giant of a man and his quiet calm manner.

A thought formed in Hooker's mind. "What do Norm and Claire call you? I mean, wouldn't it be a bit confusing to use Clair?"

"At first, it was strained, but then I just told them Sissy was good. After all, my middle name is Lucinda. But it just seemed... family, and I said it was similar to Scout... as in the book *To Kill a Mockingbird*. Then one night, Norm pinched me and said, 'Go to bed, Scout.' I jumped and squealed, Clair laughed, and Norm laughed so hard he choked. They both said he had never had the nerve to do something so improper... and they have been calling me Scout ever since."

From the way she told it, he knew she was good with the pinch, and it hadn't been abusive. "So... did you go to bed?"

She laid her head back as she recalled the night. "No." Hooker watched the long slow sigh. Her whole body now glowed through the thin shift. "I don't know who or how the conversation started, but soon, the deck of cards came out. We drank jackrabbit and chamomile tea until breakfast. Clair never sat in on my sessions with Norm, but it seemed like a group catharsis—it was when I learned he couldn't have kids."

"It sounds like many good things happened that night."

She held up her arms and looked at the strength of the phosphor glow. "Coming to accept and even love my inner light was one of them."

Hooker smiled. "Your skin doesn't seem to flake anymore."

"Norm got me on a test drug to control it. There's a little flaking—but using a sea sponge in the shower with some cream after takes care of it. We ran out of the drug once. Within a week, I was back to the large flakes. So if you ever need me to play a snow fairy in a play... I'm your girl."

She stood, and as she did, her shift came off with a wave of her hand. The thin formfitting slip allowed all of her body to glow through as she danced and jumped in the night air. Hooker hadn't watched her dance with abandon since their childhood. It was truly a release of her inner fairy or night spirit. He watched, mesmerized as she floated over the dark lawn... only where her feet came to rest did the grass turn green for a moment. And then it would return to black as the fairy of light danced back into the air, only to reveal other tiny spots of green.

She spun about in a last wild pirouette and collapsed into Hooker's lap. Her legs were curled in, and she was half the size she usually projected. Her head lay nestled in his neck as her arms and hands were folded hovering on his chest. She weighed almost nothing. He had never realized how tiny she was; she had always seemed so much larger than life.

The back screen door spring squealed softly in the night. "It's ten o'clock, Scout."

"Thank you, Papa." She softened her voice as she giggled. "It's past my bedtime... and I'd bet it's really closer to ten-thirty." She nuzzled her head down into Hooker's neck. Hooker glanced at the glowing hands on his watch. It was ten-forty-seven.

Hooker leaned his head over onto hers. "Papa?"

"They call each other Mama and Papa, and I just fell into it." She wiggled as if to get closer to Hooker. "I love my life now. I love my family and, most of all... I love the fact my family is part of my brother's family... especially my new sister."

She kissed his neck with force and then jumped up and ran toward the house.

Hooker sat, taking it all in as the moon rose behind him and lit the top of the cherry tree, creating patterns of light green and black. Dealing with his sister was much the same way—patterns of light and dark. Hooker's questions would have to wait until the morning.

THE APPLE FARM at one time was over four hundred acres. The fruit supplied the Northern Pacific Railroad as well as the commissary of the owner's little experiment into higher education—Stanford University. Over the years, shipping apples from the state of Washington and better oranges from Southern California resulted in the parceling and selling off most of the farm. Norman had salvaged the last parcel of eighty acres and bought back another hundred that had not been converted to houses during the expected housing boom of the late 1950s.

His colleagues from various colleges had led him to

convert to diverse plantings. Many of them were planted by colleges as test groves or vineyards to evaluate the region for future agricultural development. The fruits of the varied trees and soil lay about the morning table.

Hooker rested back in his chair. His head rolled over to look at his sister. "If you ate like I just did, you'll look like Dolly by next summer."

Clair snorted. "You weren't paying attention. She takes in more calories than you do. She just doesn't, and never will have, a fat neck for you to nuzzle."

Sissy smiled at her brother and drew another large slice of homemade bread from the basket and continued to layer slices of banana onto the toasted bread. When the toast was full, she drizzled honey over the banana slices.

Norm smirked as he turned to the amazed face of Hooker. "And I will have to remind her to also have a snack again before lunch. The biochemistry that produces the phosphorous burns an enormous number of calories. It mostly demands the faster-burning carbohydrates in the bread and fruits. So she feeds the production with the foods it needs, and we also slip in more of the protein she needs to produce more body mass, such as meat and beans—foods she didn't get during the last ten years. So it's a balancing act."

Sissy popped the last bit of toast into her mouth. "As you saw last night, it feeds my nightlight. But, with Norm's help, I have come to accept, and even enjoy, being a firefly. The hard part will always be putting meat on my bones."

Folding his napkin and placing it next to his plate, Hooker cleared his throat. "Speaking of bones..."

Clair pushed her chair back and stood as she took up his plate. She gave Hooker a hard look. "You waited until breakfast was over?" She held his gaze. Hooker felt his insides squirm the same as if it was her best friend, Stella.

"I didn't know—"

She cut him off. "I've been around Manny and Stella a lot longer than you've been alive. Back home, a normal Sunday dinner table topic was the best way to kill a given animal—wild or farm. I remember one Christmas dinner gathering, the men discussing the new way of field dressing and deboning an elk so a single man could pack out all the meat. We watched the local minister trying to keep his dinner down while his wife all but passed out. We found it funny and laughed for years about it. So next time you have some gory thing to ask your sister... don't wait. Now I need to make another pot of coffee... so give me a minute before you get to the goo and guts."

Hooker looked at Norm. The man nodded. "She is serious. So if the guts are first, you had better just go open the door for your cat. He's been knocking for almost five minutes."

Sissy whipped out of her chair and was at the door before Hooker could turn. She cracked the door, and as the large cat strode in, she scooped him up and snuggled her face into his side. She didn't have a huge shelf to lie on like Dolly, but as they came close, Hooker could hear the picky cat had lost himself to a fourth person.

Box's head lolled out of her arm. The single eye was already half-closed as he looked at Hooker.

Hooker chuffed. "Slut."

The cat rolled in on himself and snuggled his face into her neck—ignoring Hooker. She giggled as she sat back down, and Box's purr deepened and slowed as it got louder.

"First, you lay claim to Danny, and now you steal my cat..."

She giggled. "He started it by crawling into my bed."

"Danny or Box?"

Clair snorted as she returned with a fresh carafe of coffee. "He's got you there, Scout."

Sissy nuzzled her face down into the body of the large cat. "I rather like the idea of not designating which male. It's good to keep a little brother guessing."

Hooker snorted over his steaming mug of coffee. "The purring screws your scheme of intrigue."

Clair sat and looked at Hooker. "So, where were we about bones, and knowing you—dead bodies?"

Hooker told them about the body dump, his interview with the streetwalkers, and breakfast with Sweets. Part of the way in, Norm went to a drawer and got some paper and a pencil and two pens— red and blue. He started graphing out the information, and occasionally, a thin hand would surface out of the depths of orange fur to point to a couple of things to connect.

Hooker was relying on his sister's amazing ability to see patterns and paths where others saw only random information. By the end of the hour, Norm had redone the information in four different ways with path connections in red and blue arrows covering all of them. Hooker sat back and waited for the questions or answers to flow. It started from a place he hadn't expected.

Clair had been glancing at the growing graphs and lists, but not necessarily paying attention. She sipped from her mug and then quietly put it down. "Are all the bodies female?"

Norm and Sissy looked up and then at Hooker.

"I'm..." He thought a moment. "Can I use your phone?"

A few minutes later, he came back. "The count is thirty-two, and three are male. But the coroner is not so sure about those bones. They're older and could be just others dumped there from the days of when Drawbridge was a real town."

"So what we potentially have is a killer who only preys on women. And is probably targeting prostitutes."

Hooker looked at Claire. "But only one confirmed identity is a prostitute."

Norm took over. "Have you ever been driving in the afternoon and watched a guy at the stoplight who is picking his nose? I'm not talking casually... I'm talking about really mining at the back of his sinuses."

Hooker nodded with a smirk.

"Do you think the guy does it all the time... or did you just happen to see the one and only time he did it?"

Now Hooker snorted. "All the time and twice on his morning drive."

"In the psychological profession, we call it a pattern of one. You only observe it once, but you know it is a pattern. I think if you ask around, you will find many streetwalkers have disappeared over the years. And yet, we only have one... but the rest are also."

Sissy spoke with her mouth, barely out of hiding in the fur of Box. "I think, as they examine the bodies... well, bones, they will find no incidents of violence. No gunshots, no knives, no bats, no broken bones, no strangulations... nothing."

"Why?" Hooker frowned.

Claire looked at Norm. "Because the killer is a woman. She's only using poison." Norm nodded.

Hooker looked at Sissy. The liquid blue eyes opened and looked back, half-hidden by the fur. She nodded. "It's because it isn't violent and rude—poison is passive, clean, and dignified."

"What about Sweets seeing two people—a man and a woman?"

Sissy poured down the now aqueous cat. "According to you, he didn't." She checked one of Norm's notes. "He saw both, but they weren't separate... and he only saw one ponytail."

Hooker sat back, thinking. "So where to now?"

Sissy looked at the graphs. "You need to go talk to the older girls, the ones who have been around the longest. Try to get a feel for who is missing, and let the police go from there."

She sat back and sighed. Hooker knew what would come next was not easy for her. He knew the sigh.

"Do you know how to get ahold of Peter still?"

"Sure, he's spending more time around the parish with Father Damian. Why?"

"He used to know a man named Tess. She was a mess. She only wore a dress, but her real heart was her crest. Yes, it's a terrible rhyme, but the woman is a man in a dress. She dives garbage bins, but she also loves shrimp and crabs, so she works the bins behind seafood markets and restaurants. But more importantly for you—she knows many watermen working the flats of the south bay. She'll know about someone we called the Waterman, but he was different from the rest. He was like a ghost. But he stood in his boat when every other waterman sat and rowed—as if he was uncomfortable sitting. He moved very stiff in his body. I always thought he'd been in an accident. Maybe there's more to it."

She shifted in her seat, and Hooker knew she had just curled her legs up under her. The act was subtle, but like a snake coiling its base weight so it could strike.

"The few times I saw him, he poled a long canoe instead of rowing. But he had a certain delicate nature about him—even with the massive upper body. The one thing was he wore a few layers of T-shirts—almost like armor—even if the temperatures were climbing into the high nineties or hitting a hundred. But the one thing that always struck me as odd was his ponytail—it was more girl length than those short guy head whips."

Hooker looked at Norm, who shrugged. *It wasn't his department.* He turned back to Sissy. "Where did you see this guy?"

"Occasionally, we were up around the rim on the east side. He might be putting in around south of Fremont. With a canoe, you don't need a ramp or any other public place. It's not really a far stretch to boat, but we would catch glimpses of him when we would winter out in the old buildings on the island. There is a small ghost town out there called Drawbridge. The train trestle running across the island has no drawbridge, it's just the name."

"Do you remember what time of day you would see him?"

"Sure, the bird girls used to twitter about him being the dawn patrol. It was like he rose up out of the water with the early fog. Just as silent too. Paddling can make noise, but the pole never leaves the water. It makes a very spooky sight to watch him glide by through the soft fog wisps. Just his body was visible above the seagrasses—just gliding along."

Hooker shivered. "I think that's what Sweets saw. The

view from standing in the boat, gliding through the grasses. I'll go find Peter."

Sissy rocked on her chair and sat up straight, leaning forward as she took up her coffee mug. Her face had changed to pure glowing delight. "How is my sister?"

Hooker knew her feet now lay flat on the floor—a safe topic to talk about. Some of her old physical tells would never leave her. He smiled softly, knowing he knew her so well, and forever, the best parts would be there.

He thought about the first time he realized when they talked about scary things that she would pull her feet off the ground. In their blanket tent forts, one chair always had the seat facing into the fort. If she slithered up onto the seat, drawing up her legs, they were talking about scary things.

"She's doing great. The classes are long and hard, but she is working at Good Sam as a nurse's aide, so she gets great practical knowledge and experience. The Squirt teases her about taking so long, but she teases back—she has so much to learn about why two guys keep landing in the hospital—shot up or blown up."

Norm snorted. "Tell her it's on-the-job training for marriage."

Hooker blanched, and Norm realized he had raced well past the level of Hooker and Candy's relationship. "You two haven't thought about...?"

Hooker's gut knotted, but he remembered who he was with. It still only made it tolerable to talk, but not easy.

"We're still trying to figure out the love part. Neither one of us had the greatest of loving track records to copy. And as for my last ten years, there is a lot of love, but no examples to see how they all got there. You two, Manny and Stella, Dolly, and even Uncle Willie and Maddie have a long history at how you relate to each other. We don't have a clue how to get there. The first night Candy snuck up to my room, we were so scared we just cuddled until we fell asleep in the early dawn. We don't know what we're doing now... much less thinking about something like getting married."

Clair reached across the table and put her hand on Hooker's hand. "Honey, nobody comes to a relationship perfect—if we did, you would have to wonder what happened to the last one. In the beginning, there are many questions—you just need to find the person you are comfortable talking to. Even your Uncle Willie has answers... or at least Hank will have them for him. They are a newish couple, but they understand the loving part. The sex part is just mechanics. Hell, talk to Dolly—you two are cut from the same cloth. You just don't see it."

Hooker harrumphed. "We're nowhere near the same—"

"Horseshit." The woman cut him off. "Why do you think you sit at the head of her table on Wednesdays... because you look pretty? No. It's because you truly are an extension of her. She's not grooming you to take over when she's gone—she just wants you comfortable sitting on the throne she's built in San Jose. And from what I hear, you have already built quite a war chest of markers and chips for the big game, in your own right. Talk to her. If there is one thing I know about Stella and her sister, their hearts are bigger than their bodies."

"I'm not the one in line to take over when she's gone... but I'll talk to her."

"You talk to her, and I'll have a little chat with Stella."

Sissy giggled. "And then, you can always send my sister up here to visit me."

Hooker gave her a zombie roll of the head. "I may be dumb sometimes, but I'm not stupid."

Box poured his way back up onto Sissy's lap and leaned into her chest as he looked back at Hooker. Hooker recognized the *I'm bored with all the talking* stance, but it looked more like he was also laughing at Hooker.

Sissy pushed her face down into the neck of the large cat. The squirming stopped and then turned into a purr. Hooker knew his sister had awesome powers nobody understood. Box was a force of nature and had his own will, but Hooker had just watched him become a quiet kitty instead of the swaggering stud. They all sat quietly watching and listening to Box purr. It was like watching Mae West idling at the curb, and just as loud.

15

CHECKING IN WITH WILLIE

The barnlike garage originally designed to house large blimps stood dark. The three-story-tall sliding door was rolled back—waiting for Hooker to get home. Hooker scratched Box around the cat's single ear as they both reluctantly got out of the Speedwagon.

"I know, boy. But we can't run tow calls in the Speedwagon, and Mae isn't back together yet." They strode across the acre of floor like a couple of Wild West gunslingers. Hooker continued, "I hate the stinking dinky truck as much as you do, but it is what we've got for now. It's either the dinky toy and keep working or sit on some ugly beach in Mexico."

Hooker had never been to Mexico, but sitting on a beach was something he thought about with the summer heat. Sitting next to Candy, watching the ocean.

Hooker reached for the door to the house.

"The fun is all out here, Hooker." The matching giant door, out to the backyard, was also rolled open.

Hooker and Box both froze in the dark. Hooker didn't want to turn around. "Are you two naked, Hank?" With the summer heat, Willie and Hank sometimes enjoyed the night air in the buff as they got drunk on moonshine. Even Maddie occasionally joined them—but wore a long T-shirt. *Some decorum had to be preserved.*

"Oh, heavens to Betty in a broken Bonneville, Hooker—you are such a priss." Willie's speech was only slightly slurred. Hooker guessed they were only on the first fruit jar of moonshine.

"Well? Are you naked or not?"

Maddie giggled as she asked quietly, "Is he always this skittish, or is this something new?"

Willie moaned. "I tried to raise him up with an open mind, you know I have. But lately, it is like he is a different person. I don't know whether to chalk it up to not having Mae around, or his new girlfriend living under the same roof—"

Hooker growled, "Willie..."

Candy giggled. "We all be naked as little jaybirds."

Hooker now knew both of his legs had been pulled. Candy was barely up to being naked with him—much less being so in public. He turned and made his way toward the voices and dark shapes.

Willie clicked on a work light. They were all dressed in work clothes. Nurse, librarian, retired schoolteacher in a bow tie, and the former Navy intelligence officer in an extremely ugly plaid granny dress with burn holes and scorch marks among the grease stains. Hooker figured Willie or Hank would put the cutting torch to the rag before Willie would be let back into the house.

The small Ball fruit jars sat beside each of their empty plates with dark crumbs and forks.

"Any cake left?"

Hank rose and pointed at his seat. "Sit. I'll fix you a plate."

"I stopped for a hotdog in San Mateo, but Box could use some tuna."

Hank pointed toward the roll-around workbench. "The shine is over there. Cake for you and fillet of fish for the big guy."

"Thanks, Hank."

"Don't thank me. Maddie brought the fresh salmon from up the coast. She can have my kiss. Just save my hug for later."

Hooker sat down and glared at Willie and Maddie. The staring contest was off to a great start because Hooker was most of a fruit jar behind in the drinking. Maddie got the giggles. Hooker snorted as he thought about this giggling woman stepping off a motorcycle on the Bonneville Salt Flats at well over a hundred miles per hour.

"And you were planning to tell me about Mae... when?"

Maddie made an attempt to act serious. "Don't get your boxers in a bunch, Hooper... I mean Hooter." With each attempt at his name, Willie got closer to wetting his dress, Candy a close second, and Maddie's speech got worse. Hooker thought about revising his estimate about the amount of alcohol floating around the giant garage.

Hooker warned with only a slightly straight face, "Don't anyone light a match."

Uncle Willie was the first to recover. "We were going to tell you, but it wasn't a done deal when we left for Texas. The Challenger with the eight-hundred horse motor cinched the deal."

"You sold the Challenger?"

The door to the house opened as Hooker's mouth hung

open. Hank snorted as he crossed the garage. "You must have told him about the tinker toy."

Hooker turned and frowned. "*Tinker toy?*"

Maddie sighed. "The Challenger. We were only tinkering around with it. The drags are full of them out here on the coast, so they force them to bracket in the nines. At the horsepower we were throwing into the beast, she would have turned closer to six or seven seconds with ten percent alcohol." She lifted her fruit jar and took a sip and then held it up to look at the clear liquid. "And that's with regular stuff... just think what this would do."

As Hooker finished the last of the chocolate cake, he glanced at his watch. He looked over at Candy, who had a silly smile on her face with the rosy cheeks. "I need to go over to Father Damian's tomorrow around dinner to see if I can find Peter. Do you want to go?"

Her eyes rolled, and her smile spread wider. "Remind me in the morning what you asked me..."

Hooker knew he would have to carry her over his shoulder into the house.

Maddie patted his hand as she watched Candy start to snore. "Just put a blanket over her. And while you're at it, I'll take one too."

Hooker stood and went to retrieve four blankets.

THE MORNING FOUND the five bodies in various positions, covered and uncovered. Everyone had their clothes on except Hooker. Even Hank still had his bow tie on, but Hooker had only his swim trunks—the urge for a midnight swim in the hot summer night was too delicious to pass up.

Candy woke to find Maddie looking at Hooker. Maddie's smile was the woman's silent laugh. She looked over at Candy and jerked her head out the back door toward the swimming pool. Candy thought about how devilishly naughty it sounded. They silently rose and, padding on bare feet, headed for the large open maw of the back door.

Hank's voice froze them halfway out the door. "The kid up the hill has his Cub Scout den over, and they are all over the hill watching for birds with their binoculars."

Maddie glared conspiratorially at Candy. "Just showing Candy the area I think would make a great barbecue. Oh, and Hank," she turned, "could we have some breakfast soon? I know Hooker needs to do some work today, and I need to run up to Emeryville for some parts for the Matchless."

Hank chuckled. "Pancakes with all the fixings coming right up." He mumbled to himself, "It will soak up the hangovers." He reached out with his sock-covered foot and nudged Willie. He addressed the one open eye. "Breakfast in thirty... just in case you want to burn your dress. I laid out a nice neon-lime one earlier."

The dresses were not always about the cheap nature of buying them by the large garbage bag full at twenty-five cents a bag, but mostly, it was about the uglier, the better to tease Hooker's senses. All other kinds of teasing were either off-limits or had stopped working long before. Hank had been offended by the ugly nature of his boyfriend's taste until he warmed up to the nature of the family's inner workings. Once he understood the *take no prisoner* level of teasing—and the truth of Willie's sense of taste being much finer than the ugly dresses—he was a willing participant. Hank was a quiet, behind the scenes, and protective body of his partner—but a willing, and sometimes devious, participant.

Willie rolled back and forth as he loosened his stiff body. His eyes never left the backside of his partner. The smirk on the ex-spy, ex-POW, ex-Navy SEAL pulled jagged by the scars on his throat and neck, but no less appreciative of the devious nature Hank currently showed.

Willie's head ground around as his soft giggle only slightly shook his body. Maddie had seen the look many times.

She stretched her own scarred body as she mouthed, "What?" Candy still looked with longing at the pool—and up the hill. *Someday*.

Willie looked over at the still sleeping Hooker. "I was thinking about April first and Hank's biscuits stuffed with cotton balls... Hooker had been tired and heading for bed. He slathered butter and some jam through the side of one and shoved the whole into his mouth. The reaction came after he made it into his bedroom and wearing nothing but his angry face. He caught Hank, threw him over his shoulder, and didn't stop until they were both in the pool."

The laughter of Maddie and Willie woke Hooker, who looked at them with bloodshot eyes. He didn't participate in the worst of the drinking but was purely exhausted.

"What?"

The door from the house opening cut Maddie off. Candy stood in the opening. "Breakfast is almost ready."

Hooker closed his eyes against the pain and stood. The jolt of grimace did not escape the two older walking scar-bodies. They exchanged knowing looks and followed the younger stiff-walking zombie. Food is a motivator; good food is a powerful motivator. Breakfast cooked by Hank can raise the dead—the three filing through the door past Candy were living proof. Each received a kiss on the side of the head as they stumbled past.

HOOKER PUSHED the last piece of bacon into his mouth and washed it down with more coffee. The four were looking more alive.

Willie put his coffee mug down. "She knew her killer."

Candy thought a moment. "How can you be sure?"

Maddie leaned back. She had been around Willie the longest and had even done research for him back in the day. "Because there was no evidence of a struggle."

Willie smiled. "And you know this... how?"

"She was still dressed."

"But the dress was torn up."

Maddie leaned in and faced her mentor as the others enjoyed watching the two engage in mental tennis. "The dress wasn't the important part. The waist of her pantyhose was the only important part."

"Why?" Candy couldn't stand the drawn-out dialogue of discovery.

Willie and Maddie both turned on her. Willie was first, "If she had been in a fight, her pantyhose wouldn't be in place. How often do you pull your hose up?"

"Often..."

Maddie finished. "In a fight, her pantyhose would have come down, and her driver's license would have fallen out." She smiled. "It hadn't and was still on her hip in her pantyhose. She trusted her killer and didn't know she was being poisoned."

Hooker leaned in. "Do you think she would trust a john that much?"

Hank sat up and primped at his bow tie. "It would be highly unlikely."

"Why?"

"To acquire so much trust, the john would have to spend a great deal of time with her. By doing so, he would risk drawing a high degree of unwanted attention from the other streetwalkers. After all, girls do talk. So highly unlikely. I think you need to be looking elsewhere."

Hooker rubbed at the scars along his head. "But who else spends time with them—other than the other girls? Are we thinking one of the girls is taking out the competition?"

Hank sipped on his coffee. His eyes traveled over Hooker's face. He gently placed the coffee cup back on the only saucer on the table. "You tell me. Do you only spend time with other tow truck drivers?"

"Hardly any time at all..." His voice faded off. "But cops are a different story. There are always cops who have a beat, and they know everyone and everything they can about those people."

Willie grunted grumpily. "This isn't a cop."

Maddie turned on her oldest friend. "Why so quick to judge? Or in this case, to give a free pass?"

"Poison is not the act of a cop. They are more forthright, more direct with physical and brutal methods."

"Not all cops are brutal."

"No, but when they go off the reservation and turn to killing, they are. Their weapon of choice is what they know the most—guns and truncheon."

Hank pulled himself up. "Experience, William?"

Willie stared with a thousand-mile stare at the table. *He did not need to nod.*

Hooker broke the thick silence. "So not another working girl and not a cop. Who else would they know?"

Candy cleared her throat. "Waitress, waiter, or even the owner of a restaurant they frequent for food." She looked at Hooker. "You talked to a couple of the girls. Go ask them who they talk to and have become friends with."

"I don't think—"

The loud klaxon horn honked in the shop garage area just before the phone rang on the counter and in Hooker's bedroom. Hooker, Willie, and Candy all glanced at their watches.

Hank answered the phone and listened. "Thank you, Karen. I'll have him ready. Say hello to your wonderful mother. Good-bye." He turned to Hooker. "Your truck is about five minutes away... or less."

Hooker looked at his watch again.

Hank sunk back against the counter. "It's down here in Blood Alley—about fourteen cars and some trucks. Wear your dirty clothes, and I'll just burn them when you come back all bloody."

Hooker rose, kissed Candy on the top of the head, and turned for his bedroom. He looked at the jeans draped around his boots. He had yet to have a pair of jeans last more than three or four months. Usually, they got torn, but also, they disappeared at the hand of Hank doing the laundry. If they were only soiled, they got washed, but anything Hank didn't want in his sparkling clean machine got washed from the earth by Willie's cutting torch—the closest Hank got to tools.

Hooker's arm draped over Candy's shoulders as they

walked out into the sunshine. The five-ton truck pulled up the last of the hill and nosed into the large concrete apron poured to accommodate the much larger Mae West. The apron made the large truck appear even smaller. Hooker frowned at the size and then smiled when he saw who was driving the truck.

The Squirt slid out the door and onto the apron. Candy gave her brother a hug. "Are they giving you some time off?"

"I turned in my last paper yesterday, and it will take them about a week to sort through the eighty pages, and sixty-seven bibliographies." He smirked. "Who knew doing all those research papers for Maddie would pay off in time off?"

"How did you get the truck?"

"I ran calls yesterday while you were traveling. Also, I was up at Dolly's doing paperwork this morning when the call came in." He hugged Candy one more time and kissed her on top of her head. "Gotta go."

As they climbed into the truck, the Squirt filled Hooker in on the accident. Hooker thought about the commercial tows that would have to go to someone else. He missed Mae.

16

THE WORK IS THE WORK

Working an accident is much like triage during a war, or a train wreck—sometimes small and manageable, and other times, spread over an area the size of a football field, or larger.

Being high up in a cab of a large truck can give a better advantage to see across a large area of carnage. With the shorter truck than his usual, Hooker chose to first drive up on a small hill.

He saw no other way to get to the back of the accident, so a short stop on the way to working the accident from both ends seemed like a great idea.

"Fudge... still not good enough." Hooker hit the steering wheel.

The Squirt snorted with a smile—he understood Hooker's frustration. "Don't blame the tool; blame the person who isn't using it right."

He slithered through the window and stood on top of the cab before Hooker figured out what he was doing.

As Hooker worked his way out of his window and onto

the top of the truck, the Squirt had already started mapping the large accident. The report of only fourteen cars needed updating.

"We're going to have to take out some fence, but we need to get down at least where the white van is on its side. The best would be to use the field we used last year to stash a bunch of cars. It's only a half-mile down the road, but I remember it wasn't even half-full with seventeen cars. We can just do a pass-through and drop them as we feed through the line-up."

Hooker scanned the length of the whole wreck. "What about the other end?"

The Squirt laughed. "Do you see who the chip is?" *Micha.* "Knowing him, he'll make any of the rigs coming down the 101 grab a tow and leave. If they head up Blossom Hill and stash a car or three, they will be smarter than I think."

Hooker smiled at the kid but pointed at a distinctive auto club rig. "There's the stash king himself. How do you like Ace's new rig?" He pointed at a five-ton truck similar to the one they stood on.

The Squirt snorted with a laugh. "How big is his engine?"

Hooker laughed. "They thought they got a monster at just under four hundred horses." The Squirt and Hooker both knew they stood on closer to five-hundred and was still a wallowing pig.

The kid laughed again. "Let's go jerk some prom queens out of this barn dance."

AS THE CARS were hauled away, and the highway slowly

cleared, the day turned ugly. A rare summer squall blew in with enough wet to dampen everything. Within minutes, the clouds were squeezed dry and blew away. The sun seared the damp and turned it into mugginess as the temperature soared again.

Micha walked up to Hooker as the man crawled out from under a delivery van with its engine now pushed into the cargo hold. The paramedics had long removed what was left of the driver. Hooker had seen the man's injuries before. He knew the man would only be good for parts donation when they got him to Valley Medical.

"Hooker, what should we do with the prom queen?"

Hooker knew his friend was talking about the one vehicle Hooker would have gotten with Mae—the real money job in the whole mess. Hooker and the Squirt looked at the payday twisted in the slow lane. The truck tractor was a conventional Peterbilt with high capacity dual driving axles. The set of double trailers suffered a few scratches in the melee, but it was basically good to roll with some new paint. The Squirt had peeked into the cab after they took the driver to the hospital from hitting the windshield. It hadn't knocked him out, but his vision was blurred. The tractor still had paper license plates in the back window, and less than ten thousand miles on the odometer—even the bent frame wouldn't total the tractor. It was at least a hundred hours of work for the Fly. Hooker's cut would have paid his basic bills for the month or more.

Hooker wiped his hands on the grease rag as he thought about the larger tow rigs on the scene earlier. "Did Tri-Counties take the Mack in front?"

"They were early and only got the short-bob, and it went

up on Guadalupe. I think Miller got the Mack—and it's headed for South Bay Auto in Daily City."

"See if Karen can get Tri-Counties back here. I might be able to pull the back trailer with the tongue on the jeep, but if I can talk them into taking the whole enchilada to the Fly, then it would make my time here worthwhile." Hooker tried to look hangdog as he cocked his head, looking at his friend.

Micha shaded his eyes as he looked south toward the field where Hooker had been stashing cars for the last three hours. "And you have how many cars parked down near the rail spur?" Micha laughed as he glanced at his watch. "Dolly is there now. How about you powwow with your partner in crime while stashing this one—let her strong-arm Tri-Counties."

Hooker smiled. He knew Micha would casually tell the Tri-Counties driver the rig was headed for the Fly's repair yard. All Hooker had to do was pre-arrange the slots in the backyard.

As Hooker and the Squirt headed for the truck cab, the Squirt turned and looked back at the retreating Highway Patrol Officer. "Hey, Micha... what was the count?"

The man turned. His face was sober in the hot sun. "Four and twenty-three... so far..." *Four dead and twenty-three critical enough to be taken to the hospital. The final death toll may be another twenty-four hours away.*

The kid mused, "It would be nice if the state could find some money to put up at least a dividing barrier."

Micha nodded as he turned. "Seat belt law would have helped too... especially with the little kid."

The accident started with a couple of beers in the middle of the day. Those beers and the heat led to the man falling asleep and crossing the two yellow paint lines separating his car from the oncoming lane full of cars and big rigs.

The southbound lane was only a single lane, but the northbound was split into two lanes a half-mile before. It was natural for drivers to speed up in anticipation of entering the new freeway. The combined force was over one hundred miles per hour coming to a dead stop. The car had caromed off the short-bob truck and angled into the Mack, flipping the tractor and its long trailer full of pipes.

The pipes had split their constraints and boomeranged into the oncoming traffic. The total carnage covered a quarter-mile and spread across all three lanes. Nine tow trucks had worked the scene, along with five fire vehicles and twelve ambulances. Hooker knew the photos of the wreck would be above the fold on tomorrow's front page of the Mercury News. Hooker stopped saving clippings of the wrecks he worked long ago. Someone would be screaming for the state to do something about Blood Alley by noon the next day.

He slipped the truck into gear and watched his mirrors as he began towing the small truck down to the field. The highway was empty. Hooker knew the CHP had the entire highway blocked off to allow access for emergency vehicles. He glanced at his watch and knew the highway would be closed for at least two more hours while the last was towed away. Only then would the forensic guys wrap up the entire scene.

The four-man crew would carefully walk the length of the accident, spread across only one lane at a time. There would be three very slow trips. But first, all the vehicles had to be removed.

Hooker grabbed the microphone and called Dolly. The

day had only started, and it wouldn't be over until every car and truck was towed to where they were going. Hooker knew their day wouldn't be over until well after midnight.

He glanced at the Squirt. Hooker knew if he were hungry, the Squirt was too. On the seat between the men, Box was snoozing, but Hooker knew he would like some food as well.

"1-4-1."

Dolly sounded agitated and in rare form. "Go 1-4-1... and I better get the count."

Hooker passed the microphone to the Squirt as he pulled into the field. He drew the short truck up to the end of the row of eleven cars and three trucks.

"Four and twenty-three, Dolly... but we think the four might be only wishful thinking."

Hooker slid out of the cab. "Ask her if she can order some lunch to go at Chick-n-Ribs. We'll be there in about an hour."

The Squirt waved his hand and returned to the microphone.

When Hooker climbed back into the cab, the kid had a thousand-mile stare as he looked north toward San Jose. "What?"

"She's holding a long tow for tonight or tomorrow."

"Where?"

"Lake Tahoe... and they found another girl... stuffed behind a trash bin..."

"How many days do you have off?"

"A few... but I'll only take the tow to Tahoe with you if I also get to work the case."

"The boys in blue downtown won't like it."

"Their boss won't like it worse when we break the case, and I tell him I'm taking the job with the DOJ in Sacramento." He ground his head around as he leaned back. His face rolled into the family zombie pose.

"Did you get an offer in Sac?"

The kid held up three fingers... and smiled.

Hooker had missed the kid.

As Hooker pulled back onto the highway for the last tow, he smirked and shot the kid a glance. "Sometimes, it pays to get your hand in the way of a fork."

The Squirt held up his hand and examined the four tiny scars on the back of his left hand. "Yeah, well... it was a two-bit stunt."

They both laughed as they pulled up alongside the set of double trailers.

17

—————

WHO?

Dolly looked up from her paperwork. She heard the armor-plate front door swinging open. She glanced over at the small black and white television attached to the cameras looking out to the parking lot and at the front door. It took her a moment to remember who was driving the new five-ton truck, but the second camera revealed two leather jackets and a large cat.

Box slid through the legs and stalked into the large room. His target was sitting where expected. With little effort, he landed in the middle of the big desk and walked onto the top of Dolly's large chest. He snuggled the side of her head as she chuckled, and then he poured himself onto her lumps and into her hands. The French vanilla ice cream had been tasty, but this was worth purring about.

Dolly put her face down into the large cat's side and muttered dove coos and other messages of love. He was the only animal who got her unmonitored affection... everyone else got grief with an occasional hug.

Dolly's head leaned back as she addressed the two men. "You're late."

The two men looked at each other and smiled. In unison, they both rumbled, "We had a stop to make..."

The ice cream voices were stereo and caused the two women at the switchboard to go into instant fits of laughter. Dolly's head snapped up, only an inch from the fur, as she gave them both a hard look. Both men were constantly warned about stopping for French vanilla ice cream and then calling the switchboard. All the girls squirmed and giggled at what Dolly called the bedroom voice. Everyone knew it only made Hooker stop for ice cream more often.

"Go drink some warm water... both of you." Dolly's growl made the women laugh even harder. Everyone knew it was bluster. The girls also knew when the guys called in with ice cream voices, Dolly's work suffered for a brief while after. Dolly's right eye followed the two men returning from the kitchen. The two had scamp written all over their faces, but she was sure they had minded and washed the cream from their throats.

"How was Tahoe?"

Hooker sat next to the desk as the Squirt went over to look in the playpen at Dina's sleeping baby. Dina had made noises about staying off work longer, but Dolly had put her foot down to get back to work and bring the little one. Dolly had already bought the playpen. The kid had inherited a nickname of Dee—short for dispatch. The little bundle had become the company mascot.

Hooker stretched. "Tahoe was an easy in and out. Their new impound yard has some solid features the Fly could implement..."

"I hear a *but* in there."

"That truck is a piece of—"

"Hooker..."

"Piece of a tin dog toy."

"And it is Don's new toy, not yours."

"He'll never drive it more than a hundred miles... maybe." Hooker stuck his thumb in his mouth and pushed on his upper teeth. "Crossing Vacaville to Sacramento, it liked to shake my upper teeth loose."

Dolly rolled her eyes at his exaggeration. She looked over at the younger hoodlum. "You got a complaint too, Squirt?"

The kid looked up. "No, ma'am... but I do think my liver is where my spleen is supposed to be, and my kidneys played square-dance with a foxtrot..."

"You two whiners need to go get some sleep. Don't get up before three this afternoon, and be clean when you come to dinner."

Hooker nodded. It had been a long twenty-two hours. It wasn't until he got to the front door he remembered it was daylight and he was going home. "Box... Go time."

The sleeping cat roused and slid out of the already closing door.

Dolly turned to Dina. "Grab the kid and go home."

The young woman started to protest about not being off for another hour. Karen gave her a stern look. Dina unplugged her headset and, with a *yes ma'am*, was gone.

Karen gave it a few minutes before she turned to face her mother.

Dolly eased herself forward in the chair. "I want her to take the night off. Get Toni in here instead. Also, find Fester and get him here for dinner. Tell his commander he will be held a little late after dinner."

"Anything else?"

"Have Mike pick me up an extra twenty pounds of sausage at Chiaramontes. Call your aunt after one this afternoon and tell her I have the sausage, we need to have a Sunday barbecue. I think the Sweets would be nice to have out also."

Karen knew, even in her sister's home, Dolly had no qualms about arranging people who needed to meet or see one another. The politics of running the county from behind the scenes never stopped.

"Anybody else you want there?"

Dolly thought as she rose from the chair. "Chet... and the nice girlfriend he's seeing. It has been way too long since we've seen him... or them."

Karen thought about the mix for the night's dinner and the Sunday dinner. There were always two sides of the same investigation when it came to the police—and Hooker. "What about Willie, Hank, and Maddie?"

Dolly chuckled, her daughter was learning well. "You mean they don't automatically come with Hooker?"

"Goodnight, Mama." Karen swung her chair around as she gave Dolly one last smirking look. They both looked at the movement on the monitor. The yellow Super Bee had just pulled in. *June.*

As the new gal on the day shift, June pulled the first in slot. By seven-thirty, there would be five snake-wranglers for the patch lines on the answering service's busy switchboards.

Dolly's day finished as Karen's just got warmed up. Their long hours overlapped at both ends. Dolly would be back around three in the afternoon to start dinner, and Karen would usually run the floor and board until the dinner finished.

Without Dina, Karen knew her day would end sometime around nine or ten at night, but Dina would work long the next day while Karen had a day off.

Karen watched the monitor as her mother got into her Cadillac. She knew the last time the woman had taken a day off was when the doctors sent an ambulance to pick her up. Dina had called Valley Med and asked what to do—Dolly was at her desk, panting for breath.

Two days later, the doctor told Dolly she'd had congestive heart failure. Dolly waited for the doctor to leave and then called for a tow truck. She was back running the city after taking a thirty-four-hour vacation.

Karen waited for June to plug into the board then she toggled the shop radio. "1-4-1?"

"1-4-1."

"Your boss said to remind you not to get up before three this afternoon. You are also to be clean and presentable tonight. Where are you and the Squirt going to be?"

"The Hacienda—Hank was up to the city yesterday and didn't do wash. We need fresh shirts."

Karen smirked as she looked up at a schedule Hooker didn't know she had. Candy got off work shortly after midnight.

"Right... Hank... 10-4, 1-4-1."

She wrote a note on her 'hot-board' to call her aunt around one—to tell her about Sunday and Hooker sleeping until at least three.

Well, at least not come out of his room.

She pulled a cord up and plugged it into one of the holes. "Good morning, San Jose Plumbing…"

FOURTEEN HOURS LATER, Karen was still plugging holes on the board, and the dining room was aglow with her mother and the select participants at the table. She gathered the small stack of notepapers and blew a police whistle. She checked the roster again real fast to make sure she had remembered correctly about it being an all-men night. Without turning, she called out the messages to the men seated at the table.

"Ace, you have a commercial holding. See me. I have all the information about the tow—it is going up-country to Santa Rosa. Make sure you get your fuel at the yard.

"Mike, your wife says don't forget to bring the jerky. I think this is code for don't forget your puppy is at your brother's house, and he is holding some homemade jerky for you.

"Fester, the lieutenant said to stay for the meeting, but come see him at home after. You are rover until midnight and then will be working the 17 from the Cats up.

"Don, it was good to see you again. Hooker doesn't let you out enough. Now go home and pack. Your flight is early in the morning. Aloha.

"Steve, you have a T-wonderful. It's now twelve minutes old. You are two minutes out and looking.

"Paul, call your shop. They want you to swap trucks for the night.

"The rest of you men can have more coffee, but you might want to use the office.

"Those leaving—the yard is clear. Don't forget to hug Dolly at the door. Keep it safe."

Hooker pushed back his chair and stood. "Gentlemen..." He shook hands as the men left or moved into the office. The Squirt finished the line.

"Seems like old times..."

"Squirt, you haven't missed many dinners... but your presence has been missed." Hooker tossed his head toward the office. "Let's go fill you in."

As they entered the office, the three other men were just getting comfortable. Hooker took the lounge chair near the desk and pointed at the large desk chair. The Squirt started to object, but Hooker gave him a hard look.

"Que jefe?" The kid took the hint and sat in what would usually be the seat of power.

Hooker gave the Squirt a bland look of mild expectation as he sipped on his coffee. He was amused to see the small signs of the kid uncomfortable at being thrown into the lead position. Hooker also watched the casual adjustment with interest.

The Squirt spread his hands out on the desktop as if feeling the power of the desk and its place in the city and county, as well as its place in Dolly's purview. He looked at the stately gentleman he knew.

"Your Honor, it's good to have you down from the big city to see us again... but I have a feeling this isn't just social. Would you care to introduce your friend...?"

The Superior Court Judge nodded with a smile. "If it would please the desk, we can do without formal titles tonight." He stretched his hands up and out. "After all, we are among friends here, are we not?"

The Squirt nodded with a chuckle. "And we are gathered as brothers in the innermost sanctum sanctorum..."

"Exactly to my way of thinking, Squirt." He smiled and turned to the slight man with the pencil-line mustache, which reminded Hooker and the Squirt of Hank. "This is the man with the most titles, but it's just easiest to say Francis is the foremost authority on the marshes of the San Francisco Bay. Francis, this young man is named John but is ironically known as Squirt. Squirt... Francis d'Bois de la Champagne, of the San Francisco Bay aquarium."

The man had only a slight French accent, but his air and how he sat was very continental. "When I came here to San Francisco, I lived in the dormitory reserved for marine biology students. Because of my fear of being underwater—in a culture that is almost exclusively diving, I was nicknamed Bubbles because of my last name—Champagne. But also, a tease for the one thing I would never do—make bubbles. But you can call me Frank or Frenchie, I respond to those as well as Puddles." He hung his head. "I have a strong love for tide pools."

The Squirt snorted with a laugh. The man fit right in with the usual motif of humor among the extended family of Hooker. "I think we can be comfortable with Francis."

The judge turned with a laugh and poked his fist at the other man's shoulder. "See, Crabby, I told you they were great guys." The man groaned with mock suffering while the judge laughed. Obviously, they were old friends.

The Squirt raised his eyebrows. "And your other friend, Hack?" Feeling comfortable, he used the judge's preferred nickname.

Hooker leaned forward. "Um, Fester is family here,

Squirt. He's Dina's uncle." He waved his finger back and forth between the judge and the officer. "But you two know each other?"

"Only recently... I met Francis out in the marsh because I was the officer of record on the wreck and the resulting homicide investigation. The judge... I only met yesterday up at the aquarium."

Francis re-crossed his legs as he leaned toward Fester. "The duties of a crime scene investigator in the wetlands include taking water and mud samples. Those samples were sent to us at the aquarium for analysis. The extremely high content of cyanide was, to say the least, very alarming. I arranged to take my own samples with the help of an experienced diver. Sadly, we found the fresh samples as alarming as the original ones. Subsequently, we have spent the last two weeks taking counts and samples of the fauna as well as the seagrasses and other flora." Fester rubbed his bald head. As it turns out, the studies have been fortunate in explaining some of the abnormalities in all the skeletons. We scratched our heads about some of the decomp and raw rotting, as opposed to the chew marks we expected from the local crabs and bugs—but only found them in the older bones.

"*Oui*, it appears the poison was in high levels, and because of the stagnant nature of the wetlands, the cyanide concentrated in pockets and either killed off much of the aggressive bio population. A few of the more sensitive yet hearty beetles were driven away. Eventually, if this keeps happening, there will be no more fauna, and from lack of stimulation and diversification, the flora will also die off."

"Are there any measures of mitigation we can take?"

Hooker's head snapped around to look at the kid almost as fast as the smirk of pride washed over his face.

The kid ignored his friend and raised his eyebrows toward the scientist.

"*Oui*, stop this killer from putting bodies in the bay. But I know this is already on everybody's mind—we are just here to add an urgent reason to catching this person, *n'est-ce pas?*"

Hooker's head ground back around. "Persons—as in plural."

The judge gasped. "Two? Do we know who they are?"

Hooker and the Squirt started at the same time. "Sort of..." They stopped and snorted. *Great minds...* Hooker nodded for the Squirt to continue.

"We have a lead on the person who's dumping the bodies. Our sources suggest a man referred to as The Waterman. He has been seen in a canoe he poles standing up. Given the area, it makes a lot of sense. All we know is the area he operates in, and a description of a short blond ponytail, and muscular—or at least has a barrel chest, which could just be an abnormality stemming from chronic childhood asthma in a high altitude or several other medical conditions.

"The poisoner is still a mystery. We are canvassing the downtown area as well as putting the word out for the street workers to be very careful and work or hang out in teams. They are our best bet to watch over one another, and they know it."

"What is being done about finding this Waterman?"

Hooker cleared his throat. "Um... I have a lead... my sister gave me a... she told me there is a vagrant—goes by Tess. She dives the dumpsters behind seafood restaurants on the east side. My sister said this Tess might know more about the guy..."

The judge asked quietly, "Your sister?"

The Squirt came to the rescue. "She has many... um... unorthodox connections and sources for information in the entire Bay Area. She has proved to be reliable and instrumental in solving several investigations. It was her information that led to the wrapping up of the cold case last Christmas as well as critical aid with the mutilator and the shotgun killer cases."

He held the judge's stare until the older man nodded. "Then, let's see where your sister's information leads us."

18
———

TESS

Hooker sat on the toilet—still half asleep. His right hand curled with the two first knuckles mindlessly rubbing the solo fuzzy ear. The deep purr rumbled in the tiled bathroom. Images of the coming day tumbled loosely in Hooker's mind.

The east side of the lower bay was a hodgepodge of industrial areas. In the early years of industry in the south bay, the manufacturing relied on flat-bottomed boats and barges. The alternative to getting your goods to San Francisco entailed a long trip down and around the bay by wagon. The other involved freighting the goods on the train up to Oakland and then ferry across to the docks in the Barbary Coast. Many of the original entrepreneurial boatmen had worked in their youth on riverboats on the Mississippi or the Ohio. A wind-powered skiff or barge can haul a lot of cargo and not worry about snagging on seagrass.

Later, as steam changed boating, the channels became formalized, and centers popped up along those shipping avenues. Tiny clusters named after the original dock owner—

now became towns and cities. Between larger known towns or cities, like Milpitas, Fremont, and San Lorenzo, there were tiny enclaves named for more colorful reasons. Union City had been one of the first to ban the Bars and Stars of the rebels who had broken away from the United States. There had been no other group or town who thought to align with the new federation—most were more concerned with getting the last money of the gold rush and looking forward to what was next for the state.

Another enclave named Newark—for a castle in Scotland. Originally, a broad flatland enjoyed by the Ohlone Indians. Then came Mission San Jose, and the Indians were put to work on the same land, now claimed by the padres. The land wasn't the most fertile, but the fish, crabs, and shrimp were put to good use—mostly feeding the padres' pigs.

An enterprising young man named Mowry dug out a shallow area and diked off the water. Once flooded, he would stop any new water for a few days of hot sun and then refill the shallow basins. Eventually, the basins would dry, and he would have his workers harvest the raw salt. This salt would then be loaded into bags, ferried out along Mowry's slough, and then across to the waiting ships. The salt was sold around the world.

Hooker stood in the cool fall of shower water as he thought about Mowry's slough, and the small crab shacks dotting the shoreline. The crab was better in Monterey, but it would be a good place to start looking for a man in a dress named Tess.

"Good morning, sunshine." Stella looked at the foggy eyes as she poured Hooker a large mug of coffee. She wanted to laugh, but at a quarter till noon, she knew he was not in his usual routine. "Manny and the Squirt are going over some maps and details in the office. Do you want me to start making you something to eat?"

Hooker leaned his hip against the counter with his eyes closed. Stella wasn't sure if he had fallen asleep or just thinking. "Um... when did you plan to eat next?"

"We can have lunch in about an hour. Manny will need food then." She was timing his blood sugar levels in her head.

Hooker took the mug and gently sipped. Stella watched his shoulders relax. He turned toward the office and then turned back and kissed her on the cheek. "Thanks. I can wait, and we can all eat together."

She watched the bare feet padding across the slate floor as the zombie in a white T-shirt and jeans walked with his nose in the coffee vapors. He paused for a larger sip before entering the office.

Absentmindedly, Stella dialed the number she called at least once a day.

Karen's voice reminded her Dolly wasn't up yet. It didn't matter. Her niece would do just fine. This was just silly girl stuff anyway. "When did he become such a man?"

Karen chortled. "Hooker? You obviously haven't been paying much attention these last... what, ten years?" She sighed. "Auntie Stell, I think he was a man before he got his real truck. We just weren't paying attention."

"The one-ton Don gave him... or Mae?"

"Take your pick. I think Don knew he was underage back then. But he wouldn't have given the new Ford to someone who wouldn't respect the opportunity. I think Don always saw the man in Hooker. It just took the rest of us time to catch up."

Stella ran the cold water and stuck her left hand in the stream. "Well, I'm sure glad my daughter Candy saw the man in him. Sometimes a jacket can hide a lot of adult."

Karen snorted. "He tries to... but there is nothing he can get away with around here. Sweetie, the boards are on fire this morning. I gotta go help out. Love you."

"Love you too—" Stella pulled the buzzing dial tone away from her ear. "—sweetheart." She hung up the phone and leaned against the counter, sipping her coffee. Her sense of need had only been partially placated. She hated when the ogres of her childhood would sneak back into her heart when she was supposed to stand strong for her family.

She thought about lunch and gently poured the last of the coffee from her cup into the pot of the coleus plant hanging near the window. Even the tiny plant she bought only six months before—now the size of a beach ball—proved coffee was good for you.

Manny was calmly reading with the headphones on. Hooker glanced over at the large reels on the tape recorder. The sixteen-inch reels moved slow enough for Hooker to read the word Bach on the label. He knew Manny was truly relaxing and working hard at not being interested in the Squirt methodically going over a couple of detailed auto club maps.

"Did Manny breakout water charts for the bay, as well?"

The Squirt put his finger on where he had last studied. He looked up and smiled.

"No need. I memorized those when we rolled the train with the caustic soda. At the time, I also needed the tide flow-charts to know where the currents would eventually take the soda—and what it would end up killing."

"What a waste of time… "

"No… I knew we could roll the cars over and not leak a drop—we had done it too many times to screw up. No, I needed the information to solidify my credentials."

Hooker chuckled. "And jack the poor railroad guys up for an unwarranted payday."

The Squirt rolled his eyes as he returned to the map. "Yeah, I noticed how polished and shiny Mae looks out front. Even if she also looks like you shrunk her in the spin cycle."

Manny slipped his headphones down and turned his chair around. "Where do you plan to start?"

Hooker pointed at his chest. "Excuse me? Are you talking to the one person who hasn't got the slightest clue as to where we're going?" He pointed at the Squirt. "Why don't you ask the driver?"

The Squirt's head snapped up, and his look volleyed back and forth between the other two. "Since when do I get to drive?"

"The question is more like do you know how? I mean, you did drive the five-ton over and pick me up… but then, you could have just gotten lucky."

"I've been practicing on the skidpad at the academy if it counts for anything?" He looked at Manny for support.

Manny shrugged and mewed his lips. "I guess if the street just happens to be all hosed down with soapsuds and it's raining." He smiled at Hooker.

Hooker gave the kid a cold look. "So where are we going? Or have you worked it out yet?"

"Mostly." He grabbed one of the more detailed water depth maps and folded under the bay water section—leaving the shoreline and land. He took the auto club map and laid it out the same way. With the auto club map on top, he started pointing at the channels.

"I've been looking for areas containing small food joints which might overlook public put-in ramps or docks. In the water, I've also been looking at where the channels lead from the body dump to the east side of the bay. Now the distance by small boat being paddled or poled is quite a ways, but if the guy is on the water all the time—the distance won't matter." He washed his hand along the shoreline. "I think our best chance of finding Tess is in this twelve miles. It sounds like a lot, but I'm guessing there are only seven or eight crab shacks at the most." He sat back.

Hooker looked at the area. He hadn't wanted to start down in Fremont and work north, looking for a crab shack, sandwich hut, or food joint along the shore. He could just feel how tedious the hunt could be.

The Squirt's plan would cut to the heart of the southeast shoreline and trim the work in half or less. He looked up at the Squirt and smiled. He then looked at Manny and started to laugh.

Hooker could hear the insecurity in the kid's protest. "What...?"

Hooker put his hand up. "No, really, kid. You did great. You already cut at least half of the search area out. And in this? That's huge." He turned toward Manny. "What is your favorite most powerful weapon or tool?"

Manny started to laugh as he picked up the phone to show. "But I don't have the phone book for those areas."

Hooker held his hand out for the instrument. "No, but dispatch does. And more than that, they have phone numbers and radios straight to the guys who tow those areas and would know all of those shacks."

Stella called from the other room. "Boys, your powwow is over. Wash your hands. Lunch is ready."

Hooker nodded his head sideways. "Go ahead. I'll be quick..." He started dialing

19

FROM OUT OF THE GRASS

Lane poled slowly. The late grass grew high enough above the waterline to hide all but his head. As his canoe slid silently over the water, he scanned the grass and beyond. He rarely looked at the open water of the rivers through the grass. In the black water, he only ever saw the night sky. It disturbed him to think of the other part.

The sunshine burned on his back. The three layers of cotton shirt and undershirts, although hotter, were necessary. He picked at the binding layers with his off-poling hand as he switched the pole to the other side. The few crabs in the bottom of the canoe crawled slowly in the heat and made a scratching noise on the aluminum. Lane knew the water kept the floor of the canoe cool because his bare feet rested there. He liked to think he could feel the water flowing under the metal even though he knew it was just in his imagination. His eyes burned darkly under the long-billed hat as he watched the distant shoreline.

Lane did not need to be close to know what the bearded woman in the filthy baggy dress was telling the two men. Her fat arms waved back and forth as she pointed at the sea of grass. She pointed north where the river of freshwater came from, where the crayfish were sweeter, where Lane usually hid his canoe. Her arm moved south to where the river wound into the grass, and with three chops of her hand and arm, she told them about the three passages Lane used the most to get out to the island.

Lane watched as the woman's hand fanned out as she described the spread of the smaller streams of sweet water wandering out toward the trestle. His eyes rolled up into his head as he silently hacked up some bile and spat into the water near the grass. He slowly sank down onto the seat in the middle of the canoe. His hand slowly slid down on the pole shoved into the mud. He leaned into the pole and his hand. *That nosey fucking woman...*

Lane's breathing was raspy. He was becoming agitated. Even as a child, his mother would see him this way and take his hand, guiding him into the house and onto her bed, where she would rub his chest until he calmed down. The rubbing had been reassuring and calming as a small child, but as an older child, it became another form to cause agitation. The rubbing became more than just to calm the chest.

With a bible in one hand, scripture spewing rapid-fire from her mouth between the panting breaths that turned to moans—Lane was introduced to tantric hellfire and brimstone salvation and sex. As the body matured, and the chest grew large, the ritual took on even more grotesque machinations. None of which had anything to do with calming or religious salvation—but everything to do with sexual deviancy.

Lane's eyes rolled, and his breathing turned to panting. His pupils looked out from the edge of his upper eyelids as his head lowered. The hand on the pole pulled down as the body slowly rose. The eyes, hidden in the dark shadow of the long bill of the waterman's hat, focused across the tips of the grass. The loose hand slowly rubbed and stroked the large breasts under the binding as the one side of the mouth twitched and jerked gradually into a sardonic smirk.

Pete's voice growled deep in the throat, "Tonight, bitch... tonight."

Slowly, Lane took back his body and face. His breathing was calmer. Everything would be taken care of... tonight. Under the night sky, the same sky he saw when he looked into the water. The sky of his other half...

Unhurriedly, he crouched slightly, his head just below the level of the grass. His hands gripped the pole and worked it— silently walking the tip in the mud.

The canoe turned and drifted back through the rivers of the grasses. The sun overhead danced in the wavering heated air. The summer sun drove the crabs and shrimp to find safety in among the grasses... in among the dead... in among... the two's mother. Lane pushed on the end of the pole. Tonight would come. *Their mother would be fed.*

THE SQUIRT PUT his hand up to shade his eyes as he looked west across the grass. Slowly, his eyes panned across an area Tess had pointed out.

"What do you see, Squirt?"

He shook his head as his hand dropped. He turned and looked at Hooker and Tess. "Probably a bird or something."

Tess harrumphed. "The grass will do funny things to you. You think there is something there... and then you really look... and it's nothing." He looked at Hooker. "Or it's the waterman..."

"So you think he's in the area?"

Hooker raised an eyebrow.

"If the sun is up—he's on the water. It's always just a matter of where. Like I was saying, he moves around a large area. I mean... not large like the whole bay, but for a man in a canoe... the grass lakes are large." Tess hitched at the shoulder of his muumuu. Hooker heard the metallic sound again like muffled tin.

"You used the term before—lakes of grass. What do you mean by it?"

Tess pointed out across the bay with his hand spread out flat. "When you look out there, you see grass. When you think of the bay from here to, say, the place where the white airplanes fly—"

The Squirt cut in. "The Navy base... those are submarine chasers—P-3 Orion." He could see on the man's face that none of the information was making sense to him. He shook his open palm back and forth. "Never mind. Continue."

Tess grabbed his chest with both palms and moved his breasts or whatever was under the large dress, side to side. He closed his eyes, and as he opened them, he was looking back at Hooker. "When you think of the bay, you think of it as one large body of water. But what you don't know, unless you have been out there, is there are large areas which have water, but there are also areas of land."

"Like the island the trestle runs across."

"Yes. And on the island, there's a lake, as there are other lakes. There are paths of land between those lakes, and the only breaks are the rivers of freshwater running through everything. But the areas between the levies, pathways, roads, or just dirt, make those lakes. But when I say lake, you think of a large area of open water. But what I'm talking about is a body of water consisting of mud below, grass above, and the water between the two."

Hooker pointed at the clear water in front of them for all of twenty feet and then the field of grass. "So you are saying this area in front of us is one lake, and the one way down there is another lake..."

Tess smirked. "Almost. Way down there is just a salt marsh—not much water." He turned, pointing further north of them. "That... is another lake—of grass."

The Squirt was having a hard time with the concepts. "But why say grass instead of a lake of water with grass in it?"

"Because... the grass is everything here.

"I've been up North Bay. I've seen what they have there. Until you start up the river... there is no grass. Sure, there is some little grass growing along the shore. But no lakes of grass —not like here."

Hooker was starting to understand the weight or meaning of the grass. "So, without the grass...?"

Tess's head began to bob, and his long stringy beard crinkled and folded below his chin. "... ever'thin' be dead." He pointed out across to where he knew the ghost town was. "Dead like that there Drawbridge town." He shook with a muted sound of metal. "Dead like them women you said they pulled out from under the old trestle."

Hooker glanced at his watch. "Tess," he stuck his hand out, "we would like to thank you for taking the time to talk to us. Is there anything we can do for you... buy you some seafood from the shack or anything?"

"Don't like no fresh food. Better to get it out of the barrels —too hot otherwise. But if you have any empty cans..." He smiled and patted his hips. The muted sound of tin cans rattled under his hands. No clarification.

Hooker softly shook his head. "If we had any, they would be yours. If we come back, I'll remember to bring some... any particular size you want?"

"Naw... any size will do."

"I'll remember that."

20

NIGHT ATTACK

The crescent moon left only an eerie ghosting glow around objects. The collective trash heap of shipping pallets, packing crates, and tin cans were squeezed into what had once been a loading dock before a fire removed the old wooden warehouse. Layers of smashed tin cans littered the top of the heap—showing leaden in the soft light.

A dark figure moved from deep shadow to deep shadow. It crept along the alley, which once had been lined with busy trucks of commerce. The crumbling ruins were now a reflection of the broken dreams of better times.

The large breasts swung loosely in the shirt as Pete crept to the piled trash where Tess lived. Pete squatted to see in the low hooch.

The lumps of darker shapes in the gloom of the structure were the focus of her intent. Her hands absentmindedly snapped open the commando knife. Gripping the knife with both hands, she began stabbing the shape in a rage.

"Hey." The voice bounced muffled off the alley structures.

Pete jumped erect—frightened. She flipped the knife, face forward in her hand. The heap she dismissed before as trash rose. *Tess.* Pete charged and stabbed at the woman's chest. The knife met with hard resistance. Pete became enraged and stabbed over and over—all ending with the tip of the knife hitting a hard surface or being deflected.

Tess began hitting at the attacker's head. It wasn't the first time Tess had been attacked. But once he started making his tin-can armor, the attacks had become less successful. His fists were telling as he hit the head and shoulders.

Finally, realizing the stabbing wasn't successful, Pete focused on the head and arms. But even those became diffi-cult as the intended victim seemed adept at defending those areas not protected by the dress of armor plate.

The battle raged, crashing among the trash. The two stumbled in amateurish combat for their lives. Tess grabbed and threw trash as ammunition, most of which just bounced off the attacker. Occasionally, some trash was heavy enough to take a toll. The blood flung about as the knife slowly took its toll on the exposed flesh.

Pete dodged a large wet object and made one last slash at Tess's neck, connecting. The blade bit deep at the side of the neck and slid forward. Grabbing at her neck, Tess stumbled backward and fell, screaming into a pile of trash. Pete fled.

Gasping for breath, Tess rolled over and began to crawl. The trail of blood smeared blackly in the dim light. Tess's vision blurred, but a glow of light blossomed into a peony of yellow, and then contracted to a dim forty-watt bug light a few blocks away.

Tess knew nobody would be in the small machine shop at this hour, but she clung to the hope—*someone would at least find her body.*

FORTY MILES, and hours later, the phone rang in the sunroom. The walls were still yellow with the dawn light. The phone rang a second time as the phone in the office echoed the ring.

The third ring was cut short. "Hello?" Hooker stood naked in the office.

"Hooker?"

"Yes...?"

The female chuckled as Dolly joined the conversation. "Where are you?"

"Hacienda..."

Dolly cleared her throat. "Where are you standing?"

"In the office..." Hooker's mind was catching up to his standing and talking on the phone. "I'll be right back." He put the phone down and stalked out of the office. He resisted the urge to look down the other short hallway to see if Stella was standing in her and Manny's bedroom doorway. This would be one of those things they would never talk about.

A slender milk-white arm and hand poked out of his bedroom door—holding his pair of jeans. As he took them, he heard the door down the other hall snick quietly closed. Candy's muffled giggle was cut short by the door closing. The thick doors in the Hacienda were almost soundproof. The sound of Candy laughing hysterically was only in Hooker's mind. *Or not.*

"What?"

There was a silent dead pause Hooker recognized as Dolly's finger holding down the mute button on her desk phone. The usual static of empty air in the Dispatch office returned. "Do you have... are you wearing—"

Hooker saved both of them by cutting her off with a growl. "It is six-twenty-seven in the morning, Dolly. I don't work today, and you have woken your sister. This had better be good."

Hooker was sure he had just heard Dolly open and close her mouth at least three times in the ensuing minute of silence. He didn't care. Only now did he have any scrap of decency with his jeans on. He did not turn at the sound behind him. He heard his boots settle on the floor and something soft being placed over the back of the chair beside the doorway.

"Were..." She still had to take a moment. "Were you out near Fremont yesterday?"

"We tracked down a man named Tess..." Hooker rubbed at the large scars along his right side, where the dimes had entered and been removed the year before. The nerves were always knitting.

"She was admitted to Fremont Memorial this morning. When they found her, they thought she was dead."

"She is a he..."

"He is a she... despite the beard."

Hooker's mind skidded on strange ice. He turned slowly at another sound. The Squirt was fully dressed and leaning against the doorway.

The Squirt raised one eyebrow as he continued. "Tess is female..."

Hooker covered the phone and looked hard at the young

man. "How do you know?"

The kid, now the teacher, ran his finger down his throat. "She doesn't have an Adam's apple... therefore, a female."

Hooker grumped as he turned. "It doesn't matter." He held the phone to his ear. "We're on our way."

"Take your time... she's in surgery. But the sheriff's deputy is there and wants to talk to you. Just make sure you get something to eat—it might be a long day."

Hooker thought about the time as he hung up. "I need coffee..."

The Squirt harrumphed. "Too early. The new coffeemaker doesn't go on until eight."

Hooker leveled half an eye at the young man. "We'll get some on the way." Hooker grabbed his boots and the T-shirt as he slid past the Squirt. He opened the door to his bedroom to find Candy pulling on her espadrilles.

She looked up and paused. "Are you off or not?"

"Off... but the Squirt and I are going to the hospital in Fremont."

She stood and growled. "Oh, no, you aren't. Not without me. I'm not letting you anywhere near a hospital unsupervised. Knowing you two—you would check yourselves in."

"What are you doing about breakfast?" Hooker turned to find Stella in her bathrobe and bare feet.

"Nothing which concerns you... go back to bed. You two get the house to yourselves today." He smirked and winked. Leaning back into their surrogate mother, he kissed her on the cheek. "If I have to stay on days much longer... I'm pulling another phone line direct into here... or moving downstairs."

Stella grabbed him with both arms around his neck as she

laughed. "Don't even joke about keeping my daughter locked up down there and away from me..."

Candy kissed her on the other cheek. "I'll pay for the phone line. It can ring both places for all I care. I'm going to be wherever stinky is, anyway." She laughed and danced away toward the pantry as Hooker's hand grabbed for her jeans.

The three disappeared down the secret stairs to the garage. As the door swung back closed, Stella laughed as she heard the Squirt call back, "Don't wait dinner, Mom."

The silence settled down around her. The house was still full of the kids' noise. Stella smiled as the grandfather clock began to chime. She had hours of sleep left. She shuffled down the hall and swayed her hips as she hummed a tiny happy tune.

The Squirt backed the Granny car out of the garage. Hooker and Candy rode in the back. Candy giggled as she watched Hooker try to get comfortable. "Have you ever even been in the backseat of a car before?"

Hooker blushed. "Sure... as a kid."

As the Granny eased up the driveway to the street, Candy remembered who wasn't in the car. "Where's Box?"

The Squirt snorted. "At the curb." He pulled up and stopped at the street for only a second. The orange avenger crested over the door and stepped down and across to sit next to the Squirt. The young man nosed the car out onto the street and headed north. His right hand curled around the fur body, and his fingers found the softest fur of the cat's chest. Hooker and Candy weren't sure which was doing the purring. They leaned back and enjoyed being chauffeured in the early sunshine.

They ended at the table in the front window of the Whole Donut. As the other daughter in the family, Mai fussed over Candy and left serving the men to her husband, Ralph. "You live in big house with too many men." She moved to present her rear end just as her husband came with a plate of donuts. He knew it was coming and came to rest gently. "Just one big clumsy oaf in house enough... and sometimes too much. You take Hooker. He strong and have good teeth. He enough." She reached behind her and grabbed at her husband's crotch but only came away with a loose apron.

"Woman, you are slow. I should have used faster bait when I went fishing for a wife." Ralph sat down next to Hooker. He leaned over with a conspiratorial whisper they could all hear. "I think she is trying to kill me. She makes me run all day and then expects me to rub her feet at night. What is it with their feet?" He looked at Candy, who was now blushing.

Hooker smirked and nodded. "It's a woman thing, Ralph... it's a woman thing. I'm just happy I only have to rub Mae West's feet once every three-thousand miles."

Candy's eyes opened wide as her mouth formed a large O. "Oh, so now my feet are to be equated with big fat tires?"

Mai patted her on the shoulders. "Oh, maybe Mai be wrong about Hooker. Mai find you nice Vietnam boy. They work hard... unless they are lazy. I no find you American boy. You already have brother... if Mai have little sister—he no run far." She winked at the now blushing Squirt.

Everyone laughed at the Squirt's expense. Ralph enjoyed the moment of sitting. It was rare Hooker ever stayed more than a few moments in the back lot to pick up some donuts or the occasional stop to just say hello. The couple met in Vietnam, and when he brought Mai home with him, it was learned she was still only sixteen. They waited out the two years working in a donut shop near the VA hospital at Stanford.

Once Ralph had finished with his medical recovery, the local police and fire pooled money to buy the donut shop with its large parking lot. The police departments, fire departments, and others related to law enforcement had created pools the whole office or department had poured coins and dollars into. Once the young couple found out how it wasn't just a few special people—but the whole community who pooled together—they named the shop for the greater city of new friends.

The wall behind Ralph and Hooker was a mass of photos already layers thick of those people who helped make the shop happen, and now enjoyed the fruits of the couple's labor. Hooker's photo was in many of the photos and newspaper clippings of accidents.

Ralph leaned toward Hooker as he watched his wife and Candy. "To what do we owe the pleasure of the three of you for more than a few minutes?"

Hooker put down his mug. "We have to run up to Fremont Memorial. Someone we interviewed yesterday was attacked last night. We think they are related."

"And Candy is along to keep the two of you out of the hospital beds?" Ralph started to chuckle.

Hooker gave him a hard look. "Is my reputation that bad? That is exactly what she said she came along for."

Ralph roared and almost fell out of his chair.

"It's not funny..."

Gaining control, Ralph pointed his finger between Hooker and the Squirt. "But you have to admit..."

The Squirt rolled his eyes and raised his eyebrows. "They do have a point..."

"Oh, don't you start in on this. I can always replace you with a brick in the seat."

Ralph snorted. "Speaking of Box... didn't you bring the man?"

Hooker gave him a look. "It's a food joint."

"And?"

"It gets full of cops..."

"And?" Mai stood with her fists on her hips as she joined in. Turning, she marched to the back door where they could all hear her open the whining screen door and call once for the cat.

Box strolled in with his tail straight up to the tip where it crooked at the last inch. The front door opened. Two motorcycle cops—a CHP and a San Jose officer—walked in. The chip slowly pulled his helmet off and looked at the cat. "Good morning, Box. Where is your—" He then saw the table full of people. "Oh..."

Hooker winked. "Good morning, Bill. We're not here."

"Heck no... You're out there on the wreck on 101, with the four overturned rigs and six cars." He smiled at pulling Hooker's chain. Everyone knew it was killing Hooker to be driving a smaller tow truck, as well as pulling a standard day shift.

Hooker's middle finger mirrored the Squirt's as they slid slowly up the sides of their noses. The two officers saw the two fingers and laughed.

Ralph looked at the chest and head of the now purring

cat. He could tell Candy's hands were busy massaging the large cat. "As you can see, the regular clientele have no problem with your partner being in here. We don't see enough of any of you, so getting to see Box is a bonus."

Hooker thought about what was on many people's minds. "You two need some employees so you can come out for a Sunday barbecue."

"We have a new guy. He helps do the prep in the morning as well as the clean up after. But you know how she is about the baking." He nodded at his wife serving the two cops. "But we do talk about it. It has been six years, and we do more than enough business... and it would be good to come out to the big house and visit with Manny and Stella."

"Look, how much business do you really do on the Fourth of July?"

Ralph duck lipped a raspberry.

"Right, so you use the day as an excuse to just clean. So put a sign up today saying you'll be closed on the Fourth. Everyone will expect it anyway. Besides, you know where all of your customers will be from about eleven o'clock on." Hooker raised his eyebrow. "We expect you two no later than noon... and no donuts. Mai is only allowed to bring some hugs. Gosh knows we always have more food than we can eat... or the few hundred people who will be there."

Ralph looked at his wife returning to the table. "Honey, we're going to be closed on the Fourth of July."

"Good, you need to clean the oven racks... they start to turn brown. And, then—"

He cut her off—probably for the first time. "Good thing we will be closed on the third as well. As for the cleaning, I'm sure Manuel has a cousin or brother he can bring along. We're going to let them clean from the Wall of Fame to the street. You and I can watch or go have a nice lunch somewhere and maybe go see a movie." He looked hard at his wife.

Finally, her shoulders sagged, and she sat down. Carefully, she reached out and gently tried one cautious pet of the large cat. She watched her hands fold down into her lap. Looking up, she looked at Ralph with a slim smile. "Okie dokie, husband." She turned and smiled at Candy.

Ralph looked at a stunned Hooker. His face was a surprised relief. "Well, that went well."

Hooker snorted softly. "Noon, no later..."

"Noon."

Mai leaned over and asked quietly, "Where I make him take me for lunch?"

Candy chuckled softly. "You call Stella, and if she can't tell you—you call Dolly." The two smiled at the thought of the two powerful women in their lives, and in Hooker's life.

21

INTERVIEW AT THE HOSPITAL

"Officer Stafford?" Hooker stepped over to the officer standing behind the nurse's station. "My name is Hooker. The Squirt here and I talked to Tess about a possible suspect in the body dump out in the grasses."

"Thanks for coming out. I rolled out on the report of a dead body in the front door of a local machine shop. Lucky for the lady, machinists have a habit of working in the cool of the early morning."

Hooker pointed out the others. "This is my girlfriend, Candy, and her brother John—but he responds faster to Squirt. This isn't the first time we've worked a case."

The officer shook hands with Candy as he eyed the Squirt. He leaned in. "Is this the same snot-nosed kid who is upsetting everyone at the academy?"

Candy snorted and nodded. The Squirt opened his mouth with mock offense in a silent protest.

Hooker chuckled. "Save it, Squirt. Word travels fast."

The officer smirked. "So... making you the two-bit towing whore."

The Squirt held Hooker's hand up, and they all laughed at Hooker's chagrin. Candy smiled at the establishing credentials. "You almost sound like you're related to Dolly."

The man smiled softly. "Dispatch Dolly? She almost became my mother-in-law, but Karen ran a little too fast. But at least I attended the wedding. She graduated the year ahead of me in school."

Hooker glanced down the hall at an orderly pushing a heavily draped gurney. "Is that...?"

The officer glanced at the gurney. "Nah, she got out of surgery over an hour ago." He looked over at the nurse. "When do you think we can have a minute with her?"

The nurse stood. "Let me go check." She held her finger up. "But only a minute."

Candy snorted softly then growled. "I'll keep them on a short leash, but it is important." The nurse nodded and left.

The officer nodded. "She lost a lot of blood. The EMTs said if the machinist found her just twenty minutes later... we would be having this conversation at the morgue.

"Her wounds are all consistent with a knife attack. The lacerations are light to deep, mostly along the fronts of her forearms, so she participated in the fight. From the looks of her knuckles, our guess is she gave almost as good as she got. The final blow is the deep slash to her neck. It missed the carotid artery—but barely. Another millimeter and she would have bled out at the scene of the fight."

Hooker shifted and leaned against the desk. "So they didn't find her where she was attacked?"

"She left quite a trail. It was about two long blocks away

from the machine shop. If she had died there, she would have never been found. The blocks were warehouses back during the war—"

The Squirt frowned. "Korea?"

"Maybe as late as Korea... but it was more like manufacturing munitions to support Alameda Naval Station during the first and second war. I think it was some of the artillery stuff that started the blaze—it took out over a square mile. The area never really recovered. Manufacturing moved down into Fremont or up to Emeryville. The Navy wanted things closer, and the stuff like regular machining, tooling, and warehouses needed to be closer to the workers' homes."

The Squirt liked the history lesson, but it chaffed his cop side. "So the area is burned out and empty?"

"For the most part. There is a little rebuilding. Land is cheap, and tilt-ups are easy to build. But around where the lady set up her hooch is still pretty empty—except where people just dump stuff, which, in her case, is camouflage. It took us several minutes to realize the pile of trash, heaped in an old loading dock bay, was her hooch. The only thing that gave it away was the layers of flattened cans attached as a roof. It looked the same way she had built her dress of armor."

"Armor?"

The officer nodded. "Damnedest thing I'd ever seen. It reminded me of some of the suits of armor I saw in a German museum when I was stationed there. She had three or four layers of flattened cans held together with a network of plastic rings from six-packs of beer. We would have laughed it off like a guy with tinfoil in his hat, but we could tell by how torn up her dress was it saved her life."

"Was there anything in her... hooch?" The Squirt's face

wound into his face of not quite understanding. "I mean where she was living... anything of value?"

The officer chuckled. "Hooch... it's a term from Vietnam. The guys would stack things and make underground living shelters, much like the bums do under bridges, in doorways, old buildings... where they can feel safe and return to night or day. Some of them roam at night, and others move about panhandling and such during the day."

Hooker looked at Candy. She smiled back softly. The man was talking about family.

"There wasn't anything of real value we could figure out. But the bedding told us a lot. Whoever attacked her did so at the point of rage, but was also methodical in their attack. Most of the violent stabbings centered where a person's middle would be. It's the least defensible and the softest target. After five fast stabs—very close together, the stabs become random as if searching for a body the original attack didn't find. Under the bedding, there were some pallets. Where the original five stabs had hit, four broke the boards underneath. The power needed to do such damage tells us we're looking for a man with developed upper body strength. From my experience with knife fights and wounds, I would say we're looking for a man between five-eight and six foot. But I don't think they're really comfortable with knife fights."

"Why do you say that?"

"If you know knife fights, the blade is held down like you're using an ice pick. The edge faces away from you. This way, you can use your fist or hit and slash. Also, with a longer knife, the blade somewhat protects your forearm. But the edge cuts in the bedding were on the side toward the person kneeling there, and all the slash wounds on the woman are blade forward, edge down cuts. The person doesn't know how to fight... but they do understand a sturdy knife. Their knife did some serious damage on those boards, and the armor was bent pretty bad... I wouldn't be surprised if she has some internal damage."

"What about a waterman—someone who makes their living out there in the grass and bay?"

"Crabbies? Sure... they'd fit the bill. Pulling even small nets and poling small boats around... takes upper body strength. Shucking clams and busting up crabs takes a thick, sturdy knife. What made you think of them?"

"Call it a hunch." Hooker looked up to watch the nurse return.

"Come this way. She's still groggy from the anesthesia, but you can have a brief moment." She led the way.

"Hey, Tess..." Candy took the lead. "Hooker and the Squirt are here. They want to ask you a couple of questions. But if you start to feel woozy or tired, you let me know, and I'll send them packing."

The woman, laying quietly—more bandages than skin—waved her left arm of white gauze. Hooker leaned close.

Her voice was little more than a soft breeze rustling across the seagrass. "It was the waterman's sister..." She swallowed hard. Hooker reached over and grabbed the bottle with the straw. She took a few sips. "She looks like him. She must be a twin... but I felt her tits."

Hooker patted her on the shoulder gently. "You rest, Tess... We got all we needed. The information and to know you're all right." He leaned in close to the woman's ear. "The Mouse says to say hello." He drew back, expecting to see shock in the woman's eyes. There was none.

"I just knew it..." Softness appeared at the edge of her eyes. "You tell your sister I said hello. She always treated me with respect. She also thought, because of the beard, I was a man. You can tell her you know the truth now."

Hooker smiled and squeezed her shoulder softly. "I'll tell her next month when I go to see her."

"Is she doing okay?"

He nodded as the nurse came in. "You get some sleep now. You're safe here." He watched for the soft blink of acknowledgment. They left Tess to the nurse who pushed a syringe into the IV tube. They all knew she would be asleep before they made it to the hall.

The Squirt looked at Hooker as they walked down the hall. "I couldn't quite make out..."

"It's the waterman's twin or sister. She said she could feel the woman's tits." He looked over at the Squirt. "How big do you think they would have to be—when you can feel them during a fight for your life?"

The Squirt was almost analytical, but he had a smile. "Probably bigger than Beth's..."

Candy slugged the kid in the shoulder.

"Hey... He asked."

"Well, you didn't have to... Well, Beth is... Well, I like her." Candy grumped and folded her arms across her own chest. She knew she was nowhere near what the conversation was about—but nonetheless felt a little self-conscious.

"I like her too... but she's not as big as she likes to show. There is a little push and pad in there. Not much—but a little."

Hooker looked at the ceiling as they neared the intersection of the halls. "So, would you say maybe as big as—"

Candy cut him off. "Do you two want to catch a bus home... because, in case you didn't remember—the car was given to me?"

The men laughed and changed the subject to their favorite. The Squirt gave Hooker the eye. "Do you know where to get some ice cream around here?"

Hooker chuckled. "What do you think I am... braindead? Of course, I do." His head rolled in the zombie flop... which was mirrored by the Squirt.

"A couple of children." Candy rolled her eyes as they hit the door to the outside. She flipped around and banged the door with her butt as her head rolled back and down onto her shoulder with her mouth open and tongue slewed out. The quintessential Stella zombie roll. *She was studying her mother well.*

Hooker laughed as they spilled out into the small parking area. His eyes scanned along the strips of grass until he saw the familiar feline. "Box—go time."

22

FOURTH OF BARBECUE

The lower parking lot was full. The large doors on the food barn were wide open, and people spilled out under the large tents erected over the long tables and chairs. The canning kitchen, along the south side of the barn, was put to use as the cook stations for everything coming out of the giant barbecue trailer.

What looked like a large watering truck tank on its own set of wheels was parked along the southeast rim of the parking lot—overlooking the Almaden valley. The attending firefighters had one of the large doors up and were loading the first half of four dozen tri-tip roasts, a dozen hams, and four racks of fresh-made Sicilian sausages from Chiaramontes.

"You guys going to have enough meat?" Hooker stood with a carafe of coffee in one hand and a stack of white foam cups in the other.

The redhead, going gray, turned. The small burn patches on his face were white on his florid face. "Oh, thank the saints, Ax. The rescue is at hand." He patted the other man.

Hooker laughed. "I don't know if I would go so far as to

call it a rescue, Sparks. This tainted water is only a few minutes old. But we did start a whole pot, which will be more to your tastes in about four hours." He handed each of the men a foam cup and started pouring. Stella had known to ladle half a cow of cream and a field of cane sugar into the carafe for her two favorite firefighting brothers.

Ax took a sip and smiled. "Ah, I taste the touch of a sweet woman in these grounds." The man had never been closer to Ireland than Reno, Nevada—but Hooker had never heard him speak any other way than if he was from the green isle. *Father McBride and he must be best friends.*

"How much meat are you putting up in this monster?" Hooker looked into the large cavity and the rotating racks.

Sparks grabbed up a clipboard and glanced down the list. His lips moved as he did the math in his head. He sipped at the coffee as the totals rattled and then dropped into place. "Looks like we'll end with three-hundred-eighty or three-ninety, depending on how long the hams and sausage cook. But we filled this monster with over eighteen hundred pounds in tri-tips for the benefit last week." He waved over at the closed door. "We have the burners off on this side for a gentle heat. So we'll put the sausage and corn in there."

Hooker's smile pulled sideways as he pulled his head out of the giant barbecue and looked at the twins. "I think you two found your new careers for when you retire."

Ax grumped. "Hardly. This we do for fun... but we did buy a metal shop over in Milpitas. We already have orders for six of these. The boys down in Slow Town are drawing up plans for one to cook off well over a ton of tri-tips. They said they'd put the word out and think they can even get us some orders from back east."

Hooker continued to listen to the brothers as they talked about their favorite pastime. Inside, he chuckled. Listening to these two was almost like listening to Uncle Willie and Maddie talk about the heart and soul of a fast car or motorcycle. He thought about the motorcycle Maddie had recently let go to an undercover cop in Los Angeles. He needed a faster machine. The cop mentioned he also might need one to fit his seventeen-year-old daughter—who needed something to go to college on but also needed to keep up with dad's machine.

Hooker's attention drifted down along the ridgeline where Candy was talking to a few of the nurses she was going to school with. She seemed to be fitting into the medical world as if she had been doing it for years instead of taking care of the night creatures at the diner.

The blonde in the summer dress snapped her fingers in remembering. "Bernie, did you start reading that book yet? Because... I'm dying to read it as soon as you're finished with it."

Maddie, wandering by, perked up at the mention of a book. She swung back and gently put her arm around Candy's waist in a side hug. "Did someone say book?"

Candy laughed. "Girls, this is my aunt, Maddie. She is the head ass-kicker at the county library. And if you didn't notice the black bike over there—it's hers. And it can go over one-sixty." Maddie held up two fingers as she winked with a smile. Candy gawped. "Two hundred?"

Maddie nodded as she turned back to the nurse with the book. "Which book?"

"Sybil—about a woman who has something called multiple personality disorder," Candy explained. "One of the teachers in nursing school had mentioned the disorder and suggested the book. I haven't had time—yet."

Maddie nodded. "We have a few copies at the library. I've read it. It's very interesting. I'm not sure it's totally on the up and up, but then there are some strange things in this world. As well as stranger people... just ask Candy." She hugged the younger woman and wandered off.

The other two nurses watched her move off with her broken gait. Her affected walk made her appear older than she was.

"Wow, imagine riding a motorcycle at her age..."

Candy snorted. "Don't count her out. I think she is only sixty, but even at fifty, she was the fastest woman in the world on two wheels."

The brunette was still watching the librarian walk. "She looks like she broke her hip once."

"Probably a couple of times, at least... and her back, legs, arms, head, and even her butt." The nurses laughed, but Candy knew what she said was true and couldn't be understood by someone not in the family. At the thought, a wave of warm happiness washed through her as she realized what her thought had really meant—*she was part of a family*. She smiled as she looked over her shoulder and across to where Stella and Dolly were sitting with their bare feet up on a bench and tall glasses of iced tea in their hands. The two women were laughing and animatedly poking at each other.

"You did not... Mother came and got you..."

"Hah. It was Dad, and he was coming by in the truck while I was walking."

Stella snickered, anyway. "But you have to admit, the Taylor boy was some good-looking chunk of teen boy."

Dolly held the back of her hand against her sister's shoulder. "Which one—there were five Taylor boys, and then out Clear Waterway there were the Tailor boys..."

"Oh, God... I had forgotten about the Tailors." Her eyes got huge as she turned toward Dolly.

They both said, "Hugh Tailor..." and swooned at the same time... and then broke into a rolling round of giggles.

Uncle Willie stood with his glass of pure iced tea. His body was ramrod straight. "It would appear your wife and Dolly have started in on the moonshine a little early."

Manny rolled his eyes against his half-closed lids. "You're already up... You go tell them to behave." The moment was frozen, and then both sets of shoulders and chests started to bounce with their common silent laughing.

Hooker stood leaning on the railing. The sea of family and friends spread out below.

"Is it my imagination, or has this family grown since last year?"

Hooker looked at the Squirt with a jaundiced eye. "This time last year? This time last year, you were going in for your fourth surgery, and I could never have gotten Candy to come down then." He turned and looked back at the sea of humanity. "But to answer the question... yes, there are a lot more people here this year. You were here for Christmas—but it was cold then." They both laughed.

The Squirt snorted. "Just the right temperature for ice cream."

Hooker laughed and then looked at the couple walking down the driveway. The look on their faces was one of surprise or disbelief. Hooker muttered as he pointed out Ralph and Mai. "This ought to be interesting."

"Haven't they ever been to one of these?"

"A few years ago... back when the whole party only filled most of this deck. You remember last spring. We considered Sunday dinner to be a large party... Then last summer, things got a little out of hand. And after the Christmas party..." He turned and leaned his butt against the rail as he smiled. "The parties just got better... Hello, ladies."

The Squirt glanced over his shoulder and then turned around with a large open smile. Candy escorted Beth out through the glass door.

"We're two lost sheep... looking for a place to graze while being protected by a big strong man or two." Beth moved into a hug from Hooker before turning and kissing the Squirt.

Candy watched the heat and length of the kiss. "Well, I guess I can tell the nurses they need to start looking elsewhere."

Beth broke the kiss and fell around into the Squirt's left arm as she became even more molded to his body. "They were even looking?" She smiled. "Do I need to gouge some eyes out?"

Hooker choked. "Easy, kitten. If there is any catfighting to be had, we'll let Box do the work."

Beth looked up at the Squirt as she pushed her tightly stretched angora sweater into his stomach. "Did the cat really kill a large dog?"

The Squirt nodded.

"It must have been some fight to see."

The Squirt snapped his fingers. "It was all over in a flash..."

"Wow..." She breathed. "You were there...?"

Hooker almost choked—he couldn't miss the twin blossoms of her excitement became obvious in the stretched summer-weight sweater. He glanced at Candy who was also staring at the rapid change.

"No... but I do know Box quite well." The hitch in the Squirt's voice belied he was also feeling the young woman's excitement.

Hooker ran the tip of his tongue along his dry lips as he winked to Candy. "Maybe you can introduce Beth to Box."

The Squirt looked up at his friend with the look of a trapped animal... torn by its acceptance and eager willingness to be in the position of inability to escape. "Good idea. Let's go see where he might be hiding."

Hooker couldn't help himself. "He looked kind of tired earlier. I think he headed up the hall for a nap."

The Squirt rested his chin on the top of Beth's head as he rolled his eyes larger. Candy almost choked on a giggle, and Hooker just made a turn of his index finger in the air. *Go for it.*

As they watched the two younger ones as they beelined for the back bedroom, Candy fell laughing into Hooker's side. "You are awful. We won't see them for at least an hour."

"Or three." Hooker laughed and turned her toward the outside stairway. "Come on, mother hen. We have a party to mingle in. Someone has to be responsible around here." Hooker felt the side of her foot almost side-slap up to his butt. His boot showed her how it was done, and they laughed the whole way down the stairs.

The late evening settled in on the large group. The louder band finished. A soft trio of Navy firefighters playing a fiddle, a plucked cello, and a slide steel guitar took over. The odd mix was from Moffett field and called themselves The Black

Sheep Yeomen. None of them had been west of the Mississippi before joining the Navy. All three grew up in musical families where they considered them to be black sheep—because they no longer played classical music.

The music was natural with no amplifiers—soft and gentle. Hooker could tell Sweets was tuned into the music instead of the conversation. The man played all kinds of music, as long as it was an old-style country. The western twang of a cowboy was his love, but his appreciation ran deeper into the country's mountain music from the Smokey Mountains to the Appalachians. His expertise also extended into swamp-music or the Creole music called Zydeco.

Hooker leaned over. "You've been quiet tonight. If your toe wasn't twitching ever so slightly, I would think you were sleeping behind those shades."

The blind man remained unmoving. "I've been trying to make heads or tails about something."

Hooker snorted softly. "Let me help you out. The guy on the steel slide is Puerto Rican from New York, the white guy on the fiddle is from somewhere near Kansas City, and the cello is from somewhere up around Motor City. They all have classical training, but don't play classical or their instruments the way they were trained..."

Sweets started silently chuckling. His head turned halfway toward where he knew Hooker was. "You are the fastest mouth to wise-ass, I know. How in the world did you get this old?"

"Luck, speed, and I tease blind men who can't see where I am."

Sweets' hand was fast, and his forefinger touched the tip of Hooker's nose and recoiled before Hooker could react.

"Okay, sometimes I'm faster, but most of it came from luck." He held up his own index finger and gave Sweet's brother a mock hard look. "Don't say it, Danny... I'll break you down like a shotgun and load you up like a cannon."

Everyone within hearing broke up in laughter. The only person not laughing was Danny, whose smile was larger than Sweet's usual megawatt smile. At almost double the size of Hooker, he knew it was one of the funniest sayings to fall out of the smaller man's mouth.

"Before Danny folds you up like a cheap wallet and puts you in his hip pocket, tell me if this sounds wrong..." He paused with his hand out flat. Hooker knew the look and what could be coming.

"I have growing live grass—but it is tall and brown. There are people in the grass, but it feels like they are under the grass. The sun is hot, but my body or their bodies are cold. There is a man, but I also feel a woman. But even though I can see the sun, I know it's night. There is killing, but not there..." His voice trailed off.

"Can you see the man's face? Or the woman?"

"No, but they're the same. I can feel the tightness of a ponytail gathered tight at the base of the head. But it is the dark-light, day-night, man-woman, cold-hot thing I'm having trouble with. I'm not even sure if it has to do with you..."

Hooker closed his eyes and thought. "Have you ever told me anything you have seen—and it wasn't for me or about something I was involved with?"

He watched the black man's face. There were little twitches and muscle pulls Hooker had come to know about Sweets and his thinking.

"No."

"And it's true this time too. This all has to do with what we went over at breakfast the other day." Hooker told him about the body dump, Tess, and the waterman. He watched the man's face as he talked, waiting for a twitch of recognition or a touch on a memory.

As he spoke, Candy came and sat on the arm of Hooker's Adirondack chair. "You know... we were just talking about a new book—one that's popular..."

Hooker paused and looked at his girlfriend. He waited.

Sweets was not as patient. "And...?"

She twitched. Hooker was now sure she had indulged in more than her share of moonshine. "Um... it's called Sylvia... or something. It's about a woman who has a bunch of people living in her—"

Danny cut her off. "Excuse me, but it's called multiple personality disorder. The book's title is Sybil."

Sweets' head rolled his brother's way and stopped. Danny sighed and continued. "They are whole personalities or people who live in the one body. They don't, for the most case, know about the other people. The case study the book is written about—Sybil had over sixteen personalities."

Hooker sat up and frowned. "How does... um... a personality exist in a body and not know if someone else is in the body?"

Danny looked at him hard. He was deciding if Hooker was just trying to draw him into talking more than a few words or if he really wanted to know.

They all looked over at the wheelchair moving rapidly backward. Just before it hit them, it spun around. Manny leaned forward. "Yes, I read the book when it first became available in the library, but I still don't really understand how they don't or can't know about the other. The woman had many blank spaces in her different lives."

Danny shifted mental gears. He pointed toward the east, where the moon was just cresting the east hills. "If the moon is a dead ball of rock, how does it glow?"

Candy giggled, and Hooker chuckled and rubbed her back as she answered. "It reflects the sun."

"But the sun went down an hour ago..."

She opened her arms wide with her fingers held as if she was holding the moon and sun in a pinch hold. "They are so far apart, it all works except when there's an eclipse."

"Correct. So during the day, the moon is behind the earth... sort of. And at night, the sun is behind, and we see the moon. During those days and nights, we have the two which don't know the other exists... just for our purposes of this explanation. So if our sky is their lives, this is what they know... but don't know about the other." He looked for nodding heads. "They can't look in the mirror and see the other person—because they're both on the inside—so the mirror only reflects the same person they always see —themselves."

Nobody laughed at the idea of Danny holding forth on something as odd as this. All except Candy knew good and well Danny had gone off to USC on a football scholarship, only because it also covered his housing. The scholastic schol- arship for USC would have covered everything but his hous- ing. His walking away from a winning year—which took USC to the Rose Bowl, a shot at the NFL, and him becoming a psychiatrist or college professor—surprised nobody.

Danny came home to take care of his brother and family. It was just a different path to his happiness—not a lesser one.

In his days of waiting while his brother worked as a respected radio personality, Danny read. Possibly more than Manny or Maddie combined. His weekly order at the library Maddie ran was a dozen books of the combined librarian's choosing. If it was in the pile, Danny read it. Maddie's only concern was someday, Danny would run out of library, or librarians. The only thing Danny didn't do was written book reports.

Manny rocked forward on his elbows as he shifted his thoughts. "But a few of her personalities knew about one another."

Danny smiled. "Correct. They did. How often in the evening are they both in the sky at the same time?"

"Enough..."

Danny looked around at Hooker, and Candy laughed as she slipped down onto his lap. "Don't ask Hooker—he's a vampire and only knows about the night."

Danny snorted. "She does have a point there, Casper." Everyone laughed at Hooker's nocturnal nature.

"So... with the two in the sky at the same time—those two would know about each other."

Danny nodded as he looked back at Manny. "Exactly. Now in the book, they know about each other through inference only. One of them knew of several of the others, but the guy was a snoop and tracked down all the clothes and notes and such until he had figured out who the others were."

Hooker harrumphed, and Candy giggled. "Going back to the night and day thing... We have a person stashing bodies during the day. He is a known person in the area. But the guy or woman in the hospital swears it was the guy or his twin, but is a female because they felt the chick's..." he looked at Candy and realized she was too far gone to care, "...boobs."

"So what are you asking?"

Hooker started to talk, and then he frowned. His mouth closed, and then he looked up. "I'm not sure... but Tess swore the person who attacked her or him looked exactly like the waterman—"

"Except for teats."

"Yeah." Hooker leaned back, exhausted.

Danny stroked his chin. "You seem confused about the person in the hospital. Is it a man or a woman?"

Candy giggled. "They said she is a she... but the person lying in the bed definitely has a beard. You could put him on the cough drop box or make the Grateful Dead guy look clean-shaven."

Manny interjected. "I got the fill-in—Hirsutism. She is definitely female but suffers from extreme Hirsutism, which displays in beard and body hair."

Danny rocked as he registered the information. "It fits what I was just thinking... classic case of the sideshow's bearded woman."

He turned back to Hooker. "When was the attack?"

"At night..."

Danny was catching onto the question trail to an answer or solving a crime, which Manny usually led. "But the waterman is usually only seen during the day?"

"Only seen during the day... from what I understand."

Danny leaned back and thought. His right arm flopped out, and his finger touched his silent brother. "Which this would explain your problem of them being male and female, but the same person."

Sweets nodded. "I've been thinking about that."

Danny continued, "And if the guy you said is only around during the day—he isn't the killer personality. Which means the night personality is the one who showed up to kill your friend. Only the killer is a female personality."

Candy leaned over—or fell over—onto Hooker's chest. "So explain how the guy—the waterman guy—when the sun goes down... grows boobs." She giggled softly at saying the word boobs. Hooker knew the evening was coming to a close... soon.

"He doesn't. But during the day... she binds her chest so it looks like a guy."

The simple answer had them all nodding in silence. Sweets was the first to hear the soft little snort of a delicate snore. He started to rise. "Manny, it was a delightful party. I need to gather my mother so we can trundle her off to go sleepy bye."

"I'd get up and give you guys a hug, but I probably had a shot too many, so give me a shake, man." The blind disc jockey laughed at the old joke about Manny being paralyzed. In other's eyes, they were disabled, but they both knew and respected they were simply alternately abled.

They shook as Danny moved off like a silent ship in the night to fetch their mother. Returning, he lifted Candy so Hooker could get up, and then placed her on Hooker's body so he could carry her into her apartment a few dozen feet away. Hooker wasn't getting up early the next morning so he would stay with her. They all watched as Candy clutched with her legs around his waist with her arms and head draped over his shoulder. Her lips smacked in her sleep.

With Candy draped on his body and shoulders, he stuck

his right hand out. "Thanks for the information as well as the explanation, Danny...Sweets." He turned and gave a partial hug to their mother. "Thanks for coming, Mom. We don't see enough of you three. And you can always come out alone. I know Stella would love the help in keeping Manny in line."

"Hooker, we already made plans for Wednesday. While you menfolk have your secret dinner—we women can have some fun too." She kissed him on the cheek and let him go. She could tell Candy wasn't heavy, but she also wasn't light like a child either.

23

TO FIND THE FEMALE

Max swung her ponytail around to her back. The first time had almost caught Candy on the side of the head. The glancing blow had been a fair warning to duck when the large woman moved her head down and hitched up her shoulder—the deadly weapon was about to move. Candy hadn't noticed the series of knives secreted in the braid, but she rubbed her head and wondered if there was a hammer hidden in the braid or if the woman had too much iron in her diet. Either way, she was leery and had changed sides with Hooker.

The rust faced woman in the work uniform smiled. She could wish Candy just wanted to be closer to her, but she could tell she was definitely attached to Hooker.

"So really... all you have is the woman is blonde, built to eat oats and draw wagons, and has a rack of large bazoombas. Hell, Hooker... the only thing keeping me out of the line-up is my tiny braid is too long." To highlight her point, she tossed her head, and the long braid swept a circle in the air. Candy and Hooker both ducked. Laughing, Max stopped the cudgel in midair with her left hand and guided it down her chest.

"Not to be rude, Max... but I think you may be a little more than what we are looking for, too."

She leaned forward and planted her forehead and nose an inch away from Hooker's nose. She growled. "Are you saying I don't have a delicate girly figure?"

Candy caught her breath. "Eep." She was afraid something involving blood was about to happen.

Max's eyes shifted right and took in the frail-looking woman who, even when scared, hadn't twitched to move from Hooker's side. Her sight ground back to Hooker's face an inch away. A growl rumbled somewhere deep. "I like this one. She's going to run you ragged. You need to bring her and the cat around more often."

Hooker didn't blink. "What about the Squirt?"

Max stood to make room for her laugh. "The smartass can come by anytime—on his own time. I like a man who can remember things." She nodded her head sideways at Tawny. "It reminds me of our father. If he read it, he remembered it. He was a pisser at Scrabble. How is the Squirt at Scrabble?"

Hooker looked in surprise at Candy.

Candy shrugged. "I don't know. We've never played. But don't play cards with him. He cheats."

Max roared as she held her belly. "So do I."

Hooker snickered. "But he knows if you added a card or two."

Max toyed with her braid. "And that counts... how?"

At Candy's horrified face, Tawny leaned over. "Don't put too much into my sister's threats." Candy relaxed and looked to Tawny for her reassurance. Tawny's smile drew back lopsided. "She's only killed a few people."

Max snorted. "That you know of... and all seven deserved it."

Hooker washed his face in his hands. "Oh, God. It just keeps getting deeper and deeper."

"What?"

"Last week, you told me it was only five... and now it's up to seven?"

"This month..."

Candy pinched the bridge of her nose as she closed her eyes and gently shook her head. "Oh, my gawd—she's as bad as Willie."

Max laughed as she pointed. "She knows Willie?"

Hooker closed one eye and looked at the woman. She held both hands up and stepped back half a step before she swung her braid to her back. "Okay, I'll behave."

She splashed some brown liquid into a glass and put it on the bar in front of Hooker. He looked at it with a frown and question. Max nodded for him to go ahead. "Tell me what you think."

Hooker sipped cautiously and then slurped the rest down. "Good... very good... but it's not commercial root beer."

"Nope, but it might become commercial. A friend grew up in New Orleans, and he said this is the root beer of choice down there. He's working on reproducing the bite, which only comes from the sarsaparilla."

"Why not just get the stuff they sell down in New Orleans?"

"Because it's only made and sold down there."

Hooker thought about the strange divergence from their discussion. "So what does this have to do with the killer?"

Max smirked and leaned hard against her hands spread along the backside of the bar. "Sometimes, you have to go where the root beer is, and sometimes you have to go where the killing is." She stood back up and smiled. "And there she is."

Hooker turned to look at Shawna walking through the door.

She saw who was at the bar, and her mouth pulled up to one side in a quirky smile. "Hello, Hooker." She spotted Candy and changed the side she was headed for. She lounged her arm over Tawny and gave Hooker a smoldering look. "Who's your friend?"

Hooker chuckled at the dynamics. "This is my girlfriend, Candy. Candy, this is Shawna."

Candy smiled knowingly, and she put her hand out, but as the woman started to shake her hand, Candy drew her into a hug. "I'm so glad to meet another friend of Hooker's." And then she whispered in her ear, "We need to talk... I need some tips."

The woman froze and then softened as she realized Candy wasn't talking about the sex trade, but an open woman-to-woman talk about what to do. She drew her in fully. "Anytime, girlfriend."

They parted, but only enough to turn around as they stayed draped with an arm around the other. Hooker's eyes rose, but he knew better than to ask. He knew when he was outgunned.

Max snorted, then pulled out a glass and filled it with cola. She pushed it forward and reached for a couple of lime pieces. Twisting them into the glass, she announced, "Cola, no ice, with a twist of lime."

"Thanks, Max. I've been having fantasies about this for the last hour on the bus." She had drained half before she started to put it down. Looking at Candy, she took another sip and then put it down.

"I don't think you should take your girlfriend out slumming to places like this."

Max protested... weakly.

"We have some information, and Candy has the day off, so she's been tagging along."

"New information?"

"We had a lead for someone to talk to. After we had talked to her, she was attacked and almost killed."

"That's horrible. Do they have any idea who attacked her?"

"A good suspicion, but we have nobody who matches the description."

Max leaned forward on the bar. "That's why they're here to talk to you."

"How would I know—"

Candy rested her hand on the woman's upper chest. "Nobody is accusing you of anything... We just think you might be able to help us think of a person you and the other women might know, fitting the description. We think the person who is doing the killing is a female you girls might know."

"But we already went through this... Well, sort of. But none of us hook anything but straight-up guys looking for girls. Maybe in San Francisco, there is some girl on girl. There are certainly guys for guys, but I don't know of any girls for girls." She looked around the bar. "It's... Well, just not our style."

Hooker cleared his throat. He was still playing catch-up with Candy suddenly friendly with this other woman. "Um, we don't think it's another."

"Working girl?"

Hooker blushed and nodded. "We do think it's a female, but one who knows all of you, and more importantly, all of you know well enough to be comfortable around her. Maybe like a waitress... who works where you all go at the end of the night?"

"So what does she look like?"

"Blonde with a small ponytail. We're assuming she's about five-eight or so and muscular."

"Which would describe more than a few women I know." She looked at Max, and they all laughed.

Hooker snorted. "I said a small ponytail, not a flail attached to an anchor rope."

Shawna thought about the description and shook her head. "All the waitresses who work the restaurants we go to— or are allowed into—are my size or smaller, unless you're talking a couple who are Max's size but make her look slender."

Hooker glanced toward Max. "Well, it is someone you know, or at least, knows you. Maybe this requires some sitting and watching."

Shawna and Candy both frowned. "Sitting and watching." The words were perfect unison, and the two giggled. Candy hugged her tighter. "I knew I liked you..." And then she remembered where she was and the kind of women who were the customers. Her eyes flew open as her mouth made a small *O*. "I didn't mean... I mean... oh, this isn't going right." She blushed.

Shawna gave her a squeeze. "You're safe. I knew what you meant... and yeah, I like you too. But watch out for Tawny—you're definitely her type."

Max laughed, and Tawny snorted. "Not hardly. She doesn't have any meat on those bones."

Shawna giggled and leaned into Candy. "They tell everyone they're sisters... but really, they're girlfriends."

Max growled with a twinkle in her eye. "You want to get eighty-sixed from here?"

Hooker cleared his throat. He could feel the girl play could rapidly slip out of hand, and they had crimes to solve, and possibly people to save.

"We know the killer is someone who knows all of you. So we just need to watch all of you and see who's there—who you're so used to—you don't see them."

Max raised her eyebrows and toyed with her braid. Hooker braced to duck if she flipped it around again. He could sense Candy ready also. "So you're saying this killer is *yahoody*?"

"Who?"

Tawny snorted. "Kids these days... nobody reads, nobody respects the old poems."

She turned and recited the poem.

YESTERDAY, upon the stair,
  I met a man who wasn't there.
  He wasn't there again today,
  I wish, I wish he'd go away...

· · ·

WHEN I CAME HOME last night at three,
The man was waiting there for me,
But when I looked around the hall,
I couldn't see him there at all!
Go away, go away, don't you come back any more!
Go away, go away, and please don't slam the door...

LAST NIGHT, I saw upon the stair,
A little man who wasn't there.
He wasn't there again today.
Oh, how I wish he'd go away...

CANDY HUNG ON SHAWNA. "Sounds more like someone with hallucinations."

Shawna mumbled, "Yahoody is an old Jewish folktale about the little guy who does things nobody sees... like when you close the refrigerator door—he's the one who turns the light off."

Candy snickered. "Or leaves the toilet seat up?"

"Hey... not me."

Conspiratorially, Candy turned in toward Shawna. "It's true, he sits."

"For both?"

"For either one." They both snickered.

Hooker growled. "I'm standing right here, you know."

Max grunted. "Dude, you don't count in this conversation."

Hooker turned to make like he was leaving. "I'm going to go find a killer."

Tawny snorted. "Dude... you leave now, you ain't ever getting her back."

He turned. "The killer?"

Tawny stood up off the stool and draped her arm over Candy's shoulders—making the three a Candy sandwich. "No... someone more important."

Candy caught the drift of the innuendo and slipped out. She hit Hooker's arm and spun around, smiling. "Fun thought, but maybe another time." She winked with the eye Hooker couldn't see. The three women laughed at Hooker's struck look.

Max stood and swung her braid. "Say good-night, Hooker. Take your woman home before someone else does."

Hooker knew when he was outgunned. He spun Candy around, and they headed for the door. "Good-night, ladies." His arm waved over his head as he kissed the top of Candy's head.

He froze. He stood staring at the top of Candy's head as it rotated up to look at him. "Hooker, what's wrong?"

He smiled. "Nothing... now." He turned back.

"Shawna... around where you..."

"Work?"

He nodded. "Are there any buildings, say... two or three stories?"

"Sure. We look at a three-story office building all night. It's the Taylor building. Why?"

"Because we are going to stake it out and watch you. What is commonplace and unnoticed to you will be new to us. We'll see what you don't." His slim smile was more satisfaction for figuring out a course of action than being happy. They turned and left.

Max turned to Shawna. "What do you think?"

"I think he is one smart guy... and she is one lucky girl."

Tawny snorted as she leaned her arm on the bar and ran her fingers through her hair as she looked longing at the closed door. "I think he's the lucky one. There is something very special about her. It's very soft and subtle and still hiding from even her."

Max nodded. She made her living at reading people and saw Hooker and Candy as a great match—both damaged goods but made for each other.

24

STAKEOUT

Manny shifted in his chair. The Brahms concerto drifted from the large headphones. He studied the three young people he and Stella had come to think of as their children. He, of all people, knew the dangers of even a simple stakeout. It was a stakeout that ended his career and his ability to walk. *The stakeout... and a bullet to the spine.*

"The first thing about a stakeout is... it is—"

The Squirt coughed. "Never done alone." He had covered his mouth with his fist. He looked over the fist. The man's face was only slightly red but was rapidly growing darker. "Excuse me... a bit of dust. Please continue." The red was creeping up the young man's neck. He had forgotten he could not overstep with Manny like he could with Hooker.

Manny gave it a slow five-count, and then his eyes slid over to Hooker. "As it was so rudely put... you have to work as a team. The second you go gonzo Steve McQueen—things turn bad." He patted his chair's arms. He rolled up on his forearms as he looked at the few papers on his desk. "If you can work out the timing, I would suggest the three of you watch from the top of the building here. The last woman killed that we know of was taken from along here. Her beat was along this block, so the killer is somewhere around there."

Chastised, the Squirt was back in learning mode. "Why all three of us? Why not just Hooker and me? I mean, why put her in danger?"

Manny smiled. It was at these kinds of moments the most important lessons of police work were learned. He turned to Candy. He nodded at the Squirt.

"What can you tell me about John's clothes?"

Candy thought a moment, and then she peeked to make sure. "When we stopped for a few minutes at Willie's, the Squirt changed his pants."

"Were his pants from this morning somehow soiled?"

"On *Mister, I Aced the Academy*? Never. If they had been, he would have changed them here."

"So he soiled them later in the day?"

"Not that I observed... no."

Manny and Candy were both smiling at their knowledge and how the other two had not figured it out. Manny raised an eyebrow and looked at Hooker.

Manny motioned for the kid to stand. "Hooker, take a good look. How did Candy know the Squirt changed his pants at Willie's—instead of here?"

They waited as Hooker had the kid gradually turn around. Finally, Hooker saw it and chuckled. He leaned over toward Candy and stage-whispered, "Do you want to tell Hank, or should I break his heart?"

Candy gave him a horrified look. "Oh, there is no way I'm

telling Hank how to do his laundry. He would just put a blowtorch in my hand and tell me to have at it."

They all laughed. Hank's fondness for "laundering" very soiled clothing with a blowtorch and a long stick was infamous. Hooker had taken to carrying an extra pair of pants and a white T-shirt in his truck after a particularly nasty and filthy week of towing had cost him all but the pants and shirt he was wearing.

Hank was extremely picky about just how dirty something could be and still be washed in his sparkling and hand waxed washing machine and dryer set. Uncle Willie joked about Hank and the Maytag man being on a first-name basis, and Hank could give the repairman tips on the best wax for the white boxes of his cleaning empire.

The Squirt took one last look at his pants and sat down in wonder. "Okay, we've all had a great laugh. Now how did you know?"

Hooker pointed. "Lift your right leg and cross it semaphore on your left knee." The young man did. "Now what is wrong?"

The Squirt's left hand absentmindedly straightened the curled cuff. He continued to look for something wrong enough to see from a few feet away. "Nothing..."

Manny smiled. "What did you just do with your left hand?"

"Nothi... I just smoothed out the hem. Why?"

Manny closed his eyes as he thought about what day Stella had done laundry.

He opened his eyes. "Stella hung six pairs of jeans in your closet yesterday—please bring me two pairs."

The kid returned a moment later with a pair in each hand, still on their hangers. "I don't see it..."

Candy snorted. "She really does iron them flat."

Manny chuckled. "A dozen years of ironing my uniforms. The old habit dies hard. Well, actually, she can't stand the thought of the boys being out there looking any less than what she is capable of doing." He turned back to the Squirt. "Stella mentioned it about four minutes after you three got home. Actually, her observation was more in the vein of going over and teaching Hank how to properly do laundry."

Hooker mused. "I remember Willie being such a stickler about ironing his pants and shirts. I guess it was from many years of having a perfectly pressed uniform." He looked up. "But now he doesn't seem to care as much, except I do notice the difference when he irons my T-shirt and when Hank does. Hank only shows the bottle of starch to the shirt, where Willie gives the shirt a whole new backbone."

The kid sat down—thinking. "So with three sets of eyeballs, one might see something the other two would miss."

Manny nodded. "More importantly, Candy has a woman's eye. She might see something you two see but will assign a different importance to it... like the cuff having curled."

The Squirt looked to Hooker. "So when did you want to do this?"

"Tonight. Tomorrow is Wednesday, so the load for me will be light, and we should be out of dinner by nine." He looked at Candy.

"I'm good. I have tonight and tomorrow night off... but I work a double on Thursday. As long as I can get about eight hours of sleep before five, I'm good."

Hooker nodded. "Let's get a couple of hours rest, and then we can be on the roof by, say... nine-thirty."

Manny leaned back. "We'll wake you at nine, and Stella can have some food and a thermos packed."

They stood. "Thanks, Manny—sounds good."

Candy leaned over and kissed Manny on the top of his head as they shuffled out of the office. Stella stood in the kitchen leaning with one hand on the island. Hooker pushed his thumb back toward Manny and then put his hands together by his head.

Stella nodded. She knew she would be filled in and would have suggested they take a nap anyway.

THE TWO BACKPACKS leaned bloated against the parapet wall. The three snickered at the size of *I packed you a bit to eat*—Stella style.

"Does she ever do just a small snack like a few stalks of celery with peanut butter on them?"

Hooker rolled his head in a shortened zombie roll. "Probably the last day she squeezed into a training bra."

The Squirt blushed and mumbled as he pointed at the farthest end of the building. "I'll... um... just be down here." He grew his eyes big at Hooker and walked away. Candy snickered at her brother being still uncomfortable at the mention of a woman's undergarments. For all the grown-up he had become, there was still the boy in him. She also knew the same went for all three of them.

She wrapped her arms around Hooker's one arm and kissed him on the cheek. "I'll be at this other end." She picked up one of the bags and started toward the closer end.

Hooker looked at the two others and mumbled quietly to himself, "If anybody cares, I'll just be right here." He sat down on an old tar bucket he had turned upside-down.

Hooker's eyebrow rose, surprised at the traffic on the streets at ten-thirty at night. San Fernando ran across in front of them. From Candy's corner, she could look north up First to Santa Clara and south as far down as San Carlos. Hooker knew the Squirt worked the same range up and down Second.

From their perches on top of the bank building, they could watch most of the night action—according to Shawna. Hooker smiled at the small marker of neon green dress Shawna said she would wear. Hooker found her in his binoculars and wondered if the skirt covered anything below the edge of her bottom. As for the top, it was mostly what would be expected on a warm, humid night.

Hooker lowered the binoculars and scanned the large parking lot the bank shared with the rest of the building's tenants on the north end. There were only a few cars left parked. They looked like they would probably be there in the morning, as well. Cars moved on the street at the speed limit. The heat of the evening tempered any urgency people might feel—getting to wherever they were going.

Looking east down San Fernando, he looked for any foot traffic coming from the San Jose State housing he knew was only a few blocks away. Going for a walk or a woman could make for a nice study break. The college was full almost all year long. Summer was only a shorter semester and student load for the university. Most of the students lived at home in the area and usually took the summer off. But there was always a small group who were in a hurry to graduate and move on with their advanced education or their lives.

Three young men in T-shirts and shorts approached from the college. Judging from the arm gestures and body language, the topic of conversation started in a classroom. They were out to carry on the conversation and maybe get something to eat. Some quick sex wasn't on their minds.

The small voice in the back of Hooker's head was keeping his usual count. On San Fernando, there were three Fords, one beat-up VW bug, a Dodge Super Bee, two Chevrolets, and a Pacer he wondered about making it home. The offending gold car was smoking as if it had blown at least three of its ring sets and probably, had burned the edges of at least four valves. Of all the cars, the self-destructing Pacer, and the sanitation three-wheeler made enough noise to be heard on top of the two-story building.

The three-wheeler stopped at the garbage can at the corner of Second and San Fernando. The guy driving wore the city's loose-fitting blue jumpsuit and a Spartan's ball cap. The short ponytail stuck spiky out the hole over the size adjusting tabs. Part of Hooker's mind watched the smooth dance of the lid removed with one hand, and the other whipped around the inner can—gathering the plastic bag liner. One-handed, the worker pulled the bag of garbage out of the can.

Leaning the lid against the concrete shell, the worker kicked the bag to spin. As it slowed, they pushed down—compressing the contents and air. With a flourish, the bag was tied and slung onto the pile on the back of the cart. A fresh bag appeared from somewhere and was snapped open, hung in the can, the top turned over the can's rim, and the lid replaced.

The city worker drew a squirt bottle from where it hung

in their side pocket and with a rag, spritzed and wiped the lid down—clean and ready for the denizens of the day. They jumped back on the three-wheeler, put it in gear, and moved to the next stop. The process from stop to go had lasted less than a couple of minutes. Hooker smiled. It was all automatic —just like he was when changing a tire.

Movement to his right caught his eye. In the dark of a doorway, the red of a cigarette flared. Someone was in the doorway. Hooker raised the binoculars and searched the depth of the dark area. Shapes moved in the dark recess. Hooker wished he could get his hands on at least one of the Starlight scopes Willie had shown him a few years before. The dark doorway would have been a green light, but he could then see everything in there like it was daylight.

The cigarette flared again, and Hooker could see from the glow a man's face. He also could see the red glow lit up enough of the bobbing blond hair at the man's waist. The man was taking a smoke break and getting a blowjob at the same time. He watched to see if he could see the man's face better, but the flare of the cigarette was never enough. Hooker waited, hoping they would walk out into the street when they finished.

Hooker watched the traffic gradually become sparse. Occasionally, a car would slow, look at the girl walking, and then think better of it. One pulled to the curb, and Shawna sauntered over along with another girl called Tiny—who was anything but. If she had ever seriously been called Tiny, it was long before her chest blossomed. They bent over and talked with the driver. Tiny stood up and arched her back. Shawna stood, they conferred, and they both piled into the car. It was going to be a party.

Hooker focused on the doorway. The cigarette flared and then arched through the air out into the street. A few minutes later, the blonde stepped into the light of the street—straightening her dress. There wasn't much there to straighten. She smoothed the tight clinging material down along her hips. She waved back into the dark without even looking back and walked east along the street. Hooker saw a slight reflection as if a glass door had opened and closed—reflecting some of the streetlight. The man had entered the building. Hooker made a note of the blonde and the doorway in his book.

By midnight, the traffic was down to the occasional car. Most were passing through on their way to somewhere else. Only a rare one would slow for one of the girls. Tiny and Shawna had returned and gone at least five more times. Hooker sat watching as he quietly chewed his way through one of Stella's kosher ham sandwiches. It was she and Manny's joke. The sandwich was full of mayo, cheese, pickles, lettuce, and, of course, the ham. Manny said he would marry her if she knew how to make a kosher ham sandwich. The half-done dill pickles were the only kosher part to the sandwich. The two spears of pickle were enough for Manny.

Hooker looked in the sky to the northwest and watched the large PSA 727 letting down for a landing at the airport. The distance muted the sound of the jet engines. A Lincoln drove almost silent along San Fernando. Hooker could hear the distinct sound of the horizontally opposed two-cylinder engine of the garbage collector a few blocks away to the north. He figured they probably picked up most of the garbage from the downtown area every week. With the use of the three-wheeler, the whole of downtown would only take two or three workers.

Hooker fished through the bag looking for the thermos. Coffee sounded good right then—he noted the Squirt probably had the same idea. The young man was picking his way along the parapet.

"I thought you might want some coffee..."

The kid sat on the parapet. "Eighty-seven Fords, forty-three Chevys, nineteen Mopars, a dying Pacer, and a West-coaster garbage cart. There were ninety-one walkers, two bicycles, and a blowjob over there in the doorway." He shook his head. "Who would have guessed the Pacer would have made it up past San Carlos?"

Hooker laughed at the young man's avoidance of the blowjob. He handed him the second thermos. "How many working girls could you see?"

"Four. Shawna and Tiny here, and two more up Second... but I did find it interesting nobody is working down this block."

Hooker knew the answer, and it drew a smile from him. "What kinds of streetlights do you see out there?" He pointed toward the street.

The kid looked and then shrugged. "I don't know... some variety of incandescent or halogen, I guess."

"The color is...?"

"White...?"

Hooker nodded and then nodded toward the parapet. "And the lights in the parking lot?"

The kid glanced. "Yellow." The Squirt snapped his fingers. "Same as that place we got the burrito for the guy up in Contra Costa last year."

Hooker smiled. "They're called low-sodium. They are much cheaper to run than those halogens. The problem with them is they make a woman's makeup look like Halloween horror makeup. So you take a nice girl to dinner, and then just when you're feeling the romance—you leave the restaurant—right into a street filled with low-sodium lights. *Bam!* Your Farrah Fawcett turns into Medusa."

The kid took a sip as Hooker pointed down into the parking lot.

"So you have a nice place for kids to hang out. But because you don't want them to hang out and maybe cause some mischief, you want to discourage them. Well, young guys like to hang out where there are girls... and girls only want to hang out where they'll look good. It only takes a sixteen-year-old one walk under the yellow lights to know she's never going there again. So... no girls, no boys—problem solved."

"So how about Second and First?" Candy wasn't getting left out of a little conversation after being bored out of her mind for two hours.

Hooker turned as she walked into his arm. They tapped heads lightly. "Nobody was working the street on this block, either?"

She poured herself some coffee from Hooker's thermos as she shook her head. "All I saw on First were the two working the west side up toward San Carlos. There was nobody down here."

Hooker continued. "The bank owns the building. They paid the city to put in the yellow lights all around the three sides, just to deter people from hanging around hoodlums or hookers." He took the last sip from the cup-top of the thermos and poured the last little bit. He looked at the bag Candy had taken.

She shook her head. "Long gone. I'm up past my bedtime —I needed some coffee."

The Squirt was still studying the parking lot. "So it really works?"

Hooker nodded. "Well enough—the city is considering retrofitting all the streetlights downtown to the low-sodium."

"But why—would the energy savings be enough to justify the retrofit?"

"It doesn't need to be. Even if each light could save them, say... twenty-eight cents a week... it's enough. What they really can't say is—they are doing it to discourage the girls from working the city."

The Squirt looked out at the lime green dot across the street. "So a guy gets a blowjob in a dark alley or some motel room. Who really gets hurt?"

"Well, why we are here is maybe a real wild card—but we still don't know how many women were taken from these streets and killed. On the other hand, there are drugs, pimps, and a whole handful of other crimes that circle around the simple blowjob in the doorway. But the biggest crime—in the city's eyes—is it's a business they can't collect taxes on."

Candy smirked. "So much for capitalism and the American spirit of entrepreneurialism."

Hooker bobbed his head slightly. "I'm just like Shawna and the rest—but they can tax me, so I'm allowed to still hook." He looked out across the street. The two girls got into a cab without its light lit. He knew they were calling it an early night. He looked back at Candy.

"Did you see anything of note?"

"Nothing really stood out. When the girls got picked up, it didn't look like they knew the person. It was very strange to watch. We are raised not to talk to strangers and don't get in the car with a man you don't know, and yet, this is the very nature of their business."

"So nothing stood out?"

She shoved the thermoses in the bag as she thought. She stopped, and she cocked her hip and head. "There was one thing. How often do you think the garbage person comes by?"

Hooker splayed his face. "Once or twice a week, maybe. Why?"

"Do you think it would always be the same guy?"

"I don't know." Hooker looked at the Squirt, who rolled his shoulders.

"Because one of the girls waved to him."

"Calling him over? Soliciting? What?"

"No... just a wave... like a hello or something."

Hooker looked at the kid. The Squirt shrugged and poked out his lower lip. The nod was one Hooker recognized as *I need to think about it...*

25

MEETING CRICKET

Hooker unwound the chain from around the axle of the service truck. The driver had said there was a loud whining noise that turned to gravel-in-a-cement-mixer—right before the back of the truck crashed to the asphalt after the bump in the road where Snell and Blossom Hill crossed. Hooker didn't have to look at the street to know the dip had shattered the last of the axle. The six-inch dip, designed for rain run-off that almost never came, had claimed many differentials, oil pans, engine mounts, and mufflers. As a small truck tow driver, Hooker almost wanted to kiss the designer of the dip for keeping him in constant money. But while driving the small truck, he was also susceptible to the same design. He had never consciously noticed the dip when he drove Mae, but the first time he hit it in the small truck at real speed, he hit his head on the ceiling. Lately, he had taken to wearing the seat belt.

"What you got, Hooker?" The short Japanese woman was third-generation American born in Watsonville, but the Fly found she could get away with more if she only spoke in pigeon English.

Hooker just shook his head before he turned around with a smile. "Fly, you aren't going to believe this... but I finally brought you a piece of shit. You slap a new rear end under this heap, and she will be as good as last Thursday."

She eyed the three or four-year-old service truck with her accountant's eye. Hooker almost swore he could hear the abacus beads clicking back and forth.

Finally, she waved her finger at the truck. "You take truck out. You go beat it up. Truck driver, he bad driver. You go sideswipe a few telephone poles then you bring back. Fly no want just rear-end job—no money for new shoes."

Hooker laughed. "I think Dog was parting out one of these service trucks just last week. Same year and model—heck, same company... but it was the one who got hit in the nose." He silently referenced the rear end still being good. He knew she would still charge for a new one.

"Okay, you leave here. Dog come get. I have car. It need go to Palo Alto. I only give you half—it a forty-dollar jerk job."

"North Palo Alto or south end?"

"Palo Alto—what difference?" Hooker knew full well she knew the difference was a ten-mile spread or a forty or fifty-mile tow. The difference could mean five to eight gallons of gas.

"I'm getting low on fuel..."

She glared at him, but the twinkle was always there. They knew each other too well. He knew she would always try to chisel, but he also knew she had a warm spot for him in the place her heart should have been—if it hadn't been replaced by the abacus.

She flipped her hand in the air as she turned back to the office. "Go fill up. But I only pay you twelve."

"Eighteen and a full tank it is."

She never turned around as she opened the door. "I said only fourteen—"

"Sixteen and a tank it is."

They both knew he would get paid fifteen.

Hooker chuckled as he threw the chains on the working deck and ran the boom up. The sparring on price and pay had started the first day they met. Hooker was new to the job and a fifteen-year-old filled with enough bluster to pull off making everyone believe he was nineteen or twenty. Nobody had warned him about the woman known as The Fly. He had pulled in a wrecked but repairable year-old Cadillac. The bodywork alone was worth at least a grand, but there was also damage to the front axles that could add another grand. It was a cherry piece.

The Fly looked over the new kid and read him the riot act for dragging in a total wreck only worth fifty bucks to her. Hooker stood quietly. She had no idea he was scared. He blinked a couple of times, quietly turned, and got back in the truck.

She watched in amazement as a thousand-dollar job rolled back out the door.

Hooker drove around the corner to a phone booth he had seen earlier. He called his boss, Don.

"What do you want me to do with this Cadillac, Don?"

"Are you sure it's repairable?"

"Don, it got smacked on the left front quarter panel. It moved the grill and bumper. All of it has to be replaced. I think she could even sell a whole front clip. The damage to the front left axle will need a complete front suspension along with a new rim and tire. She might even sell a new right to balance the alignment that could be affected. Jeez mareez, Don, Willie could have this back on the road in a week for under two-hundred in used parts and a paint job."

Hooker heard the radio in the shop and his truck squawk at the same time.

"Just a minute, Hooker. She's on the radio. I guess she forgot you had a shop radio too."

Hooker listened to the radio conversation. If he didn't like Don before, he did after the conversation.

"Don... your new idiot... where he take my Cadillac?"

"Fly, you said you didn't want it... it was a total."

"I maybe figure something out... where he go?"

"He hauled it over to Capital Cadillac."

"You tell him to bring back now. I no want Capital get my wreck."

"I think he already dropped it, Fly."

"He not that fast. He new idiot. He no last. He stupid and don't know where he supposed to go with wrecks. He no good for you, Don. You call him and tell to bring car back to Fly, I make it worth you while."

"Well, Bill already called and said he would pay me three-fifty for it. There may even be something on the back side."

"You know Bill have no back side. Only Fly have back side. You bring back car."

"I don't know, Fly. My boy is probably in the office, and Bill is counting out seven Grants into his left hand right now."

"I know drivers. You call him. You get him back. I do better."

"How much better, Fly?"

"I pay you boy eight Grants."

"Well, let me see what I can do, Fly."

Hooker heard his main radio squawk, and then the shop radio rattled with static proceeding Don's voice. "1-4-1?"

Hooker slowly walked to the truck and leaned in. Grabbing the mic, he keyed the talk button. "1-4-1, go ahead?"

"What's your status on the Cadillac...?"

"I was just walking into the office to get the four hundred and eighty dollars. When he quoted you before, he didn't realize how new it was."

The silence on the radio was deafening. Hooker knew Don was laughing four miles away.

"Umm... 10-4. Umm... hold on a minute. I need to make a phone call before you get paid."

"10-4. Standing by. 1-4-1 out."

The Fly squealed the radio as she was nearly swallowing the microphone. "Don, you tell you boy bring it back. You no more play games. I give you ten Grants. He be back here in ten minutes."

Don ignored the woman. "Um, Hooker, how are you set for fuel? You might have to haul the Cadillac down to Gilroy."

"Let me see, Don... but I think I was down under a quarter tank... you know how these Chevys love to just suck gas."

The Fly was almost apoplectic. "Don, you no fool around anymore. You tell him bring to Fly. He be here in under ten minutes, Fly pay six hundred."

"He needs fuel too, Fly."

Hooker could almost hear the woman choking in the silence.

"Yeah, yeah... fuel too. He have nine and a half minutes left."

"Cash, Fly. And he gets the whole ten minutes."

Hooker took the turn onto San Jose Avenue. "1-4-1, show me 10-97 at the Fly body shop."

Hooker backed the car into the same spot it had been in only thirty minutes before. He got out of the truck and stood with his hand out. He expected the woman to come out screaming mad. He did not expect the woman who came out with the cash in her hand.

"You good. What you name?"

"Hooker."

"No, I know you a whore in a tow truck. What your name... what I call you?"

He stared her down, thinking about how much he would give away. "Horatio Octavius O'Keefer." Their eyes were locked.

"The Hor fits, but so does Hooker. You're smarter than you look. Why are you towing for Don?"

"Your pigeon English is slipping. You make a lot more money than you let on... so why are you trying to bust my chops? Don's a nice guy. He told me about his arrangement with you. If I bring you a piece of shit dog bone, you don't have to pay me. I'll try to pass those somewhere else. If it makes you money, you'll get it. But you treat Don and me right. The day you screw me or Don is the last day you will see a wreck on the end of my truck."

She smiled. "I knew it. I grew up in Watsonville. My great grandparents came here from Japan. I was born in Watsonville but learned how to talk in the camps." She wagged a finger back and forth between them. "You keep our secret, we get along."

"Deal. Now, where do you want this brick of gold, and where do I fill the tank?"

She pointed deep into the yard. "Stick the Caddy next to the white Ford truck, and the fueling is over near the gate. No more than twenty gallons. I'm not made of gold, you know."

Hooker smiled. "I'm only about half down. You got lucky today."

Hooker chuckled about the Cadillac day over ten years before. He clicked the nozzle a few times and topped off the second tank. The Fly had never let her pigeon English slip again—except when they were alone. She had always haggled with Hooker, but never maliciously. They had always worked to better both of their bottom lines.

He walked into the office and sat down next to the desk she was sitting at. He knew she moved around the six desks in the office just to throw other people off. Hooker knew it had nothing to do with him.

"How bad?"

"I took thirty-four gallons."

"No... the truck."

"Like I said—three or four hours. Pull the rear-end off the other service truck. There is no way the insurance will ever sign off on fixing it. So the busted rear-end will fit right in with the rest of the scrap."

She always marveled at how much Hooker knew about fixing cars and how he could size wrecks up in a glance. She knew almost all of his knowledge he learned from his adoptive uncle. "How's Willie doing?"

"He's great. He and Hank just got back from relaxing up

near Lake Tahoe. There is a small lake with some cabins. They like the rustic stuff."

She snorted. "Is rustic the code word for no room service?"

Hooker laughed. "Not after midnight."

"So the new man is working out okay for Willie?"

Hooker nodded with a soft smile. "Yeah, Hank is good for Willie. I think he has a good calming effect on him. I also haven't heard about Willie having the nightmares like he used to have."

She mirrored his smile. "He deserves some good in his life. He is one very special man. When are you seeing him next?"

"I need to take some paperwork up to him this afternoon. He's going down to Texas, and they want the specs on the new engine."

"I thought the engine had survived the explosion?"

"It did, but these friends of his want to put some new experimental oversized engine in her. They figure she's going to be a great test bed, and I'm a good test monkey."

The Fly knew her men. "How big of an engine?"

"Bigger than the sixteen-hundred I had before." He rolled his eyes huge and smiled.

She laughed and slapped his shoulder. "Oh, crap, Hooker. How we ever going to keep you down on the farm when you done seen the elephant?"

Hooker stood. "You won't, and I'll let Willie know you owe the swear jar fifty-cents."

"Only a quarter, but you give him a big hug for me."

"Should I kiss him behind the ear too?"

She laughed and shook her head. "I'll do the kissing part myself. Now get out of here so I can get some work done."

He was almost out the door when she added her usual money-grubbing line. "And you bring Fly more wrecks."

"I bring you all there are."

"Then you go make some more, Hooker. You slacking off."

He let the door slam before he started to laugh.

HOOKER NOSED the truck up onto the oversized concrete apron the size of most backyards. He eyed the two motorcycles parked in front of the giant door to the barnlike garage. He had never thought much about how his world consisted of large items. The scale of the two motorcycles heightened the domination.

The garage originally was designed to hold large dirigibles at the start of the century. The Navy built two of the larger hangers at Moffett Field, of which only Hanger One still stood. The eight smaller hangers, which were only an acre in footprint, were never erected. After Willie's retirement from the Navy—and feeling a need for a large indoor space to work on many auto projects at one time, he pulled strings and bought one of the hangars, which had been mothballed for well over twenty years. Almost burning down his house only led to the excuse to build an entire remodel of the structure.

The construction started with an old buddy with some old toys bought at a government auction. The D-8 Cat had made quick work of what was left of the house, and the man's new company of ex-Seabees soon had the property prepared for the new structure. The two items left in place and in working order were the swimming pool and the propane barbecue newly rigged to a five-hundred-gallon tank. The rest was just home remodeling.

The concrete pad for the new house was nothing more than a bump off the acre of twelve-inch thick concrete for the approach apron and the garage. All the concrete had suspended loops of copper pipe, which were eventually filled with hot, warm, or cool water—depending on the temperature needed for comfort and the season.

Once the concrete was ready, the area flooded with young sailors from the base who knew about construction. Some had erected one of the hangars before. Ostensibly, they were there to erect the hanger and leave—a job which should have taken a couple of weeks. The presence of a nonstop barbecue and a ready swimming pool had a delaying effect lasting the entire summer. Nobody cared if they were swimming in their undershorts or commando—Willie liked the look either way.

Willie's being well-liked on Moffett Field helped with the young Seabees and engineers borrowing needed materials from the base as they needed them. The base commander turned a blind eye to the requisitioning of material from the other four hangers stacked at the end of his runway. As a control measure, he also found time to come supervise from the shade of the large tent erected along the pool and next to the barbecue. A pint jar of clear liquid or a set of tongs for turning steaks was usually close at hand.

The acre of backyard had turned into a tent city of canopies. There were plenty of cots for those who took part in the clear liquid and spent the night.

By the first rains, the three-bedroom house was snugly overshadowed by the garage with giant doors forty feet square at both ends. By Halloween, the temperature in the garage was a toasty seventy-two degrees provided by a floor whose temperature neared ninety. Willie and Hooker were happily in new beds in a new home much to their liking. The true celebration for William Knight and his best friend Maddie Robinson was in the proper living room—an acre of concrete, filled with everything cars, trucks, and motorcycles.

Hooker parked the tow truck next to the motorcycles. As he walked toward the open door, he studied the motorcycle he had never seen before. The motor was a Triumph, but the frame was all wrong. It was low-slung like an older Harley or Indian. The back had a spring set-up providing a softer ride. The whole was modified and on the verge of being a hybrid of a racer like Maddie's Matchless and a chopper—right down to the short sissy bar on the back. There was a small roll tied down over the small front light, and a larger pack affair bungee strapped to the sissy bar. Hooker knew it wasn't one of Maddie's motorcycles because of the road grime that looked over a week old.

Willie's voice echoed in the garage, "We have shine..."

Hooker could tell Willie was already rosy-cheeked deep into the moonshine. Whoever had come with Maddie obviously didn't care if Willie was in pants or his usual dress—ugly, paisley, with burn holes from sparks picked up from welding or body grinding on one project or another.

Hooker took one more look at the black with red flames Triumph. He tucked the engine schematics under his left arm and rested his hands in his pockets as he walked into the dark garage. From thirty feet away, Hooker could tell the dress was one of the more offensive ones Uncle Willie had dragged home from the Goodwill store in a long time.

"Interesting new motorcycle you dragged over, Maddie. It looks like it was designed by Datsun and Leland but built by Fiat. Does it actually run?"

"Be nice, Hooker. We have a guest."

The young woman rose. Hooker was wondering where they made cute looking miniatures of Max. From the black cowboy boots to the white T-shirt over the jeans, she could be Hooker's relative. But the leather jacket stuffed into a cutoff jean jacket with patches screamed biker. The softly held reddish-brown ponytail fell just below her shoulders. Her face was young with a hint of freckles, but her stance was of someone much older—experienced.

He stuck his hand out. "Hi, I'm Hooker."

"Cricket, Cricket Street... happy to finally meet the topic of our conversation."

Hooker groaned. "Don't believe anything these two tell you. It's probably all true, but blown way out of proportion."

She snorted. "Yeah, I bet that's just as much bullshit as what they were slinging."

Hooker stopped pumping her hand. "Do you have a quarter?"

"Sure..."

"It goes in the swear jar."

She held his gaze as she thought for a moment and then pulled a wallet from her hip pocket. Pulling a hundred dollar bill out, she handed it to Hooker. "I live with two bikers who are undercover cops. About a hundred cops and firefighters wander in and out of our house twenty-four seven, and the place is a sea of high-test macho testosterone. Besides which, I sleep with a fourteen-foot-long snake who outweighs me by at least sixty pounds. I don't think I'll be changing my language anytime soon. If this doesn't cover everything by the time I leave, let me know—I have more where that fucking came from."

Hooker broke her gaze and looked to Willie. The man was unfazed. He simply nodded his head toward the door to the house as if to say *Go stick it in the jar. You just got one-upped.*

Hooker took the bill and turned for the house. "I'll leave the schematics in on the table."

Maddie stopped him. "Just leave them here. I want to go over them before we eat. Hank is out on the barbecue. Go say hi after you change the filthy shirt."

Hooker pulled his shirt around and looked at the large grease mark. "Damn..."

Cricket giggled. "You can take the quarter out of my hundred."

Hooker looked back at her and saw no malice. He bobbed his head. "Thanks."

The plates were cleaned, and the five sat around the large table made from a tail wing off a P-3 Orion sub chaser. The gift came from Moffett field flight wing as a belated retirement memento, and a thank you for the continuing friendship Willie showed the base and all who worked there.

Cricket pushed her plate a small bit forward and sipped on her lemonade. "Wow... the food was perfect, Hank. And I finally got a whole steak to myself."

Hooker frowned. "Why don't they let you have much meat?"

She laughed. "We have a big-assed commercial refrigerator-freezer at the house. The freezer is stuffed with steaks and some fish or hamburgers for the wimps."

"Then why not have a whole steak?" Hooker noticed the other three were holding their mouths—trying not to laugh.

"Because I always end up sharing it with the snake I sleep with."

"You were serious about the snake..."

Both Willie and Maddie nodded. "We've seen her. And she wasn't exaggerating about any of it... not the cops, not the refrigerator, and certainly not about the size of Gertie."

Hooker's mouth fell open. "What kind of cage do you keep her in?"

Cricket wagged her head as she chuffed a laugh. "The house and yard. They are hers to roam. She has never crossed the street or gone over the fence. The people who feed her are where she is, and the kids in the neighborhood come to her in the front yard—so she doesn't have to chase them. She is happy where she is."

"Does she eat the kids?"

"They don't taste good. She just stretches out on the grass after we mow it, and the kids love to pet her."

"What do the mother's think about her? I mean... she is one big snake."

"For the most part, they don't come close. Gertie is a lesbian... a very aggressive lesbian. She loves the smell of females, which is why she sleeps with me. I also think she would protect my father or me if she needed to."

"You mentioned your father before..."

"He's an undercover special investigator for the US Attorney General in Los Angeles. He just looks like a six-foot-six three-hundred-pound biker."

"Which would explain your bike out front and..." Hooker slowly waved his hand up and down pointing out her clothes.

"Both carry a certain understanding."

"Nobody asks you out?" Hooker snickered at his teasing.

Her face was anything but amusement. "Exactly."

He thought for a moment. "Seriously..."

Maddie slurred only slightly. "Why not. She's cute and obviously alone... and she will be going to a big college next month..." She left the obvious hanging in the air.

"So you're just up here taking a break before school?"

"Visiting Maddie and learning..."

"Library stuff...?"

Willie broke his silence with a hacking laugh. He looked at Cricket. "Can I borrow some of those hundred dollars?" She nodded, so he turned to Hooker. "So there, my boy is where you just screwed the pooch."

Willie's swearing set Hank to laughing. Hank's laughing set off Maddie, and as much as Hooker liked seeing the three have a good laugh—he knew it was at his expense.

He looked at the only other person—and she wasn't laughing. "Obviously, I misspoke."

"It's okay. That is exactly why I dress like my dad and ride the most kick-ass bike I can get my legs over. Perception is sometimes more powerful than reality. You see the wild chopper and the hard-assed biker bitch... and then just assume..." She smiled sweetly, and Hooker realized he had misjudged her age.

"You're not my age at all." He glared at the other three who were still trying to get themselves under control.

"No, I'm not. I turned seventeen only two months ago."

"And... my mistake was assuming you were learning something feminine from Maddie—such as working in a library." He put his face in his hands as she nodded.

Maddie snorted a half-drunk growling laugh.

"Without my boots, Maddie is four or five inches taller than me. I'm only five-foot—with two pairs of thick socks. I weigh just under ninety-four pounds, but I'm working on it with many steaks and weight training. But no... I don't want to work in a library. I'm challenging as many courses as I can at UCLA, and I hope I can start law school next fall. I'm sure I will have to take a few classes before then."

"Wait... you're challenging four years of college courses?"

She laughed. "In high school, I was a straight four-point-oh student. I have already taken some advanced placement classes at Pasadena City College. But my future uncle challenged all of his high school in a summer and most of his undergraduate work in the fall. He started med school at age sixteen. I have a great tutor to prep me."

"So what do you want to do?"

"First, I want my law degree..."

"And then what?" The other three were now working hard to learn about this enigma of a young girl.

"I don't know. My dad has his degree—he even finally took the bar exam—but is still doing what he did before."

Willie cleared his throat. "Undercover." She nodded. "I met him when he was fresh out of the Marines. He bought Maddie's old bike the night I met him. He took it for a test ride up the LA River toward Sylmar."

Cricket snorted. "I hate those tar seams. They liked to tear me up the first time I ran the Triumph up there."

Maddie smiled. "How fast?"

"First couple of times I kept it around ninety. The speedometer was the original off a Norton and only went to one-twenty. When I made the last run, I broke it."

Maddie nodded. "What's Roscoe building for you now?"

Cricket smiled. "Of course, you would know Roscoe and Honey. He has a bottom end of an old K-1, and he's casting new heads to make it around eighty-inches with Shovelhead tops. He's doing some horse-trading to get me a late forties Indian Scout frame and front-end. He thinks by stretching it about two inches, he can shoehorn it all in and add an oil radiator. It should be good for about one-seventy or one-eighty— good enough to keep up with Dad and Uncle Rabbit."

Hooker snorted. "You're here to learn how to ride fast bikes."

The freckled cheeks pooched up with her smile. "Actually, I'm here to learn how to crash safely."

Maddie nodded soberly. "Any fool can go fast. The real trick is knowing how to survive."

"Like stepping off in the salt flats at a hundred miles-per-hour."

Cricket chimed in, "Roscoe said it was more like one-fifty."

Maddie mumbled something as she waved her hand in dismissal.

Willie, without thinking, added the definitive answer. "The crash froze the speedometer at one-eighty-seven."

When Maddie backhanded Willie's chest, Hank knew it was time to put them all to bed. He stood and drew Willie up. "Cricket, if you would, Hooker can help you bring the motorcycles inside. You can use the Squirt's bed, and Maddie can use Hooker's. I washed all the sheets yesterday, so they are nice and clean." He straightened and blinked to clear his vision. "G'night." They stumbled off.

Cricket sat and watched Maddie follow the two men into

the house part of the complex. She turned back and frowned at Hooker.

"You sleep with Maddie?"

Hooker chuckled once softly. "Not hardly. I live in two places. My other family and bed are across the valley." He realized what he was saying was even more complicated. "It's complicated, but nobody is really *family*. Uncle Willie more like took me under his wing than adopted me. A couple of years later, things were kind of rough around here. I was taken in by a couple—Manny and Stella. Manny was a detective on San Jose Police. They took me in because I wasn't given a choice. Stella's sister is, if anyone is, my mother, and she demanded I go live there. Maddie can explain it all sometime when she's sober... or better yet, if you're still around this Sunday, we can have a family barbecue out at the Hacienda, and you can meet the whole family."

"Whose?"

"Whose what?"

"Whose family?"

Hooker sat back. He had never thought about it. He thought about all the connections, and the only single lynchpin was him. "I guess... it would be mine. But we are all one family."

"So you're adopted, but not legally?"

"I was just going on fourteen when I tried to hot-wire Willie's DeSoto. He smacked me on the butt with his mail and told me to scoot over. He took me to lunch because if I were trying to steal a car—I must be hungry. It was the most official we ever made it."

"And the dress?"

Hooker put his face in his hands. "Oh, gawd. He always

chooses the ugliest ones. He does it because he thinks it bothers me—it doesn't. But he buys them by the garbage bag full at Goodwill. They cost him about a quarter each. He pays rag price. So when he burns one up, it's not a big deal. A pair of bib-overalls cost about three dollars and jeans are two."

"Makes sense."

"If I remember right—and possibly don't, but the cop who got Maddie's bike down in LA is not much older than me..."

Cricket smirked. "So how does he have a seventeen-year-old daughter?"

"Yeah..."

"It's more complicated than you and Willie... but he adopted me two days after my seventeenth birthday. The same day I got emancipated from my birth parents." Hooker could tell by her face, the original family was not a pleasant affair.

He nodded gently. "My sister and I grew up in the dark side of foster homes and were sold from abusers to abusers until we ran away. My girlfriend, Candy, and her little brother, Squirt had the same—I guess it's why we understand each other so well."

"Abuse, beatings or..."

"All the above."

"I'll be around for a couple of weeks. Your family is the kind I think I would like to meet."

Hooker stood. "Just don't bring the snake."

They laughed as they went to move the motorcycles.

"So only five-foot, huh?"

"I hear you have a big truck... when you aren't blowing it up."

"You're going to fit into the family just fine."

"That's what Hank said."

"Hank is a smart man."

"So tell me about the scar on Willie's neck."

"You can ask Maddie about the medal just inside the door when she's sober in the morning."

"So what were they drinking, Vodka?"

"Worse... White Lightning. Maddie's family makes it down Salinas way."

"I think I'm liking this family more and more..."

"They grow on you."

"I've got room to grow."

26

OUT ON THE DECK AT THE HACIENDA

The heavy metal of the industrial barbecue was ticking as it cooled down. The dinner, for the most part, was done. Only the watermelon-strawberry mousse dessert was left to serve and eat.

Stella came through the door with a small tray of only six cut-crystal glasses. "Here we are... Mom's famous all summer mousse." Each of the delicate glasses full of the whipped pink mousse had a pair of handmade chocolate antlers stuck in the pudding.

A few of the diners looked at the small tray of only six delicate crystal parfait glasses with longing faces. Stella ceremoniously set one of the glasses in the center of each round table of eight dinners. "First person to touch one of my masterpieces of delicate work which took me all day to make... has to wash the dishes."

All eyes snapped back to the door with Danny's booming rumble of a voice. "But who wants some dessert?" His arms were spread wide with a large serving tray filled with larger bowls. Each heaped with the fluffy delight, which some risked putting coins into the swear jar by calling pink farts. As delightful the taste, there seemed the whipped gelatin desert had no body to it—but it did taste like summer. Maddie and Candy jumped up to help pass out the large colorful Fiestaware bowls. Cricket wasn't sure if it was her place but joined in. As she started to place the dessert in front of certain people, they laughed and covered their placemats. Finally, she noticed they would take it from Maddie or Candy... but instead of getting mad, she asked Manny why he wouldn't take it from her.

Manny laughed and reached out and grabbed her waist. Reeling her in for a hug, he started pointing out the guys who wouldn't take it from her. "He's a cop, he's a cop, he's a cop, he's an ex-cop, he's a fireman, he's close to being a cop, and the Squirt we're not sure about." He looked up at her and smiled. "I'm diabetic, and if I'm going to eat one, it's going to be the tiny centerpiece. But those guys... no cop wants to be served by a lawyer—even if she is years away from being one." The party erupted in laughter.

Being a good sport, she leaned over and gave him a hug. "Thanks. I guess I broke the first rule of litigating. I didn't know the answer before I asked the question."

"You're going to be fine. Now leave the bowl and go tell on me to Stella so she can bring me some insulin. Tell her I snitched both antlers off the centerpiece."

"But they're both there..."

"Not for long... so run along." He swatted her bottom, and she giggled. As he watched her wend through the crowd, he thought, *another kid.* It put a smile on his face.

Paul looked down at his bowl and spoke as much to the

dessert as he did to his old partner. "There is a lot to like there..."

Manny nodded. He knew their conversation was theirs alone as their low voices were lost in the rest of the conversations. "Ever think about not having kids?"

"I used to... but not anymore."

Manny looked over at the county supervisor and closest friend. "Why not now?"

He gently smiled as he nudged his jaw toward the young girl returning with the insulin kit. "Because when I feel like having some, I know I can borrow some of yours." He chuckled silently as he turned and smirked at his friend.

Cricket stopped and held onto the kit. "Where do you want it... butt, thigh or arm? I can do it between your toes also."

Manny frowned. "Are you diabetic too?"

"Nah, but a few of the cops are. I was thinking about becoming a doctor, so they thought it was good practice. Actually, most doctors don't even know how to give a shot or draw blood. I know how to do all three."

Now Paul frowned. "Shot or draw blood is only two. Where do you get three?"

She counted on her fingers. "Shot is one, draw a blood sample is two, and..." Her right hand flashed to her belt just right of her buckle, and there appeared a thin four-inch blade in her hand. "And then, there is spilling blood."

Manny and Paul both looked at the blade and the implication of it even being secreted on her body. Her only being seventeen spoke, even more, volumes about the nature of the defensive tactic. The way she had produced it showed this not to be a childish show-off trinket or whimsy.

Manny rubbed his chin. "I'll take the needle in the arm, please. How many knives do you have?"

She stepped over and took out the already measured syringe. She peeled open the alcohol patch and rubbed down his deltoid muscle toward the back. As she stuck the needle in, she answered softly. "Only the one... for now. A guy across the street is a Marine but used to be in a street gang. He's been teaching me how to use the knives and throw them. He's working on a belt that will give me four, and maybe I'll get some boots made giving me four more."

Paul rolled to one side to better look at the small young woman. "Is there a need?"

She sat down and closed the insulin kit. "I don't know... but it's a feeling I have. It is the same sort of feeling, and why I'm up here learning how to crash and ride fast from Maddie. I mean... who learns how to have an accident?"

"It's not learning to have one. It's learning to be prepared when one occurs." They all looked up at Hooker and the Squirt. The Squirt leaned over with his hand out. "Hi, we weren't introduced earlier. My name is John, but everyone calls me the Squirt."

She smiled. "The fucking new guy."

He nodded. "But it just seemed to fit. So I'll probably be like the seventy-year-old guy they call Junior or JR."

She screwed up her face with her eyes closed and began to recite a long string of numbers. "One point six, one, eight, zero, three, four." She opened her eyes and looked at him.

He smiled. "It was the Golden Mean of Euclid as confirmed by Aristotle. Leonardo De Vinci called it the Divine Proportion. Later, it was used to define the Golden

Rectangle, which is the most pleasing proportions to the eye in architecture and shape of a painting."

She smiled and shied her face in query. "But...?"

He laughed. "The modern painters' canvases are the right proportions, but when you put them in a picture frame, the proportions are destroyed."

"Eidetic memory is very rare. Maddie showed me the paper you wrote on the Golden Rectangle... it was impressive. I wrote a similar one a year ago... I got my knuckles rapped with a ruler for heretic ascription for one of God's beauties." She rolled her eyes. "Someday, you will have to come to Los Angeles and meet my future uncle. Do you have to read the address or can I just tell you?"

He smiled. "You can just tell me. What does he do?"

"He just started med school."

"So he's Hooker's age..."

"No, he's my age. He challenged all of high school and most of his undergraduate work. He has been prepping me to challenge at least the first two years of undergrad work. But he is visual, so he has to read it or at least see it. He learned most of the American Sign Language in two days."

The men all gave a low whistle. She nodded and then gave the Squirt the address and phone numbers for the house and the restaurant.

Hooker cleared his throat. "Listen, you said something the other night—about perception."

She nodded. "About it being more powerful than knowing... yes, I remember."

"Well, we have this case we're working on—"

She cut him off. "The body dump in the bay. Yes, Maddie

spoke some about it, but we also stopped in to meet Dolly. There was a bald Sheriff's deputy—"

"Uncle Fester. He was the first responder. Well, he was there for the wreck... then we found the skeleton together."

"But there is another person who is the killer?"

Hooker held up his finger and looked down a couple of tables. He clicked his tongue and watched as Sweets' head jerked around as well as Danny's. Hooker crooked his finger at Danny. Danny leaned over and spoke to Sweets. The two rose as one and came over.

"Sweets, Danny, I think you met Cricket earlier. Pull up a seat. We're going over the case and what we know and observed. I hope she can see what we are not seeing." Sweets turned and gawped at Hooker in mock shock.

Hooker growled. "Oh, shut up and sit down. I'll go get Candy."

Cricket snickered. "Make mine chocolate, please."

Hooker scowled at her in misunderstanding. And then rolled his head in zombie fall and walked off.

Cricket turned to Manny. "What was the head and dead look thing?"

Manny rolled his eyes. "It's shorthand around here for a stupid question or not realizing the chocolate and Candy reference. Some of us have been damaged enough, and so we don't like smacking ourselves in the forehead. Ask Hooker. It was something he and his sister started as small kids."

"With a family gathering this big—I expected to meet her."

"She'll come down for Christmas. She lives with friends about a hundred miles north of here."

Cricket slumped slightly. "I think we are going to be in Brazil then."

Hooker and Candy returned holding hands. Cricket sized up the body posture. It wasn't your usual relationship handhold. It had a lot more *us against the world* than just lovebirds. It was as if they drew strength from each other's presence. She could relate, and her lap suddenly was missing the heavyweight of her snake. Hooker sat, and Candy snuggled between Hooker and her brother. Cricket recognized a wall of force when she saw it.

"So, we will start with what we know, and as we go through it, stop us at any time and ask questions or make suggestions."

Manny pushed up on his chair. "Wouldn't it be better to have the whiteboard?"

The Squirt jumped up. "Good idea. I'll get it as you go over the initial discovery."

Soon, the large gathering had pushed tables around and rearranged the deck so they could all see the whiteboard and the rapidly growing lines of information. Cops, firefighters, or those just loosely associated with law enforcement made up most of the gathering. No matter their job, the detective work and how it developed through Hooker and the family was of interest to all.

Cricket pulled her legs up into the large chair as she leaned forward. "So wipe out all the cars driving by. What we need is who stopped—someone they might know—regular customers. And what is a Cushman?"

Candy looked back and smiled. "It's one of those little three-wheel carts like a golf cart. Only, instead of golf bags, this one has a truck bed kind of thing the garbage man puts the bags of garbage in and takes them to a larger collection place."

"Oh... Thanks. I think it's the same system they have in San Marino. They have a fleet of little carts running up the long driveways of the mansions—so the rich people don't have to haul their trash to the curb or suffer seeing their neighbor's garbage. Okay, so we have someone getting a blowjob while they have a cigarette break. Some people from the college walking around. Several cars driving through the area—few stop, and a garbage man collecting the day's trash before it starts to stink up the area. But no one they seemed to know."

Candy started to put up her finger... but her face was still screwed up trying to work out what it was Cricket had said... wrong... or not quite right.

Sweets' head suddenly twitched, and Danny jerked and studied him. Sweets reached out and held on to Danny's arm and just softly hummed to himself. Danny knew he was working through a memory or something he had seen in one of his visions.

Sweets' head swiveled. "What did you just say?"

Candy jumped. "I didn't..."

"No, the other... Cricket. What did you say about the garbage man?"

"I said he drives around and puts the garbage in the cart and hauls it away?"

Sweets was disturbed. It wasn't right... he searched. His head swung about. "Squirt?"

"Yeah?"

His head swung around and locked on. "What exactly did she say?"

The Squirt's eyes rolled back, and he searched for the

right moment. "The blowjob, the cars, nobody stopping... and then a garbage man collecting the day's trash before it starts to stink up the area."

Sweets rolled his finger and hand in the air, "But after... "

"But no one they seemed to know..."

Sweets pointed. "Which... is wrong. Candy said the garbage dude waved to the girls on First."

Candy stiffened. "Oh, my lord. The one girl did wave back. But it seemed so natural. It was like a side wave from her hip. It was a... a... friendship wave, not a flirty wave."

Sweets leaned back and smiled. "And I told you about the smell. It was the same as when Danny took out the garbage from under the sink every day... it's fresh..." He pointed directly at Cricket. "Before it stinks up the place."

"But how would you know about the smell?" Cricket furrowed her brow.

Manny leaned over and rested his hand on her arm. Quietly, he muttered, "It's a very long story for another time."

Sweets smiled. "Because I smelled it before. There is your killer—the garbage dude."

Hooker wasn't convinced. "What about what Tess said about the Waterman having a female twin? She was the one who attacked Tess."

Chet looked up from where he had been quietly enjoying the evening with his blonde date. "Maybe there is a third person in this party..."

Cricket had talked with Chet and the shrink for a while when they first arrived. She liked the man and his lady friend. "Captain, do you have any female officers?"

Micha snorted and called out to his boss. "She sounds a lot like Dolly."

Chet rolled his eyes and nodded with a lopsided smile of agreement. "We are implementing new guidelines from Sacramento with some of the new recruits from this new hiring cycle."

Cricket swung around. "Candy, are there any male nurses or female doctors?"

"Both."

"So why assume a garbage collector you only saw from... what? A block away—is a dude?"

Paul's one eyebrow rose as he looked past Cricket at his old partner. But he addressed the young woman. "Are you sure you want to become a lawyer? You think more like a cop."

Her head ground around as she growled. "I'm also only five feet tall. And they don't make bulletproof vests in size zero."

"Pity... I'm just saying."

"You change the requirements and give me a call. The Squirt has our number at the frat house."

"Frat house?"

Manny leaned back and looked to his partner. "The house she lives in has a commercial coffee pot and a large freezer full of steaks and no lock on the back door. The local LEOs are in and out around the clock."

Paul smiled. "Frat house."

Hooker cleared his throat and pointed at the whiteboard.

Cricket nodded. "Any way to find out who the garbage person is?"

Stella stood. "On it..." She padded into the house. Six minutes later, she came out reading from a small piece of paper. "Her name is Petunia Scarsdale, like the city in New York. She goes by the name Pete."

Later, as the party was breaking up and people were leaving, Hooker sat down next to Cricket. "It's a shame you aren't staying. You do have a good mind for this stuff."

"I think you're selling your family short. I don't think any major crimes unit in any large city has the experience, talent, and special skills of the team or family you have surrounded yourself with. Manny told me about Sweets and how he sees things. That is amazing enough, but then you live with the Squirt and Manny, which is not to dismiss Willie and his intelligence background."

"Don't leave out Maddie..."

"I've adopted her as my official aunt. There is a lot there that I'm sure most of us will never know. My time here has been amazing."

"When do you head back?"

"I'll catch the train tomorrow night."

"Why so soon?"

"Roscoe said he will have my new chopper ready Wednesday. And you can only crash a Triumph so many times. The last one this afternoon—the asphalt and wall won. Maddie didn't think there were any parts to salvage... but you never know about Willie and his creative welding."

"Are we going to see you again?"

"I'd like to bring Dad up. I think he would enjoy spending some time picking Manny's brain. And the ride was nice."

"We have room to put you guys up, downstairs. When I'm here, Candy doesn't spend much time in her apartment. So you two can stay as long as you want. If it's cop talk and investigation, the time would be good for Manny, as well. Just don't bring the snake."

Cricket snorted a giggle. "Gertie doesn't travel. She has a house full of cops to keep straight. But the family may soon be four or five of us."

"Well, you are welcome anytime. Two or six... we'll find room here or at Willie's."

"So you really do float back and forth?"

"Not as much as I used to. I like being here with Candy, and the Squirt has pretty much made his nest here too. But I still stay over at the boy shack enough to keep Willie and Hank on their best behavior."

She gave an amateurish zombie roll of her head. "Right, but at least the dress tonight wasn't one of the ugly paisley ones."

Hooker lowered his one eye. "The jean patchwork dress was the Squirt's idea. He told Willie it had more of the go-to town look."

She laughed. "Panache."

Hooker looked at his watch but then remembered it was Sunday. Shawna probably didn't work, and it was too late to go by the Stick and Balls. He would swing by Monday evening.

27

BUT FIRST

Hooker was a mile away. Fewer than five minutes even with the traffic. The right turn was in his sight.

"1-4-1, I'm holding a multiple-vehicle pile-up... Southbound 101, just south of Blossom Hill, but Micha says to forget trying to get there from Blossom Hill. He suggests dropping to Santa Teresa and come back. You will have to come up on the southbound lanes as the northbound is already jammed up halfway to Coyote."

Hooker had reached for the switches for the lights and siren before he realized those were only in Mae West. His right hand pawed useless on the smooth metal under the dashboard.

"Oh, hell." He grabbed the mic as he took a right. "10-4, it's going to take a while. I'm in the pig."

"10-4, Hooker—we feel the frustration from here. Chet just called and said Almaden to Santa Tee and out, was clear, but to please keep it under sixty or so."

"Thanks, Karen. Tell auto club I'm probably done for the day."

"We already told Motorbody and the club dispatch. Don is picking up the Chevy just in case. There are a couple of elephants in the zoo, so I called Jose, and he's on his way up the back way. He said to get started, and he'll be there in an hour."

Hooker straightened out on Almaden Expressway and switched on his rotating yellows and the flashers. "Micha, have a count...?"

"Rapid read was double arms and three legs. We have seven meat wagons coming to the party and fire is just arriving. Five known log-outs so far."

"10-4." He hung the microphone. He turned the volume down on the auto club radio. He knew the only radio he wanted to hear was the shop. It was the only one Dispatch, and he could talk freely on.

The double arms meant over twenty cars with the legs being larger trucks or buses. Seven ambulances meant there would be many injuries and five dead bodies with just the first look-over. The elephants or large trucks were usually double trailers, which could mean some serious money. Late in the summer, the crashes are few, and real money starts to look like something a tow driver won't see until the rains come. This large of an accident on clean hot pavement was rare and always serious.

Every tow driver out there feels for the people involved, but to keep it from becoming overwhelming, they only think about the money and how to tow what, and how many they can get. Hooker had once even watched a driver hook up the back end of a CHP car with the light bar lit up. The guy tried to explain he had been tired and wasn't paying attention.

Hooker wound through the traffic and crossed Blossom Hill. Two lights further down, he would then turn left.

"1-4-1, pull over."

What? He snapped the mic up and keyed it. "1-4-1, say again?"

"1-4-1, we didn't say anything."

The siren behind him blipped. Hooker looked in the mirror. He realized the talking wasn't over the radio at all.

"Pull over, Hooker."

He nosed to the curb. In his right rearview mirror, he saw the Squirt jump out of the squad car. He ran to the passenger door and jumped in. "You thought you could go to a big hoedown without me?" Hooker liked his smile.

Hooker cleared the mirrors as the squad car pulled out in front of them with lights and siren.

"Bill is going to clear Santa Teresa for us, but the new rules say he has to keep it under eighty."

Hooker snorted as he jammed the gears into third. "Man, I hope this pig can keep up."

The Squirt grunted. "So have you thought about stepping on the gas pedal?"

Hooker blew a raspberry with his lips as he watched the creeping needle claw its way to the midpoint marked with a large sixty. He knew the manufacturer had been dreaming or just laughing when they installed a speedometer marked to one-twenty.

"When does the new rendition of Mae West rise from the ashes?"

"They decided the new Desert Eagle engine wouldn't

perform as well with the new configuration of triple axles—so they're building an engine from the ground up. They won't even know what the true horsepower is until..." He paused as he wrestled the truck around a large sweeping curve he had driven Mae around many times with a single finger. "This pig wallows like a whale... I sure hope Don likes it." He downshifted as he saw the patrol car turn left to head for the highway. "So they have to get the engine in Mae and throw it all on some giant dyne-o-tune machine to even find out what the horsepower is at the rear end."

"What are they hoping for?"

A FEW MILES LATER, they slowed to turn north onto the southbound lanes of the highway. They both glanced south. They could see over a mile of standing traffic. People stood in small groups—talking and looking north.

They had seen this before. "It's going to be a long day."

"Maybe it won't be so bad."

As they came around the one last jog in the highway, their view was of static mass pandemonium. Hooker let out a low whistle. "Dante painted this."

The Squirt's eyes danced over the mass and calculated cars, directions, towing lanes. "No—right idea, just the wrong painter. This work is pure Hieronymus Bosch."

Hooker glanced at the Squirt. He wasn't sure if the kid knew his true name... but he didn't put it past him. He smiled and returned his attention to the officer waving them down. "Yeah, I should be more mindful of keeping my names straight."

They pulled alongside the black officer sweating like a pro

basketball player in the final minutes. "Hey, Micha, I thought you were used to this heat."

Micha bit his lower lip. Hooker noted the strained look around his eyes. He had a job to do and would never shy from his responsibility, but Hooker saw his friend was now hurting.

Hooker lowered his voice. "How bad?"

Micha glanced north into the carnage. "Too many prom queens, and this one... we have a baby... the mom was holding it in her arms."

Hooker knew the dynamics of an eight-pound baby becoming a one-ton projectile at the sudden stop from thirty or forty. He could only imagine what would happen with a car traveling at sixty. He scanned over the field of twisted metal.

"Where did it end up?"

"On the dashboard... of the camper they rear-ended..." Micha's voice was shaky, and he looked away. He and Hooker had too much history for his hiding his tears, but...

"Where do you want us to start, Micha?"

The man indicated their area and south. "We need to build a buffer zone."

"10-4." Hooker cleared his mirrors and started backing to turn around. He backed onto the side and turned the truck south. As they came to the last damaged car, he pulled onto the shoulder.

Both dropped open their side compartments and pulled out the large boxes of thirty-minute flares. "Stuff your pockets, but let's hold off lighting them up. We'll turn this herd around and head them back toward Coyote Road, and the Chips can set up the detour later."

Hooker took the newish Ford pickup truck with the

young couple in work clothes. The Squirt in his uniform took the white Cordoba and its beefy driver with an angry red face. Reluctantly, the line started making the U-turn and headed south to the exit.

As they slowly walked south, waving the retreating line into a continuous U-turn, they continued their personal conversation.

"Is it possible to get that much horsepower out of a standard-sized engine?"

"You tell me. Maddie had you do some wild research reports."

"Nothing I ever ran across. The stuff I was researching sounded more like the racetrack crazy Maddie and Willie would be doing. Those monster engines are built for speed—but with short lifespans."

"I don't know... it is beyond my understanding too. Maddie went over the schematics the other night and again the next day. She talked to her brother Ben... and they seem comfortable with the whole idea. Either way, we will always have the Eagle here as a swap-out backup."

"Hmm..." The Squirt stared at the woman in the Corvette, who seemed to have a hard time understanding why she couldn't just drive straight. After all, she was headed to San Jose or San Francisco... and she was in her expensive car, with her hair all done up in the new style giant Dutch-boy flip...

Hooker was holding the VW, waiting on the Corvette as she finally huffed and puffed herself into turning around... but she wasn't going to like it.

"Did you hear anything new this morning up at the office about finding the garbage collector?"

"They went to the address she had on her application and her driver's license—"

Hooker snorted. "Empty building, wrong person, or no such address...?"

The Squirt chuffed. "You've been at this way too long—electrical transfer station."

"So what now?"

The Squirt glanced over at Hooker and gave him a smarmy smile.

"What?"

"CHP and the Sheriff want to throw it back into our hands."

Hooker took a double-take. "Are you serious?"

"We do have a certain reputation... and we don't care about county lines or jurisdictions..."

The CHP cruiser pulled out from Coyote Road and onto the shoulder. The officer stepped out and opened his trunk. Grabbing a box of flares, he walked over to Hooker and the Squirt.

"Hey, Heinz, did they wake you up or just call you back from fishing?"

"Neither. The wife's cousin wound up at Good Sam early this morning with some kind of woman issues, and so I was there with them." He handed the box to the Squirt and jabbed his chin up the highway. "How bad...?"

The Squirt turned around so the man could pull the four flares out of his back pocket. Hooker growled softly. "You don't want to come up. Just stay here in the sun. You'll be better off tonight."

The man grabbed the four out of Hooker's pocket as well.

"There are six more boxes in the trunk—leave me at least two."

"I'll leave you four. You're going to need them before midnight."

The officer sighed. "Thanks."

Hooker was wrong. The traffic finally started crawling by in restricted lanes shortly after two in the morning. The Squirt sat on the running board. Hooker gave up and simply stretched out on the highway. There was a problem, and they couldn't hook onto their last car until the fire guys cleared it.

"Do you think we can come get all those stashed cars later this morning?"

Hooker smiled. "Don has already got us covered. He's having the two new hires shuttle everything up to the Fly for us. It's actually kind of smart. They get a week's worth of experience blowing-and-going with turds they can't damage—and we get paid for the tows."

"What about those six pancakes needing a dolly?"

"The sleds too."

The kid leaned back against the door. "Wow... Sleep..."

"Someone here order some French vanilla ice cream, triple-scoops in sugar cones?"

The two men looked up at a paramedic holding two cones. Her smile was as refreshing as the ice cream looked.

Hooker rolled up and stood stiffly. "Hello, Holly. You look like an angel standing there." He took the offered cone.

The Squirt stood with a smile. "Hello, Chuck."

She blushed. "You promised you wouldn't call—"

"I promised not to call you Vomit Comet." He ran his tongue around the top scoop and smiled at her.

Hooker snickered. "Hmm, Comet Chuck... has a certain ring to it."

She turned on him. "And this coming from a certain man who has a reputation for being a quickie?"

Hooker smiled drunkenly tired. "Yes, ma'am."

She growled.

The Squirt talked around the last of the top scoop. "Thanks for the first aid. How do you like working the ambulance?"

She blushed. "I like the siren. I like being out."

Hooker and the Squirt looked up as they saw the other driver walking up. The woman was shorter than Holly but blonde with a nice shape, which did good things for the uniform.

Hooker smiled. "And you like your partner?"

Holly blushed and looked back. Turning, she looked at Hooker and gently nodded. Hooker gave her a wink. *Good for you.*

She looked at the Squirt. He nodded a small nod and smile. He also approved of the partner.

"Am I interrupting?"

"Kam, this is Hooker and the Squirt. Guys, this is my partner, Kam—and behave."

Kam leaned over with her hand out. "Mr. Quickie and Mr. Scar tissue... Yup, I've heard all about this team." Her smile was disarming. She looked close at the Squirts' hand. "How is the paw?"

"How do you know about his hand?"

She smiled. "Where you forked him to the counter?"

Holly looked at Hooker. "You did what?"

Hooker waved it off. "Old story and it was nothing."

Kam laughed. "No... that came later. What? About two bucks of dimes shoved in you?"

Holly blanched.

"And you are...?"

"My cousin is, um, what do you call her... Cynthia Eye Candy?"

Hooker and the Squirt both laughed. "Yeah, then you would know about all the stuff."

"Yeah, Cyn and I go way back on the stories about you bringing in body parts."

"Do you ever talk to Max up at the Stick and Balls?"

The woman didn't even flinch. "Her hand is doing pretty good. At least it didn't stop her from riding the motorcycle... but she can't throw the knives two-handed like she used to."

"I wish I could have seen that."

"She'll still whip your ass at darts if you don't make her use darts."

They all turned at the sound of the shrill whistle. The fireman in the dirty yellow turnouts was winding his finger over his head. Hooker waved and headed for the cab of the tow truck. "Duty calls. Thanks for the ice cream, Holly and nice meeting you, Kam. Maybe we'll run into you two at the Stick and Balls some night." He jumped up in the cab and started the truck.

Kam looked back, and Hooker watched her in his side mirror as she smiled and then told Holly something as they walked back to their rig. He would miss Holly at the Thrifty's when he stopped for ice cream, but he was glad she had found her niche.

28

GETTING WET

"You two were out late last night." Hank sat sideways in the chair as he leaned over the morning newspaper. His socks were on, but no shoes. His chinos had knife-edge creases as crisp as his starch-stiffened white dress shirt. Hooker knew the bow tie and freshly polished shoes would be the last items to go on. Hooker shuffled to the coffeemaker.

"We wanted to give you two enough time alone to be nasty and run around the shop naked and go skinny-dipping." He turned to find a single eye drilling holes in him. He grabbed the carafe and held it out. "More coffee?" He hoped his smile appeared disarming.

Hank moved his coffee cup as he pretended to read the Dear Abby column. "You need to show a little more respect. Your uncle is getting up in years. He is no longer capable of running wild through the garage." He softly turned the page. "We creep."

The Squirt kissed him on the top of the head and silently

sat down, burying his nose into his coffee mug. Hooker watched—afraid he had fallen asleep and might drown.

Without looking up, Hank reached over, and grabbing a handful of hair, lifted the head out of the mug. Coffee dripped from the end of the nose. The zombie mumbled, "I'm good..." and returned to sipping his coffee.

Hank closed and creased the Mercury News. Shuffling the parts back together, Hooker could have sworn it had never been read.

Hank took up his mug and rose. "I can hear the grizzly bear crashing about his cave, so I'll start breakfast."

Hooker looked at the clock. Two-forty-three... there had been much creeping going on the night before. "Do I need to vacuum the pool this afternoon?"

Willie's voice croaked with the early morning dryness affecting his scarred throat. "No need to be crude, Hooker. We have a new pool boy for that. Augustus is a respectful, quiet, young man who doesn't make vulgar comments about his elder's nightlife." He wandered past Hank and grabbed his butt. The other man jumped only slightly and nodded at the coffee. Willie poured his own mug full and topped Hank's off as well.

Willie parted his bathrobe to reveal standard white Navy swim trunks, and sat heavily. "Maybe Augustus can come tomorrow instead."

Hooker's one eyebrow moved. "Is Augustus feeling under the weather?"

Willie looked at him with only one eye over the top of the mug. "Just old..."

Hooker closed his eyes and then stood. Silently, he walked into his bedroom, and a minute later returned. In his hand, he held a large pink envelope. He kissed Willie behind the ear and laid the card in front of him.

He whispered with a laugh, "You thought we forgot..."

As Hank stood behind him, Willie opened the birthday card. The card folded out to over four feet long. Whatever had been printed on the inside—had long been written over with signatures. His laughter sounded like a coughing lion after swallowing a driving range bucket of balls. Hank patted him on the back and kissed him on the forehead as he looked up.

His eyes were wet as he looked up at two blurry blobs across the table. His smile crinkled and finally, he just sagged back. Nothing needed saying.

Hooker mopped up the last few bites of pancakes and eggs as the phone rang. The Squirt, standing closest as he poured more coffee into four mugs, answered the phone.

"Good evening, Chez Menz."

He stood for a second and then turned and looked at Hooker. "10-4, we'll take it in the truck. We're out in three... I need a shower." He hung up laughing. "The new girl." He checked to make sure Hooker had his boots on. Both had taken advantage of the warm summer night and bathed in the swimming pool at quarter past three in the morning.

Hank patted the air. "Leave it all. Go..."

He found himself talking to the air as the fire-rated door to the garage slammed shut.

Hooker started the truck and nosed it off the apron and down the street. The Squirt looked around. "Where's Box?" Hooker slammed on the brakes. They sat in the middle of the afternoon street thinking.

Hooker grabbed the shop mic. "Karen, is Box there with you?"

"Negatory, Hooker. Do I need to check if he is out running calls in another truck all by himself?"

Hooker knew she could barely keep from laughing.

Hooker pinched the bridge of his nose. He left the mic unkeyed and muttered to himself or the Squirt, "What day is this?"

The silence was deafening. The small tin speaker rumbled and vibrated with Dolly's voice. "You left him here when you ran out so fast on Wednesday night. If you have missed a step or six... this is Saturday."

Karen's voice bled in, "Squirt?"

The Squirt took the mic. "Go ahead."

"See Fester at the crab shack near Tess's camp. And from what I gather... you need to step on it."

Hooker dumped the clutch and the truck shot forward two feet and stalled. He turned the key and restarted the engine. The silent growl was enough. The Squirt didn't even smile. He rolled down his window and hoped for some cooling. They were four minutes away from the freeway.

The Squirt got an evil look in his eye. The truck lumbered down the hill. Gaining speed, he and Hooker both knew could not be used in a drifting slide to make the left turn at the bottom. "Um... 10-4... Show our ETA at four hours and twenty-eight minutes."

"10-9?" Dolly's voice had an edge to it.

The Squirt still wasn't done. "We're in the High-Speed Wonder, not the svelte demure Ms. West."

"The High-Speed Wonder... 1-4-1, which vehicle are you

in?" Don must have been listening on the shop radio or out running a call.

Hooker grabbed the mic from the Squirt. "Your new baby... and when you get her back, you too will be wondering where they hid the high-speed gears."

"They said the truck could hit at least one-twenty..."

"Capable and able to do so are two different universes. They travel in deep space on TV, but us getting there is another story."

Hooker glanced at the Squirt before he stomped on the breaks and manhandled the truck around the turn. "Before you get it back, Don, you might want to let Willie have it for a few months."

The radio was silent as they rode the distance to the next sharp turn onto the freeway on-ramp.

"Calling the reservation into William right now..."

"You might make it for after the holiday wrecking party." Every tow truck driver knew from the first rains until a week after New Year's Day, all moving trucks were busy.

"That's what Willie just said."

The two in the tow truck chuckled. Hooker tossed the mic in the air, and the Squirt caught it as he watched Hooker muscle the right turn. He keyed the mic. "Willie's a smart guy."

"I think it runs in the family. Don out."

Hooker and the Squirt cleared their mirrors as they settled into the long drive to Fremont. Hooker tried to push the truck past seventy-five, but the shimmy affected the steering, so he held it at seventy and relaxed in the wind of the window.

Hooker left the yellow flashers off. Nobody would have

paid attention, and the drivers were all lethargically numb from the heat and driving on autopilot. *Sunday and a hot afternoon—drones going nowhere.*

Fester checked his wristwatch when he spotted the medium-sized yellow blob of a tow truck turn the corner four blocks away. Dispatch hadn't been far wrong. This was not the fast truck Hooker got his reputation with. They were only off by a couple of hours.

The Squirt dropped from the truck first. "What have we got?" He held the double-barreled sawed-off shotgun at his side.

"Suspect went out on the water about two this afternoon. The witness, who called it in, said they thought he had a large and long garbage bag over his shoulder. Could be we have another body."

Hooker came around the nose of the truck. "Who's the witness?"

Fester pointed to the crab shack. "Waitress named Joan or Joanne."

Hooker and the Squirt looked out across the miles of grass. They both had seen aerial photos of the fine spider-web of freshwater rivers running through the grass like streets in a crazy laid-out city. If you didn't know where you were going, it would be easy to get lost—*or hide.*

"We have two fast-assault pontoon boats coming down from Alameda. The SEAL teams come down here to train so they won't get lost."

Hooker looked up the long street to the north.

Fester laughed. "Are you kidding, Hooker? I said SEAL."

The Squirt snorted. "They're on the water." He turned. "I'm going to go talk to the waitress."

Hooker looked at the kid. "Yeah, coffee sounds good."

As the three walked to the shack, Fester glanced at Hooker and the drained look of his shoulders. "What time did you clear the wreck yesterday?"

"Three... this morning... "

"I'll buy."

THE WAITRESS HAD nothing more to add, except some carrot cake. She said she and the owner were like many of the people in the area. At first, they were leery of Tess and her strange habits, but then they got to looking after him. Hooker didn't think it his place to set her straight about Tess being a woman. He could tell the young woman really was protective, if not fond of her.

Hooker assured her Tess would be back, but not until it was safe.

"Gentlemen, it looks like your rides are here."

The three turned to look out the window as the two insertion boats nosed up onto the launch ramp. The heavily muffled engines were noiseless through the window. Hooker was pretty sure they would have still been surprised if they had been sitting out on the deck.

Fester passed a ten across the counter, and they left. The waitress sang them out with a longing call to three good-looking men, "Y'all come back soon now. Ya hear?"

The SEALs had chart maps showing all the rivers or lanes as they called them. Hooker and Fester showed them where the body dump had been. The two team leaders quickly assessed the route to go in and see if the suspect had gone home to what he knew. They also looked at a pincher assault to Bridgetown by coming in from the south and north. This would be their search area B. If both of those failed, they would start a quadrant search and call for some air support from Moffett. If night fell, they would switch to Hueys with spotters using infrared and starlight scopes that could spot the heat of a man.

The temperature drop surprised Hooker the moment they left the shallows and ran along the grass line just offshore. The twin outboard motors were quieter than most cars with their windows closed. The team members wore a dark-water camouflage Hooker had never seen before. Each man intently searched the grass and lanes as they glided down the waterway. Even though Hooker searched also, he felt like a billboard in his white T-shirt and also felt out of his league in the search department. Tell him to find the dead AMC Pacer in the middle of a fifty-car pile-up, and he's your man. But grass, water, the sun, and looking for someone who lives in this condition—Hooker felt like a tourist.

They turned west and ran down a narrow lane, which let out onto a wider lane Hooker would have called a freeway. The two pontoon boats ran side by side. With all eleven men searching, the drivers ran the boats up closer to thirty. Hooker could feel the boat rise out of the water and assumed it now only ran on the narrow part of the V in the bottom. The ride had become as smooth as Sweets' Lincoln Town Car. The water seemed like a flat glass mirror of the summer's dead air. The grasses along the north side seemed darker—like they held a secret.

As Hooker looked forward, he spotted the trestle and knew why the grass seemed so foreboding. *Because the secret was death.* He turned to the driver and patted his hand down in the air. The driver throttled back as the other boat responded the same. Hooker pointed to the car trunk with the police ribbon still attached. The team members started spotting the fiberglass orange marker sticks standing six-feet out of the water, and a foot or so above the grass.

The other boat surged ahead. It threaded through the trestle and around the corner. The radio squawked. "The Sheriff said the body dump extended back to the next lane. We're going to work the north end," the driver responded and then turned the boat around.

"This is all clear, but there's a narrow alley back there we can get up."

Hooker nodded. He knew, eventually, they would probably drive up, down, through or around every acre of the south bay. This tedious crime-solving he didn't usually do—usually, it came to him.

As they slid tightly through the grass in the narrow alley, Hooker slumped down into the bottom of the boat. He rested against the round of the pontoon. The low hum of the engine and the hiss of the boat slipping past the grass created a powerful sleep aid. The heat from the sun didn't help. The radios were turned down and became only a small distraction as Hooker drifted in and out with the heat.

The boat slowed. The pressure of the grass pushing against the sides had become a large drag. If need be, the SEALs will start hacking back the grass to clear a passage, or just push harder. Hooker slid down further and finally rolled over onto his side.

His head had just dipped below the edge when the other men started yelling. Hooker's eyes flew open—looking at a knife, tied to a pole, thrown like a spear. A few seconds earlier and the knife would have been in his back or neck. As it was, the jerry-rigged spear stuck into the side of the pontoon.

One of the SEALS dove to the floorboard and grabbed a small kit. He drew out a rubber patch and peeled the tape off. Pulling the spear out, he inserted the patch and worked it with his finger. He withdrew his hand, and the sound of escaping air stopped. The man rolled over.

"Are you okay?"

"I'm good." Hooker's guts were shaking, but he knew he could function.

The boat had slid to a stop, but nobody moved. The driver quietly spoke into his walkie-talkie, "We just took assault from out in the grass to the east of us and south of you."

The radio squawked. "Roger, we're coming down the north border lane."

Hooker watched as two of the SEALs rolled over the side of the boat and slid into the water and grass without a splash or rustle. Hooker sat on the bottom of the boat and leaned against the other side—his shoulders covering the patch. His head swiveled as he kept watching the grass for something, anything. His mind worked in overdrive with more than just a hint of panic. A part of him started expecting another spear to fly out of the grass and pin his chest to the side of the boat.

He was wrong.

The hand came from behind him. Before he could scream or anyone knew what was happening, he was pulled up and over the pontoon. He had a second to take a last breath.

Under the boat, a murky person attacked Hooker. As they fought, the silt clouded the water. Old nightmares of drowning flashed through Hooker's mind. The beast in front of him would give him even more. The light-colored shirt wavered in the water and left the impression of an indistinct shape—maybe a human or maybe a shark. Hooker struck out with his fist.

Nothing there.

A sudden pain shot through his thigh. As he looked down, he could just make out a dark trail leaving his leg. The warm water numbed the pain, but he knew it was either cut or stabbed. He feathered his legs, turning his body in place. The water swished—too deep to stand up.

Out of the corner of his eye, he saw a movement of light color. He fanned his hands up and pushed his body down. The knife aimed at his throat was a glancing slash across his forearm. *Another trail of blood in the water—are there sharks in the bay?*

Hooker punched up with his right fist. He struck something soft and forgiving. He didn't think it had any effect. He tried to grab a leg or arm or something to no avail.

Hooker touched the bottom, but his attempt to push off only resulted in his boots sinking deeper into the mud and silt. The suction stopped him from leaving to the air above. *He stood floating in the water—trapped.*

The white shark came out of the dark murk. Hooker bent sideways away from the knife glinting in the water. His right foot slipped out of its boot. The pain in his back spun him around. The feet were kicking as the body moved back into the murk. Hooker lurched right and released his left foot.

He pushed off as best he could in the direction the fiend had gone. He clawed at the water as his lungs clawed at his chest—he knew he needed air. As he cleared the shadow of the boat, he grabbed the grasses and pulled himself up in one desperate lunge.

The water in the grasses ruptured as Hooker gasped for air. A thick rope struck him around the shoulders. "Grab the rope..."

He wrapped the rope around his arm as he felt it being pulled back to the boat. In his blurred vision, he could see the two seamen hauling him in.

Just as he cleared the grass, the form reared out of the grass and fell on his legs. The right hand drove the knife into Hooker's back. The hilt of the large knife slammed to a stop on his shirt. Hooker screamed and letting go of the rope, twisted around to try to remove the knife. His right hand fanned at his lower back as he sank back into the water.

Against protocol, the second SEAL dove in after Hooker. The team leader stared, helpless. He had no idea where his other two SEALs were. Now, it was just him. He called out. Nobody answered.

The SEAL clawed through the muddy water. His eyes stung. He looked for anything that could be Hooker or the other thing. As he looked down, he thought he saw a foot disappearing into the grass. He folded up and dove after it.

The other boat maneuvered into the alley, hanging nosed in with the other half out in the wider lane. The four SEALs and the Squirt stood in the boat looking into the grass. They could see movement in the tops. Fester finished getting his pants off and his tech-belt on. He checked the knife on each side and then dove out into the grass. Two of the SEALs followed. They all knew with the water muddied, they could end up swimming right over who they were looking for.

Fester stuck closer to the bottom as he pulled his way through the grass. His head swung a constant pendulum of motion. As he slid toward where they had seen movement, he saw a light shape. Grabbing the grass to his right, he pulled his way down to the body. The SEAL hung in the water suspended—motionless—a foot or two above the silt. Fester recognized the position of the short stick protruded from the man's back. A small area of silver hung at the man's skin. Fester knew it would be duct tape, holding a blade to the end of the short spear. The loop of the surgical tubing attached to the end had provided the propulsion of the handheld spear. He had used such a rig for years instead of a spear gun. He rolled the SEAL over. The man's throat gaped open—*coup d grace.*

Fester gently pushed the man up toward the light and air. Breaking the surface, he found himself turned around in the grass. "Call out..."

"Over here."

Fester started swimming in a sidestroke as he dragged the body. He got to the boat, and the SEALs leaned over and silently pulled in their teammate. Their mutual silence spoke volumes. Fester turned to go back.

In the grass, someone thrashed and a scream—mixed with gasping for air.

The Squirt called out, "Hooker, this way. Over here, Hooker. Swim to my voice."

They could hear the grass whipping about as the person thrashed toward the sound of Squirt's voice. The movement and sound were not smooth but the sound of desperation.

"Keep coming..."

One of the SEALs stood with a hank of line ready to throw. As the grass parted, he threw it hard. Most of the hank hit Hooker on the back and the back of his head. His one arm swung up and wound around, trapping the line around it.

The SEAL pulled hard. Hooker surged out of the grass as an arm swung through the air. The short spear was buried into Hooker's ribs. The knife still protruded from his back. The fiend grabbed the knife and hung on as the SEAL pulled Hooker's body up onto the pontoon.

Fester surged from the side of the pontoon where he had been hanging. The knife in his hand flashed as he buried it into the armpit of the white shirt. The fiend screamed and bared her teeth. The eyes were wild with bloodlust. Her hands worked on Hooker's back. Her left grabbed into his shirt as the right pulled the knife from his body and drove it in again.

As she pulled the knife out again, she rose. She looked into the bottom of the boat. Her eyes locked with the eyes of the Squirt.

He smiled. "Oh, hell no, bitch…"

She looked down at the large openings of the shortened twelve-gauge shotgun. The Squirt rested the end on the top of Hooker's head as his thumb moved the selector to the middle.

"You're going straight to hell…" He pulled the trigger on both barrels. Her head—a foot away… disappeared.

29

THE HOSPITAL AGAIN?

The headless body floated half in the grass. The body still convulsed with muscle contractions as the heart worked pumping life-sustaining blood to a head no longer there.

In the boat, the men worked rapidly. "Stay with us, Hooker. Just hang on, buddy. We're getting you to a doctor."

The radio squawked. "SEAL two, go ahead."

"This is team leader Chief Sanchez, requesting immediate medical evac. I have two men in their mid-twenties with multiple stab wounds. Both have lost a lot of blood. BP is dropping. Pulse is rapid but thready. Helo can set down at the crab shack parking lot. We will clear it."

The team leader turned to the driver. "Get us the hell up there now, Chief."

The boat surged and straightened in the lane, as it began to hydroplane, the chief switched the radio. "Team two to team one."

"Team one."

"We have Hooker and the Squirt. Hooker is badly

wounded. Roberts is dead, say again, Roberts is dead. We are making our way to the shack for dust off. Round up the rest and meet us there."

"Roger, team two. We have just Porter to get in, and we'll be right there. The sheriff will need the evac, as well."

"Roger."

As the driver ran the pontoon up the launch ramp, the chief looked up. The helicopter came across the grass tilted forward. He figured the pilot kept it at fast attack angle the entire way from Alameda.

As they hoisted Hooker, the helicopter flared and started to settle on its skids. The side doors opened, and one medic jumped to the ground.

The other medic shoved out a stretcher, and they laid Hooker on it and shoved it back in. The diver with the arm wound rolled in.

The other boat raced out of the lane, already turning. The driver aimed for the launch ramp and the helicopter. The boat slid the entire length of the ramp—coming to rest twenty feet from the helicopter.

The two SEALS grabbed Fester and ran him over. They rolled him onto the chopper's floor as the one medic yelled, and the machine lifted off. It turned in the air and nosed over. The hospital was four minutes away with a ticking clock.

"Where to?" The Squirt stood watching the helicopter become a dot in the sky.

"Moffett is the closer of the two." The man pointed where the helicopter had gone—out over the grasses. "It's straight across. Alameda would be another five or ten minutes. But because Hooker's a civilian, they will probably take him straight to Stanford."

The Squirt mused as he watched the now empty sky. "With stab wounds, why not straight to Valley Medical?"

"Even five minutes can make a difference. Stanford will at least stabilize him and then later move him either down to Valley or up to San Francisco. Either one is expert when it comes to stabs and gunshot."

The Squirt turned and looked at the SEAL. "What about your guys?"

The guy shrugged and waved his hand in dismissal. "As soon as they got in the chopper, they probably handed him a roll of duct tape and put him to work."

The Squirt snorted. "Yeah, sounds like something Uncle Willie would do..."

"Rear Admiral William Knight? Cutthroat Willie?"

"I think he was only a captain. But the cutthroat thing fits."

The guy was excited. "You're talking about William Knight who builds fast cars?"

The kid grunted with a smirk. "And drinks moonshine, wears a dress, and is Hooker's uncle."

"The gentleman is no captain. I don't know what he's told you, but the man saved my uncle and a couple dozen other guys from a POW camp. They made him a Rear Admiral and got put in for a Medal of Honor. The guy is a legend." The guy stopped. "What do you mean he wears a dress?"

The Squirt smiled. "If Hooker survives this one, we'll have you guys down for a barbecue. The medal and citation hang by the door into an acre of garage. Next to it, hangs a picture of him in the hospital with tubes everywhere, and the President shaking his hand and looking like an idiot. The dresses are just cheap and burn up or get greasy a lot."

The man laughed. "He always did march to a different orchestra..."

"But he followed regulations. Give the man a penny-whistle and a place to walk, and he's happy—which is all we care about." The Squirt felt in his wet pockets in panic and then relief as he pulled out the key to the truck. "For a moment there, I thought I had given the key back to Hooker after I got Betsy Ross." He held up the shortened shotgun.

The man looked at the wild pistol grip 12-guage shotgun. "I saw the head disappear—double-aught buck doesn't act like—"

The Squirt held up the shotgun he had become so entwined with. "No, but a buck-forty of dimes in each barrel does—especially from a foot away."

The radio squawked. "Helo six-eight to SEAL two."

"SEAL two, go ahead."

"Hooker and the sheriff are down at Stanford. We'll take your diver back to Alameda. He says he wants to sleep in his own bed. Helo six-eight out."

The SEAL nodded at the Squirt. "Roger six-eight. Franco just got married last month. I will advise Hooker's partner, and thanks for the lift. SEAL two out."

He gazed across the grass to an unseen distant hospital. Looking back at the Squirt. "You won't know anything for several hours or tomorrow even. We'll round up the Coasties... the body is in the bay, and they will want to see it. We probably need the sheriff out here as well. They get whiney when you move a body and don't tell them."

The Squirt tossed the key in the air and caught it. "I'll handle the law enforcement end while you get the Coast Guard down here. I'm sure the sheriff has several questions for all of us... even if they didn't want to do their job in the beginning."

Both men nodded with grimaces. The diver pointed his radio up at the young woman watching them from the deck of the crab shack. The Squirt nodded. He would join them in a few minutes.

"1-4-1."

"Go ahead, Squirt." Dolly's voice had a strained edge to it. It was not going to be a good night.

"We're going to need some sheriff out here. They need to send the crime scene unit. I also think it would be best to advise the Transportation Department—the body is under the trestle and in the railroad easement."

"10-4, Sheriff and Cal Trans... on their way."

The Squirt looked out across the grass. The late afternoon's golden light was just starting to settle in over the waves of tan grass—turning it to a warm fire in the late summer heat. He didn't want to think of anything at the moment. He slid out of the truck and walked across the parking lot.

The closed door muted the radio, but the tears came anyway.

"1-4-1... Where is Hooker?"

"1-4-1?"

"1-4-1... Are you there?"

"Squirt...?"

30

JUDGE'S CHAMBERS

"We won't know for a while. He was in surgery for sixteen hours the first round..." An exhausted Squirt looked over at the Superior Court Judge.

The man lowered his glasses from the top of his head. "Have you slept at all?"

"I've dozed a bit at the hospital..."

Hack leaned back in his chair. "So I'll take it as a no..."

The Squirt shrugged his eyes and nodded.

"So what now... for you...?"

The young man hesitated, and then his hand unclasped in a manual shrug.

The judge eased forward and looked at the large pile of files open and spread across his desk. "I've been going over... well, for no other word for it... your resume."

"Resume?"

"If you could boil down a couple of years of taking down killers, solving cold cases and murders, and the bombing, and anything else you two did... outside the academy. And then there is the impressive work inside the academy..." The man gently pulled his horned-rimmed glasses from his face and tapped the files.

Laying the glasses down, he leaned back in his large chair. A thin knife of light through the vertical shutters traced a line across the thinning hair. He closed his eyes as his left hand gently scratched the length of his nose.

"Can you actually picture yourself in a uniform for the years it would take to make detective?"

The Squirt sat back in his chair. What had once been a fantasy for a career had been made available as reality. But along the way, it had become other than what he found interesting or exciting. His joke of going straight to detective was just that—a joke. He knew in his heart that he would have to serve the trial of being a uniform and serve out his time as well as test for the position. He also knew his activities of solving major crimes had created some ill feelings toward him. And he knew those ill feelings could cause political roadblocks on his road for future advancements.

He bit his upper lip as he rubbed his thumb over the four small scars on his left hand. *Four tiny dots... where everything had started—a lifetime ago.*

He sighed as he looked up. "I'm adrift... if you have any suggestions."

"I spoke with Russell over at Department of Justice in Sacramento... He said you have received more than a few offers outside the Bay Area—apart from his office. But anywhere you go, they all would involve a uniform of sorts. Even if you landed with Russell, you would be in a uniform suit with a tie and tight shoes."

The kid nodded. "I've been thinking about all of those things this summer."

"Which is why you have delayed graduating from the academy by taking all the higher courses? Courses which others return over the years to take?"

The Squirt's lower lip pushed up against his upper in a shrug. His eyes wandered over the judge's wall of legal reference books.

Hack slowly closed the files and stacked them. The final pile was several inches thick. He rested his folded hands on top. "I think you have already found your place—we just need to find a legal way to use that unique position and resource."

The kid looked up through his eyebrows. His head gently rose in interest.

"How soon is the giant truck getting back on the road?"

"Last we heard, they were putting the final pieces together down in Texas."

The judge glanced at the small calendar on his desk. He ran the edge of his index finger along his curled lips. "Maybe we need to send you down to Texas to oversee the final construction—and learn how to drive her."

"Who, exactly, are we...?"

"For now... my office. It wouldn't be the first time you worked for me. But, for the future, we'll figure it out when the time comes."

ALSO BY BAER CHARLTON

<u>Novels</u>

The Very Littlest Dragon: NEW 2019 Editions
(Newly edited editions available: an all-new full-color ebook, a paperback with coloring
pages, and a full-color Collector's Edition hardback)

Stoneheart
(Pulitzer Nominee 2015)

Angel Flights
What About Marsha?
Pirate's Patch
Dry Bridge of Vengeance

—

<u>Southside Hooker Series</u>

Death on a Dime – Book One
Night Vision – Book Two
Unbidden Garden – Book Three
Boomtown – Book Four
One Day Under the Grass – Book Five

Southside Hooker Series: Books 1–5 Box Set
(Collector's Edition hardback & ebook available)

—

<u>Thorny Wallace Series</u>

Death in the Valley – Book One
Light to Light – Book Two

BAER CHARLTON

ABOUT THE AUTHOR

BAER CHARLTON

Baer Charlton graduated from UC Irvine with a degree in Social Anthropology, monkeyed around for a while, and then proceeded onward with a life of global travel, multi-disciplinary adventure, and meeting the memorable array of characters he would come to describe in his writing. He has ridden things with gears, engines, and sails, and made things with wood, leather, and metal. He has been stitched back together more times than the average hockey team; his long-suffering wife and an assortment of cats and dogs have nursed him back to health after each surgery.

Baer knows a lot about many things in this world. History flows through his veins and pours out of him at the slightest provocation. Do not ask him what you may think is a simple question unless you have the time to hear a fascinating story.

You can find more about Baer at his website.
www.baercharlton.com